'A super-smart, hotly competitive Asian-Australian
YA gamer rom-com that celebrates burning your
own path through life. This nerd *loved* it.'
Rebecca Lim, award-winning author of *Tiger Daughter*

'An utterly gorgeous and heartwarming debut about
family, creativity, ambition and believing in yourself.'
Nina Kenwood, bestselling author of *Unnecessary Drama*

'A warm, witty and big-hearted novel that effortlessly
weaves together breathless game playing, epic trash
talk, slow-burn romance, complex family dynamics
and true friendships.'
Leanne Hall, award-winning author of *The Gaps*

'Hilarious, genuine and wonderfully geeky, this
book perfectly captures how it feels to be a young
Asian-Australian person navigating career dreams,
family expectations and first love.'
Grace Chan, author of *Every Version of You*

'A gloriously nerdy debut about family, culture, passion
and ambition. A love letter to games and puzzles of all
kinds, including the biggest puzzle of them all – life.'
Tobias Madden, bestselling author of
Take a Bow, Noah Mitchell

TWO CAN PLAY THAT GAME

LEANNE YONG

ALLEN&UNWIN
SYDNEY • MELBOURNE • AUCKLAND • LONDON

First published by Allen & Unwin in 2023

Allen & Unwin
Cammeraygal Country
83 Alexander Street
Crows Nest NSW 2065
Australia
Phone: (61 2) 8425 0100
Email: info@allenandunwin.com
Web: www.allenandunwin.com

Allen & Unwin acknowledges the Traditional Owners of the Country on which we live and work. We pay our respects to all Aboriginal and Torres Strait Islander Elders, past and present.

A catalogue record for this book is available from the National Library of Australia

ISBN 978 1 76106 337 4

For teaching resources, explore
www.allenandunwin.com/resources/for-teachers

Cover and text design by Mika Tabata
Cover illustration by Lucy Wang
Author photo by Myles Kalus
Internal images: (video game controller) © Polina Tomtosova/iStockphoto; (card paper texture) © Abstractor/Shutterstock; (card border frame) © Tartila/Shutterstock; (card heading frame) © Cute vector illustration/Shutterstock; (pixel art hourglass) © Kaleb da Silva Pereira/iStockphoto; (glowing orb) © klyaksun/Shutterstock; (meat and knife) © thkatefox/Shutterstock; (cloning icon) © T VECTOR ICONS/Shutterstock; (hands reaching) © Viktoriia_M/Shutterstock
Set in 12/16 pt Perpetua by Midland Typesetters, Australia
Printed and bound in Australia by the Opus Group

10 9 8 7 6 5 4 3 2 1

www.leanneyong.com

To Daddy, who taught me to fly.
To Mummy, who made a safe space to fall.
And to Nat Nut, who kept me going along the way.
This is my love letter to all of you.

CHAPTER 1

Future Devs Showcase: 28 days left

Another day, another asshole dude-bro gamer who's simultaneously trying to pick me up while explaining to me why, as someone lacking a physical pair of balls, I'll never be a 'real' gamer like him.

'If you need someone to help you with the bosses in *Negatory*'s Super Hard Mode, I made it through without a single death,' he says, his smug look an obvious invitation for the adulation he believes is his natural right.

It's been like this since he turned up at 5 am at the GamesMasters store, and I've had enough of him trying to impress any girls in earshot. I roll my eyes and turn away — not that there's anywhere to escape to in this crowd of a hundred-odd people, and not that I'm giving up my prime position to rush into the GamesMasters store as soon as it opens. *Especially* as there's no line, just a general crush of both masked and unmasked people.

I don't think the store expected this many people to be excited about a game by a small independent developer, so they never bothered with crowd control. Everyone's shoved tightly together, the days of social distancing relegated to a past everyone wants to forget.

The guy mutters something about 'fake' gamer girls who only game so they can get guys, as though he wasn't the one who started talking at me condescendingly.

He's the kind of person who, if I was actually with a guy, would assume I'm here to 'support my man', as though I couldn't possibly be a gamer in my own right. It would probably blow his mind to know I won awards all throughout high school for being so damn good at coding and got accepted into a scholarship program at Queensland University of Technology because of those same skills.

Not to mention the indie game I'm creating at the moment, *Vinculum*, which is my true pride and joy. Uni hasn't started yet, but I already know this much – scholarships are for schmucks who want to get a degree so they can get a boring job and get rich. Real artists? They follow their vision, wherever it leads.

Even if that's standing outside a store at 4 am on a Saturday and defending your position at any cost.

I check my watch again. 8.59 am. One minute till opening. I'm so close to picking up a special limited edition of *Negatory*, the best indie game ever made. They all contain a golden prize:

a ticket to an exclusive Art of Game Design workshop held by the *Negatory* developers at PopSplosion, a major pop culture convention.

For most people here, it's a super-exclusive chance to meet their idols. For me, it's the key to my future.

My watch flips over to 9.00 am. Still no movement. I shift from foot to foot, desperate to grab one of the thirty or so bundles available instore only. There are three hundred copies total, divided between the flagship GamesMasters stores in each state. Most were sent to Sydney and Melbourne thanks to population density, while we here in Brisbane are fighting over what feels like leftovers.

An excited chatter rises from the front of the queue, and I push my glasses up so they sit firmly on the bridge of my nose. Then the crowd surges ahead, me with them. Although I started in a promising position, people somehow manage to flow around me till my initial advantage is lost.

'Excuse me, sorry, if I could just—'

No one's listening, of course. So I bend forwards and *push*. Under this person's arm. Threading through the gap between those two peoples' bodies. If I can't be tall enough to see over everyone else, then my small Asian frame should at least be useful for something.

I navigate the crush and get to the table with the special edition boxes. There are only two left, and I grab for one. My hands close around it.

I AM GOING TO THE WORKSHOP, BABY!

Except . . . Someone else has their hands on my precious.

Another lucky person snatches up the remaining box, so the one we've got is the only one that remains.

We both yank, and we both manage to hold on. In those first frantic moments, all I can see of my opponent is a *Stanley Parable* shirt (a gaming shirt I would compliment the owner on in any circumstance save for this one). On the opposing side, long callused fingers grip the box as tightly as my own.

Then I look up. My first reaction is relief that it's not the dude bro from before. My second is surprise that I recognise the boyish face currently set in a determined scowl. I've never spoken to this guy before, I don't even know his name, but I've seen him around at some of the Singaporean and Malaysian social events my parents are always going to. His dad also plays badminton with mine sometimes. The way his eyes widen, it's clear he recognises me as well.

Then his eyes narrow again and I'm reminded we're in the middle of a war. *This bundle is* mine, *damn it.* I didn't see him anywhere when I queued up at four, so I should obviously have first dibs since I was here earliest.

'Please let go of *my* box,' I say as politely as anyone can when their teeth are gritted.

'I could say the same thing,' he replies with an identical level of civility.

'I got here before you, and my hand touched the box first.'

I'm not giving way. I *need* to attend this workshop with the Farrows, who created *Negatory*. They're super supportive of indie game developers breaking into the industry. Not only would this workshop be an intensive with the duo who made me believe I could make games – I might even be able to pitch *Vinculum* to them.

I spent the last year developing my game every spare moment I had. During lunch at school, after school, over school holidays. Since the start of high school when I watched the Farrows' developer streams on Twitch, I've known for sure that creating video games is all I want to do with my life. Since graduating high school two months ago, I'm even more desperate to prove it.

The guy in front of me might not know it, but I need this workshop ticket way more than he does.

He gives me a smile that's a little twitch of the lips, like we're partners in crime. 'How about we make a deal for the bundle? I'm sure we could come to an agreement.'

We're the only ones remaining in the store. Everyone else has seen the empty table and left in disappointment or frustration. I want everything in the bundle so badly, though I'm keeping my eyes on the prize. I can live without the special edition game as long as I get the workshop ticket. I'm even willing to pay for the lot as a last, desperate play.

I nod once, slowly. 'What were you thinking of?'

'Well, I—' He yanks the box from the grip I relaxed ever so slightly. 'I changed my mind. Bye!'

He runs for the counter, weaving through the crowd with efficient, practised movements. *Great, so he has the reflexes of an athlete, too.* I'm left empty-handed, heart sinking. Were it anything else I wanted, I'd walk away with my fury and resentment, and find a way to move on. But the special edition and the ticket within – that's my future he's stealing! If I was contemplating murder before, now I'm deadset on it. This jerk is *not* getting away with such a lowball move.

I wait outside of GamesMasters, keeping one eye on him as he pays. Meanwhile, I search through my parents' friends on Facebook until I find a picture of his parents, then go through their profiles to find his name.

Jaysen Chua, huh? Well, Jaysen the Jerk, you've just made an enemy.

I confront him the moment he steps out of the store. 'Don't want to face your victim, Jaysen?'

He stops and spins around. 'I can't believe you haven't learned the harsh reality of this world yet. You snooze, you lose.'

'Very mature. Now, here's my proposition for you—'

'I don't think you have the room to propose anything.' He hugs the box to his chest, the white, plastic GamesMasters bag crinkling against it. 'I don't even know you, and the limited edition of *Negatory* is mine.'

'You're a terrible liar.' I hold up my phone, showing his dad's profile page. 'My parents know your parents, and we've seen each other around at their social events.'

'You know my name. So what?' He takes another step back. He's cornered, and we both know it.

'So, *my* parents know *your* parents.' I pull up a series of profiles, one after the other. 'That's me, these are my parents, and as you can see, they're Facebook friends with your parents. If I were to tell *my* mum what you did, you know it's going to get back to *your* mum, and then you'll have to explain to her why you scammed such a "nice girl", and an aunty's daughter to boot.'

What I don't mention is that it's a bluff. My mum would never make a fuss just because I missed out on a video game. She low-key thinks they're more of 'a boy thing' and something I'll grow out of.

Jaysen glares down at me, taking advantage of his extra head of height. 'Oh, come on. I don't even know your name, and you're threatening me with the Asian Gossip Network?'

'You thought you were so smart with your sneaky move,' I reply. 'Well, two can play that game. Before the day is out, every single aunty and uncle in Brisbane will be whispering about what you did to poor Samantha Khoo. Gosh, what *would* your parents think about losing face like that?'

'I'm still not giving you the bundle,' he says, watching me carefully as he runs his hand through the spiky black mess that passes for his hair. 'Let me guess, Samantha, you want the workshop pass? So do I.'

'I didn't expect a jerkwad like you to do the decent thing.'

'Just because you lost, that doesn't make me a—'

'You deliberately got my guard down when I was willing to negotiate in good faith. That makes you one hundred per cent a jerkwad.'

There's a hint of a squirm, yet he doesn't release the box. 'I saw a chance and I took it. Anyone would.'

'Tell that to your mum.'

His gaze drifts to the bag, and I can tell he's weighing up whether it's worth a serious scolding from her. In his place, I'd take the scolding, redeem the code for the workshop ticket, and offer the rest up to placate the aunties and uncles. I can't let him walk away with my future.

'Look,' I add quickly, 'I'm not asking you to hand it over without a fight.'

'I already—'

I point at his shirt. 'You're also a gamer, right? Then do you have the courage to fight me to see who deserves the ticket more? We'll settle it with a competition of indie games.'

It's a desperate ploy, and honestly, I don't expect him to take me up on it. He has more to lose than I do.

To my surprise, he eyes me with interest and says, 'A competition, huh?'

I have no idea what that would even entail. If he's biting, though, I'll run with it. 'If I win, you give me the box. If you win, you keep it and I never tell a soul about what you did this morning.'

There's an expression on his face I know all too well. The kind of feeling where you're about to tackle a game and it's going to be the kind of challenging that makes you want to throw your controller at the screen, except it's also exciting for the exact same reason.

He looks at me, at the people giving us sideways glances. 'We need to discuss the conditions, but I'd say you've got a deal.'

CHAPTER 2

Future Devs Showcase: 28 days left

Jaysen and I end up in the back corner of The Greatest Outdoors, an outdoor and camping gear store, to work out the details of the competition. He clutches the white plastic bag with the game tightly against his slim frame the whole time, ready to run. *So paranoid.*

We're here because there is almost no chance of running into anyone from our Singaporean and Malaysian communities, who will certainly make very wrong assumptions about the situation if they see us. I don't date jerks, even if they have good taste in games and in shirts.

I especially don't date people I plan to thoroughly destroy.

'Here should be safe enough,' I say, gesturing at the random camping gear I could never hope to identify, and Jaysen nods in agreement.

We stare at each other in awkward silence for what feels like forever but is probably only a few seconds, sizing each other up. At any other time, I'd dismiss him as another gangly Asian boy. Now that I'm assessing him as a potential threat I can spot the corded muscles that run lean, and a sharpness to his gaze.

I wonder what he sees when he looks at me. Although there's no way he can spot Samantha the developer, does my *Negatory* shirt say 'fake gamer girl' or 'fellow fan'? It's a pity I can't make my thick-rimmed glasses reflect the light so that they become opaque, the way anime characters do. I wouldn't mind channelling that mysterious yet menacing air.

'What kind of competition were you thinking of?' Jaysen eventually asks.

I came up with a few ideas as we were walking here, and I think I have something that will work. 'One classic indie game. Single-player, so there's a variety of game options. Person who finishes the game the fastest, or gets furthest in the game within the time limit, wins.'

He purses his lips, drumming long, tapered fingers on the box against his chest. On *my* box, though he doesn't realise it yet. 'One game? Then it's also down to luck as to what kind of game it is. There should be a few rounds.'

Ugh, this is gonna take more time than I thought. 'Three, then?'

'Make it five. That'll give us the chance to have a proper variety of games so it's fairer. Picked from a pool of games we both chose.'

I hate to admit that his idea sounds the most workable. Except, five games is a time commitment away from developing

Vinculum . . . I remind myself that this is still time spent furthering my game, just in a different way.

'Fine, but we should—'

Footsteps approach. We both turn to opposite sides of the aisle and pretend to browse. Plastic rustles, and I take a quick peek to see that Jaysen's now holding the bag in one hand while the other holds a small cardboard box from the shelf. I quickly look back at the array of . . . portable camping espresso machines? . . . in front of me as a shadow appears around the corner. A tall brunette walks past without giving us a second glance, and I let out a huff of relief as I turn back to face Jaysen. He's frowning down at the box he was pretending to examine, and holds it up when he notices me watching him.

'D'ya think there's a difference between camping chopsticks and normal chopsticks?' He tosses it at me, and I catch it. 'Other than a twenty dollar price tag and a storage pouch.'

I stare at the box in disbelief, but he's right – these are a pair of so-called camping chopsticks that unscrew in the middle and come with a canvas pouch that has a carabiner attached. So you'll never lose them no matter how rugged the conditions, I suppose.

Tossing the box back to him, I shake my head. 'Definitely targeting white people. What self-respecting Asian would spend that much on something you can get for a few dollars at Daiso?'

You can get just about anything at Daiso, including cutely shaped sausage cutters (exactly what it says on the box), illuminated earwax diggers, finger massagers and more. Chopsticks you can dismantle are par for the course.

He places the box back on the shelf. 'That's why we're hashing things out here and not there. I mean, have you even been in this store before today?'

I glance at the back wall, which is stocked with portable camping toilets, and try to imagine my mum going anywhere near one of those. Nope, can't do it. Let's be honest, I can't even imagine either of my parents sleeping in a tent. Or most of the uncles and aunties I know.

'That's why I suggested coming here,' I say, gesturing at all the items around me.

His eyes narrow. 'Excuse me? You just said we should go somewhere no one we know would spot us. I was the one who listed stores like Valleygirl and City Beach.'

'I was the one who pointed out The Greatest Outdoors.'

'As we were walking past it. You got lucky.'

'I think you mean I'm good at strategising on the fly.'

He stares me down for a few moments longer. 'If we're doing this competition, it should be in-person so we can keep an eye on what the other person's doing in real time. Proof they're actually playing and not a stand-in, as well as checking for cheat programs on demand. We can find a neutral location far away from any nosy aunties and uncles. You've got a laptop that's good for games?' When I nod, he continues, 'Great, then we can meet up for a few hours each weekend.'

'That works. After all, if anyone should be worried about cheating, that would be me.'

'You mean if anyone should be worried about losing to me again, it's you.'

I don't mind him acting smug, because it means his guard is down. Before he can react I snatch the bag from him and dangle it in front of his face. 'You sure about that?'

He holds out his hand, snapping his fingers demandingly. 'Give it back.'

I intend to – doing anything illegal would mean losing all leverage on him – but I'll let him sweat a bit longer.

Then he says, 'Steal it, and you'll have nothing to use against me. If anything, it'll be my turn to take advantage of the Asian Gossip Network to let everyone know how you stole from a gwai zai like me.'

Hah. 'Good boy' my ass. Even if his Cantonese pronunciation is perfect, ugh.

I slowly and deliberately place the bag right in front of his feet. 'You think I didn't know that? It was a reminder to keep you on your toes. Go right ahead, be arrogant. That gives me an advantage.'

His left hand snaps out towards the handles. I grin. It's amusing to see him so unnerved. When he sees my expression, he draws his hand back and leaves the bag where I placed it.

I hold out my hand. 'We have a deal?'

He glowers – sulks, really – for a few more seconds before he reaches out with his own hand. Instead of taking mine in a handshake, he places his palm on the back of my hand. It's how the secret society of magic users in *Negatory* create a sacred oath with one another. He's testing me. I flip my hand so it's palm-down. He brings his hand around so it's beneath mine and moves it up so our palms slap together. Then we grab each other's wrists in a monkey grip.

'Badras methilin,' we say in unison, and release each other.

He lets out a small huff. 'So you've played the game.'

After the asshole this morning, having to prove myself again is just too much even though I've been doing it my whole life. 'Oh, so now I have to prove I'm a "real" fan because I'm a woman and women can't possibly be gamers, huh?'

His expression is legitimately mortified as he draws back, I'll give him that.

'No! That never crossed my mind, or I'd never have agreed to the competition with you.' He pulls up the browser on his phone and shows me an eBay search. 'It's because people are already selling these workshop passes for thousands of dollars online, and I don't trust anyone's intentions but my own.'

'Scalpers can go to hell.'

He actually laughs, and his eyes crinkle in a way that makes him seem almost nice. 'You can say that again.'

Let's see what information I can squeeze out of him. 'Why do you want the workshop pass? What's in it for you?'

'It's for someone important to me.' His answer is evasive, so my guess is to impress someone he likes.

He changes the topic. 'How do we decide the games?'

I've no clue. All I know is that I don't want to give him more proof of how impulsive my challenge was. 'I'll come up with rules tonight. You can be sure it'll involve classic indie games.'

He leans back against a shelf. 'I'd suggest *Portal*, but . . .'

I nod in understanding. 'It doesn't reaaaally count as an indie game because it's a Valve game, even though it feels like one.'

Portal is the holy grail of puzzle game design, and anyone who says otherwise can fight me. I've studied the game backwards and forwards while designing my own games, and I have no doubt I'd win that round. So it sucks that it's technically out.

Jaysen nods emphatically. 'Same with *Flower* and *Journey*. I mean, maybe they could be included because everyone calls them indie and ThatGameCompany is small, but they're published by Sony who are one of the big guys.'

It's criminal, someone like him having such good taste in games. Especially when his eyes light up and he gestures emphatically as he mentions each name. I have to remind myself that less than an hour ago, this guy lied to me and promptly took advantage of me when I tried to compromise. Behind that smooth-talker lurks a cold, calculating monster.

I fish out my phone from my pocket. 'Let's exchange numbers. We'll do the first round tomorrow, where we can also decide on the games and how they're chosen. Gives you less time to find a way to rig things.'

He shakes his head. 'You have to trust me at some point, like I have to trust you. There's a million ways to cheat this.'

The nerve of this guy! 'Trust? Coming from the person who abused mine?'

He flushes. *Interesting.* Could that be a shred of conscience? Maybe there's hope for him after all.

Then he opens his mouth: 'You were the one who suggested the competition, not me.'

'I thought it was preferable to doing a snatch-and-run or shanking you in the parking lot. Imagine what all the aunties would say if I got thrown in jail.'

His lips quirk up in a half-smile. 'Aiya, that Samantha lah, so hopeless wan. Make her parents so sad, sit on wrong side of lawyer table.'

Jaysen mimics the tones and cadences perfectly, just like an aunty or uncle at church disguising gossip as concern for said party. I cover my mouth to muffle my amusement.

There's a self-satisfied look on his face as he says, 'Made you laugh, even though you were trying not to.'

Argh! That's it; I'm not giving any more satisfaction to this over-competitive oaf. I set my face into a blank mask, create a new contact on my phone and swap it with his. He has one of the latest non-mainstream models that are only sold online, because of course he does. If he's going for an edgy-pretentious vibe, he's succeeded. Not that I'm jealous or anything, my three-year-old model is great.

There's a small crocheted phone charm dangling from the bottom of his phone case, at odds with the entire image I have of him. When it spins around, it reveals the 'Reflect' rune from *Negatory*, which casts a spell that deflects certain attacks. When paired with the 'Reinforce' rune, the two spells form a powerful combo. The charm would make sense as one half of a couples' set, though I've never seen anything like it sold anywhere.

When it comes to my entire future versus him wanting to impress whoever he's going out with, it's pretty easy to see who *should* get the spot at the Farrows' workshop.

I enter my details into his phone and save them. I'm not thinking, and automatically tap the home icon at the bottom of the screen as I would if it were my phone. Everything minimises to a clean screen with no icons or widgets. The background image is Jaysen, a younger boy who I assume is his brother, and his parents standing at a lookout on what I think is the Great Ocean Road. He's got one arm around the boy, and the two of them are laughing.

It's a little adorable, like the crocheted phone charm, but nowhere near enough to redeem all his personal and moral failings.

Then the phone is plucked from my hands. 'Gawking at my photos?'

'If it's meant to be private, don't put it on your home screen.'

'I wasn't—' He sighs, returns my phone and picks up the plastic bag. 'Whatever. One-thirty tomorrow afternoon work? I've got church in the morning.'

I stuff my phone back into my pocket. 'I've got church too, so that works. I'll find a place we won't be interrupted, and text you. We done?'

'We're done. All things considered, I'd say this was a triumph.'

I incline my head. 'Huge success.'

'Beat you tomorrow, Samantha.'

Too bad the one-finger salute would be inappropriate. 'Don't let my skills hit you on the way out.'

CHAPTER 3

Future Devs Showcase: 28 days left

The hesitant plunking of a piano greets me as I open the garage door and lean on the frame to kick off my shoes. My mum's Saturday morning students are all little kids, and while they can be adorable, the continual off-notes and weird rhythms really grate on my nerves. They're the reason I spent too much money on noise-cancelling headphones.

I hurry past my mum's closed studio to the kitchen, where my dad's dumping everything into the sink. He cooks on weekends because she's teaching all day, but he never cleans up after himself, which she says is worse than him not cooking at all.

'Have you eaten yet?' is the very first thing he says in Cantonese as I slump into one of the chairs by the counter. Because of course it is.

'Nope.'

As he takes out a frying pan and the carton of eggs from the fridge, he asks, 'You didn't get your game even though you went so early?'

It's not worth explaining the entire saga of Jaysen – or Jay, as he entered his name into my mobile – to my dad. 'It was sold out.'

'That's a pity.' He puts the frying pan onto the stove and pauses. 'What do you want for breakfast?'

I glance at the eggs he's taken out. 'What are you making?'

He points at the pan. 'French toast or special egg.' He names them in English, but says them with a Cantonese inflection. 'Or I can just make you toast.'

It's not even a question. 'Special egg.' This is his 'secret recipe', invented as a poor Malaysian student studying in London. I grab two eggs from the carton and hand them to him. 'Please.'

My dad laughs. 'Don't let your mummy know how many eggs you're eating, she'll nag you about your cholesterol.'

I grin. 'Thanks, Daddy.'

Childish as it seems to call my parents 'Mummy' and 'Daddy' when I've already finished high school, it makes much more sense in Canto, with a Canto inflection where the first syllable dips, then the second syllable rises and is dragged out a bit. It becomes a bit weird around Westerners, who seem creeped out about it.

As he cracks the eggs into the pan, I add, 'I saw the son of one of your friends at the shopping centre today. Jaysen Chua.'

Sizzling fills the air. 'Oh, Edwin's boy. He's a year older than you, I think. Studying chemical engineering – didn't get a scholarship like you, though. He's a good boy; takes care of his parents and brother.' He glances at me. 'Did you talk to him?'

They know nothing about his true face, dammit. 'I said hi, that was it.'

'Ah.' Does he sound a little disappointed?

'The store was very crowded, and everyone was rushing to grab a special box so there wasn't time to say much.' I'm such a good liar, I even surprise myself. 'I'm sure I'll see him around again.'

My dad flips the eggs, lets them cook for a while, then tips them onto a plate. He measures out one tablespoon of soy sauce, one tablespoon of vinegar and two tablespoons of sugar into the frying pan, then tilts it over the fire so the sauce pools to one side. I hop around the counter to stand beside him so I can watch everything caramelise as the sugar melts. He puts the eggs back in and spoons the sauce over them, then empties the lot back onto the plate.

'Scrape *all* the sauce off,' I tell him. This is the kind of sauce where you lick the plate at the end. 'Don't waste one drop.'

He shakes his head then does it anyway. 'Happy?'

I eye the pan, but black sauce on black coating makes it hard to see. 'It'll do.'

'You're not meant to take after me when it comes to eating, it's bad for you.' He puts the pan in the sink. 'Remember to wash this up before Mummy comes out for lunch. You know how she hates it when we leave everything there.'

I glance at the pile of plates, pots and cutlery already filling the sink. 'Wait, why me? You know I have to work on my game. The Future Devs Showcase is in a month and there's so much to do.'

He grins. 'I cook, you clean. Seems fair.'

'Daddyyyyyyyy.'

'You haven't even started university yet, you're still on holidays, so you have enough time. I don't care if you got a scholarship; you still have to wash up.' Before I can protest, he's sliding open the security gate to the backyard. 'Time for me to water the plants. It's better to do that in the morning.'

My dad's rule for the garden is that everything we plant must earn its keep. That is, if we grow it, it must be edible. Ideally items you can't run out to the supermarket to buy, to make them worth the effort. We have a small patch of banana trees, a mango tree, a lychee tree and a calamansi lime tree. There are a few small poles by our fence supporting dragon fruit plants. We also have a veggie patch where we grow okra, pandan leaves, mint, a few different types of chillies and lemongrass. They all thrive in Brisbane's almost-tropical weather. My dad tried a rambutan tree once, which died a miserable death for reasons we couldn't fathom.

I finish the eggs and check that my mum's still in the studio with her student before licking the plate clean, angling it just so to avoid my glasses. One of her students walked in on me doing it once, and I don't intend to let it happen again. Especially when the little brat laughed at me and pointed out the sauce on my nose and my left cheek.

Washing-up is a precarious game of Jenga-meets-Tetris as I rinse off each item and pile everything in the right basin. Plates below bowls, bowls in pots, larger pots to one side, all the cutlery gathered inside one of the pots, mugs squeezed around everything else wherever there's room. The problem comes when soaping the dishes, because everything ends up piled in reverse if you don't have someone rinsing as you soap. I've nagged my parents to replace the basins with deeper ones for years. Their latest answer is that they'll use the money they've saved on my university fees to buy a dishwasher . . . eventually. Which means never.

They're so excited because not only am I the oldest kid out of all my cousins and therefore the first in our generation to go to uni, but I also won a place in a fast-track scholarship program. My parents hustled to make sure they could send me and my younger sister Eva to one of the best private schools in Brisbane so we'd receive the best education, and be well-placed to do any uni course we wanted.

So I don't know how to tell them that after looking at the course list . . . I'm not interested. The first year courses are either simple programming, advanced math, or more general engineering. Even the later courses are more about the study of various programming methods, algorithms, data analysis and so on. The degree itself will help me find a well-paying job in some corporate company, but absolutely doesn't help me with what I really want.

I just.

Want.

To make.

Cool.

Games.

If I choose to reject the scholarship and take a gap year instead where I can work on creating games full-time, it has to be for an even bigger and better opportunity. Such as having a super popular game with a publisher that's sold a ton of copies. My game *Vinculum* will be that breakout hit for me. It's as polished as any game out there, and everyone I've shown it to on the various indie developer Discord groups has said something like: *I can't believe a high school student created a game like this!*

I have a simple two-step plan. First, score publisher interest at the Future Devs Showcase in a month and leverage that interest (a Legitimate Big Company wants to work with me!) to convince my parents to let me try full-time development instead of uni for a semester. Second, attend the Farrows' workshop at PopSplosion in June, introduce myself to them, and pitch them my game for a shout-out to their fan base . . . which leads to becoming popular enough that there's no reason to return to uni.

In that scenario, my parents — hell, their entire *community* — would understand why I'd choose to ditch the scholarship and the degree. In their eyes, instead of a could've-been dropout, I'd be a successful entrepreneur.

I stare down at my sudsy hands. *More*, the voice inside whispers. *You need to do more. You need to prove that you're enough.* I balance the last rinsed cup on top of the dishware in the drying rack. It leans precariously but doesn't topple.

Done.

When I return to my room and check my phone, there's a
message from Aneeshka waiting for me, demanding I let her
know when I'm home. She's been my best friend since we met
in Year Seven and discovered we were both total video game
nerds. We were the ones who'd be holed up in the library with
our laptops at lunchtime, learning how to make our own games.

We've done everything together – we chose all the same
subjects in high school, discovered the real-life version of video
games in the form of escape rooms, and most importantly,
developed our own games with the hopes of breaking into
the industry. If it wasn't for her, I don't think I would've even
considered a career as a game dev.

Except now Aneeshka's headed to Sydney for university,
and even though we chat every day, things don't feel the same.
But it's fine. She's always wanted to move to a bigger city. As
her best friend, I'm so happy she got into an awesome software
engineering course down there. When my game makes it
big and I earn enough to move out, I'll join her. The current
situation is only temporary.

Not long after I message her, my phone rings with a video call.

'Did you score a workshop ticket?' Aneeshka's excited
voice blasts through my speakers before her camera flicks on.

It's perfectly positioned as always, pointed down from
above because apparently that's the best angle. Her brown skin
is flawless (as usual) in the sunlight that streams into her room,
while her wavy black hair is tied up in a practical ponytail,

which means she's busy programming. After years and years of seeing her every day at school, it's strange to now only see her through a video call every few days. Sure, it was similar back during the periods of lockdown when we were doing remote learning, but we knew that would end sooner or later.

I prop my phone up on my desk and show her the tiny gap between my fingers. 'I was so close! *So* close!'

'Nooooo!' She throws her hands in the air, dramatic as always. 'Remember last night we talked about shivving people if you had to? Where was the shivving?'

Leaning back in my gaming chair, I sigh. 'I have so many regrets.'

'If I wasn't fighting with half the population of Sydney to find a rental that's actually affordable, I'd be there to do the shivving for you.' She shakes her fist at the camera. 'Why must my parents want the move to be sorted so early?!'

I never realised how much I missed her exuberance till it wasn't in my face every day. 'Yeah, it's *totally* your fault.'

She grimaces. 'Talking about being unfairly blamed, remember that creepy dude who tried to hit on me in the dev Discord then said I was asking for it?'

As a female dev with cool-girl vibes, Aneeshka attracts a lot more attention, both positive and negative, in the community. I don't envy her that. At the time, she came to me totally creeped out. She wouldn't let me tell anyone though, because if her parents found out they would've cut off her access to Discord.

'I unfortunately remember that piece of air pollution. What'd he do now?'

'He didn't do anything to me; it's fine.' Aneeshka sighs. 'But he was in the Australian indie dev server on Discord talking about how he got tickets to the Farrows' workshop from an industry insider. Think anyone will mind if we steal his tickets?'

That guy is a prime specimen of 'guys I'm going to gleefully talk down to when I'm famous'. He's some trust fund kid down in Sydney who's rich enough to pay for expensive coding courses, win charity auctions to meet famous devs, wrangle tickets to exclusive events . . . but of course, any success is due to his innate talent. Which apparently we, as women devs, will never have in the same quantities as a guy.

I raise my eyebrows. 'Wait, the guy *actually* has industry connections? I thought he was pulling shit from his ass when he trashed our games to talk up his.'

'It gets better. He was also gasbagging about how it was "a close friend of his" who got him one of the Future Devs Showcase booths near the entrance. So his connections might be legit.'

'Gross.' If I got angry every time this kind of thing happened, though, I'd be perpetually angry. I'm used to shoving it down. 'We better trash him good with our games. I want to throw all the publisher offers or press coverage from the showcase into that arrogant face of his.'

It sucks that he's representative of a whole group of human trash in the gaming world. I've been following all the news closely since I decided I wanted to make games, and it's strengthened my case for why I want to be an indie dev instead of working for the huge studios. So many stories of women being harassed and discriminated against. Don't get me started on the GamerGate stuff – that really terrified me as a young kid dipping her toe into the gaming world. Thank goodness for Aneeshka.

Aneeshka lets out a loud groan. 'Why are you reminding me how much work I need to do? I'll have you know you've just sent my stress levels skyrocketing, right when I should be enjoying my newfound freedom and starting a life that includes going to bars and discovering the wild and wonderful world of cocktails and spirits.'

'Tell me if you discover any good ones,' I say, even though I'm not that interested, really. Aneeshka's always been the curious one, eager to break into the 'adult' world despite her parents' best efforts.

We talk for a bit longer about how things are going for her – they'll be much better when her parents head back to Brisbane in two weeks, apparently – and then I start telling her about the Jaysen debacle.

The first thing she asks, to no one's surprise, is: 'Is he hot?'

It's something I've struggled to understand since we hit puberty. Suddenly, people started falling into categories of 'hot' or 'not hot'. To this day, I don't understand how a certain face or physical features can make people feel things, but I go along with her hotness rankings and all that because that's what you do for a best friend.

'Uh . . . I don't know. He didn't look bad? I was more focused on the fact that he, you know, *stole my ticket*.'

'You need to get your priorities straight, Sam.'

I'm partway through explaining the competition with Jay when she's pulled away to breakfast by her parents, so I promise to message her with the rest of the details later.

Putting my phone aside with a sigh, I stare at my desk, where my dual screens stare back with equal blankness. Time to start my work day and get my game good enough to leave all those arrogant jerks in the dust. I power up the PC tower and the colourful lights on my keyboard and mouse blink on in tandem. It boots up quickly, as a $3000 computer better damn well do.

On one screen I pull up the development console and the editor for my code, while on the other I pull up my online tracking board for outstanding issues. There are columns for severity, and one for all fixed bugs. They're colour-coded by type: technical bugs and design issues. Unfortunately, my details for a lot of the design issues boil down to 'Something isn't right with this level'. Very helpful, past me.

I lean back against the headrest of my chair with a sigh, and stare at the awards on my shelves. Top five in the Australian STEM Video Game Challenge for high schoolers two years running, with a second place last year. Awards from the many game jams I've attended over the years. A finalist in the Emerging Developers category in the Junior Australian Game Developer Awards, an under-eighteens spin-off of the main awards. And more.

Aneeshka was right there beside me, placing just above or below me, or winning other game jam awards I didn't. Every photo I have of these events has us side by side, arms over each other's shoulders, both holding certificates or medals or trophies. *The dynamic duo*, everyone called us. But she was always counting down the days to graduation, to attending uni in another state and getting away from her parents so she could have some measure of independence.

All these awards are proof that I can succeed on my own merits and make this a career. I have the skills, I just need a chance.

I turn back to my game with slightly less stale determination. *Vinculum*'s plot is about two sisters thrown into separate dimensions, both seeking a way home. Level by level they must make their way through their separate worlds, collecting fragments of memories of the cataclysmic event that caused the separation.

The idea behind the game is that your controls move both characters at the same time. However, things the older sister does on her side will affect what happens on the younger sister's side, such as opening a path when there previously was none, and vice versa. I wanted to use the mechanic to represent, thematically, how despite being in separate worlds with the spectre of past events looming over both, they still affect one another. They still need each other to get home.

Even the name of the game, 'Vinculum', means *a unifying bond*.

This needs to be a work of art. It won't get any publisher interest or press interest otherwise, not as a plain old puzzle game. I pull on my noise-cancelling headphones and focus on my screens, where *Vinculum* demands my attention. I'm sick and tired of looking at the levels, at the code that's never quite right, at a game that seems excellent one day and terrible the next, till I can't tell what it actually is anymore.

My brain is fried from the early start, so I settle for fixing the technical bugs in the 'Severe' column of my to-do list. There's something satisfying about being able to step through code to trace a bug to its origin. It's like using clues to solve a complicated puzzle, similar to the puzzle games I love best (though in some cases the 'complexity' is a missing semi-colon somewhere).

The Future Devs Showcase is in five Saturdays from now, in Sydney. Only a hundred creators under twenty years old were picked for the showcase. It's an industry-only event where publishers and studios big and small will be attending, and looking for interesting games to pick up, or games they'd like to partner with the devs to make. There'll be press to report on any interesting games, which can set you up as an indie dev if you have enough public interest.

Being invited to the showcase was yet another confirmation that I have what it takes to make my own games for a living. Perhaps I'll manage to get a big-deal company to support my game, the ones who produce multimillion-dollar games alongside smaller games? Though that does mean you lose more control over your game and aren't *really* indie anymore. But if I could get a deal from a small boutique publisher like Fellow Traveller or Blackbird Interactive, who are known for hugely successful yet niche indie games? Attention, all players: Samantha Khoo has been SLAIN!

First, though, I need to get *Vinculum* up to scratch. I throw on my soundtrack for kicking ass and work through each of the bugs, striking out each one as it's fixed. Today turns out to be a good day, where the music and everything else fades away. I'm able to fully focus on the code instead of getting distracted by online announcements from other devs who are doing so much better than me.

The next thing I know, I've been working in silence for hours. The summer sun is in the mid-afternoon phase, and I'm *starving*. The sound of a strummed guitar comes from the room next door.

My younger sister Eva has my mum's love of music, and an innate sense of rhythm that passed me by entirely. Thanks to her, the music for my game is completed.

I hum along a bit to 'You Should See Me in a Crown', 'Gravity' and, finally, 'No Interlude' by her favourite band, Wild February. Eva even has all of Wild February's CDs. A sixteen year old with CDs, in this day and age – proof of how obsessed she is with the band. At least she hasn't progressed to vinyls yet.

She's involved with both band and choir at school, and is going on a tour of Europe to perform in cathedrals later this year. It's one of the many opportunities our parents paid an obscene amount of money to send us to a private school for, which I never took advantage of. I asked her once if she wanted to become a professional musician.

'It's a hobby,' she had said, 'so I don't want to do it as a job. Who wants that kind of pressure?'

It's such a waste of her talent and I don't understand it,

but I suppose it's up to her how she wants to live her life. She partly inspired the story of *Vinculum* – how we're connected in so many ways that it'll always be us against the world, yet there are still these fundamental divides in how we see it that neither of us knows how to breach.

My phone buzzes, and I pick it up to see I have a new message.

Jerky McJerkface

I've got a few ideas for where to meet tomorrow, all no-aunty-no-uncle zones, open late afternoon on Sunday

Yes, I renamed Jay's contact in the car park before I drove home.

Yes, it was childish and unoriginal.

No, I don't have any regrets.

His message is followed by a long list of cafes and addresses dotted all around Brisbane. They are notably *not* in the suburbs down south that are Asian Central. I thought we'd agreed that I'd be the one who found a place, even if I completely forgot. It's a little annoying that he'd butt in, though if he wants to do all the work that's fine with me. I pick one at random on the north side.

Sam

Three Birds Cafe in Strathfield

His response comes back half a minute later.

Good choice, reviews said they do good drinks and stuff. Don't forget your laptop. I assume it's got Steam installed?

This . . . this smug asshole dares to insinuate that I, *a gamer*, wouldn't have THE major gaming platform installed on my computer?

I don't even dignify his question with a response.

CHAPTER 4

Future Devs Showcase: 27 days left

As soon as the Sunday church service ends, I slip out to my car. The plan is to arrive early at the place where I'm meeting Jay, and set up first. If it adds some psychological pressure on him to see me already good to go when he arrives, even better.

No one from church will miss me, at any rate. Most of the other kids my age have already coupled up, and they have a lot of social events together. They do invite me, but there's always so much to do for my game that I end up turning them down most of the time. Because I managed to win all those awards in school, if I don't turn up they all assume I'm studying, getting better at coding so I can ace the accelerated uni course, or something that's equally 'important' in their eyes.

I've almost made it to my car when Eva comes running up. She's dressed in a loose cotton top with mid-length shorts and a simple belt, cool enough for a Brisbane summer but at the same time modest enough to avoid any whispered commentary from the aunties and uncles. Her long ponytail swings about with her arms as she waves at me to wait.

'There you are,' she says. She's fit enough that she's not even out of breath. 'I can't believe you're already sneaking off. Mummy said she and Daddy are having lunch with the aunties and uncles today, so you'll have to drive me to the other church. I'm meeting up with Tamara and a few other friends for lunch before we prep for youth group stuff.'

Eva attends another church, which she considers her 'main' one. It's mainly white Australians, with a tiny smattering of other ethnicities. Their church camps involve tents and sleeping bags, unlike ours where the bare minimum for accommodation is individual cabins with private bathrooms. Our social events tend to revolve around food, such as yum cha or having a Hong Kong-style barbeque at someone's house. Theirs tend more towards outdoor activities like hiking or going to the beach.

Eva actually enjoys those activities, whereas my preference is to stuff my face in a place where I don't need to worry about being attacked by ticks or getting sand out of my clothes. There's a major trade-off, though, which is that the members at Eva's church are completely uninvolved in the gossip and politics of the Asian community. The only reason Eva still comes to my church is because she knows it makes our parents happy that our family attends services together.

'All the aunties and uncles were talking to Mummy and Daddy about you, as usual,' Eva says as we pull out of the parking lot. 'How happy they were you got the scholarship, what tuition classes you were sent to so they can send their own kids, and of course—' She gives me a teasing grin here, '—hyping up their sons for your consideration. Apparently Aunty Angela's son Andrew is single and likes computers.'

I roll my eyes. 'He also likes the idea of a girlfriend who doesn't mind that he spends his spare time playing games, and will do all the things Aunty Angela currently does for him, like cooking and cleaning. And, presumably, taking care of her and Uncle Geoffrey as they get older.'

'Yeah, he doesn't have the kind of drive you do,' she says. 'Honestly, it's a relief to be around church people who don't know our family. I don't have to worry about being set up with some random aunty's son, or that everyone will be asking if I'm going to get a scholarship like you did.'

I've somehow, inadvertently, ended up as the poster girl for what so many of these aunties and uncles want their kids to be – the high achiever making their parents' sacrifices worthwhile, and representing their family.

Wonder what they'd say if they knew I wanted to throw it all away.

'A scholarship is nice and all, but the important thing is what you want to do,' I say in the end. It sounds big-sistery, at least.

'Yeah, Ethan said he wants to take on an apprenticeship at TAFE, even though he'd do fine in any courses, even specialist maths if he wanted,' Eva says. 'And Tamara said she's going to take a gap year after we graduate.'

Although we go to an all-girls' school (so we aren't 'distracted', hah!), Eva's group of close friends includes a few guys who she came to know during combined events with one of the all-boys' schools. They're also all quintessentially Australian, which I suppose gives her a different perspective on life. At the very least, her friends aren't set on the 'go to uni, find a decent paying job' track. Yet another one of those divides between our two worlds.

'How about Linda and Liam?' I ask.

She shrugs. 'They're not sure yet. But there's two more years to work something out. I think they want to enjoy school life and all their extracurricular stuff for now. Liam's pretty sure he's a lock for the string quartet they handpick from the seniors, and Linda wants to get into the national track and field championships again. She's still upset she missed a year because of all the lockdowns at the start of high school.'

Oh, to have that kind of freedom. To not feel the constant pressure to prove yourself in some way. Our parents have never been the type to expect straight A's, but there's a definite sense of pride when we do well. Or in my case, when I tell them I've been offered a scholarship.

Every time I try to find the words to tell my parents that I don't want to go to uni, the words stick in my throat, held down by the weight of expectation. Held down by the fear of disappointment in their eyes, in the eyes of everyone around me.

I have to show them that I can still be amazing when I go my own way. If my game's successful, all my choices will be vindicated and I won't lose their respect. They'll still be proud of me.

Jay better watch out, because I'm coming for him and that ticket.

Driving Eva to her church ruins my plan to turn up to the first competition early, since I have to detour east before heading north to where the cafe is. It's part of a row of old timber houses that have been renovated into shops and cafes. There's a small verandah over the footpath so they can put one or two small tables outside. A few people are seated inside at a bench along the wide window that runs along most of the front face, chatting over coffee. I can't remember the last time I went out for coffee with friends. There's always so much to do on my game.

I push through the swing door to find Jay already seated at a table in the back corner, playing something on his laptop. That thing is a beast, a gaming laptop with backlights that change colour and cooling fans I can hear from where I stand. It's so try-hard, I can't help snickering at him as I make my way over. His *Hollow Knight* shirt, at least, is more understated, with a simple image of the main character's mask. I plonk myself down in the seat across from him.

He glances up. 'You're right on time.'

The way he says it, with the slight raise of his eyebrows and self-satisfied tone, makes it sound more like, *I beat you here, ha-ha.*

Which, I'm sure, is exactly what he meant. And exactly what I intended to do to him until things were derailed.

'You skip church or something?' I ask.

'No way. My parents would've killed me, and I had to talk to some of the guys in my Bible study group anyway. I know all the shortcuts around Brisbane, that's all.'

Smug jerk. To my dismay, I notice he has one of the same stickers on his laptop as I do: a *Negatory* one, of the rune that binds all things together. It's infuriating, having similar tastes to this guy.

Which reminds me of his phone charm. I wonder if whoever has the other rune minds that he's meeting alone with a girl? I'd like to reassure them that all I want is the workshop ticket, and then I'd be happy to never see this guy's face ever again.

I pull out my laptop. It's slim compared to his, with no dedicated graphics card or anything fancy. It does, however, contain an i7 processor and heaps of RAM, all the better to compile code with, and it runs most of the games I'm interested in. For everything else, there's my desktop computer. I remind myself that I don't need to prove anything to him, just like I don't need to prove myself to anyone who immediately assumes I couldn't *possibly* be a serious dev or gamer from a single glance.

All I need to do is beat this guy.

I pass him a sheet of paper. 'Here are my proposed rules.'

He hands me one too. 'And here are mine.'

Again? I told him I'd pull the rules together too, yet he's still gone off and done his own thing. It brings back crappy

39

memories of when I first started messing around with games and there were people I met on Discord servers who were all, *You sure you can do this coding yourself? You sure you don't need someone to do* [insert one of the thousand things needed for a game] *for you?*

'I said I'd come up with the list of suggested rules,' I tell him snappily as I pick up his list.

'I know,' he says, 'but I thought it wouldn't hurt to write down some of my ideas to throw into the mix.'

I look at his list. It's a lot shorter and more bullet-pointed than mine, so maybe he's not lying.

- Indie games with clear collectable items
- No randomly generated levels; require too much luck for a competition
- Game pool to pick from (twenty games?), each side selects ten games
- Pick/ban stage for game pool
- Five rounds
- Game picked at random each round
- First to finish game wins the round.

It's rather similar to mine, and fine, there are *some* good ideas I hadn't thought of like including bans when selecting potential games. When I look up, Jay's nodding as he finishes scanning my rules.

'Agree on the three-hour limit where the person who's furthest through the game wins,' he says when he notices my gaze. 'Only ten games in the pool so things don't get too overwhelming – that's fine. Classic indie games that both sides know makes sense. I don't want to be saddled with a game I've never heard of before, that you know inside out.'

I guess I can give a bit as well. 'While I like the pick/ban idea, this isn't a full-on esports competition. Let's keep it simple and say each side can nix one game the other person puts forward.'

He thinks it over, and nods. 'And no randomly generated levels too – you didn't write that down.'

'I assumed I didn't have to write down all the common sense stuff for you. Now I see I should have.'

'Never assume common sense when it comes to battling strange girls,' he says, so deadpan I would laugh if it wouldn't mean him claiming another victory. 'Or did Udina teach you nothing?'

It's another test to see if I really am the indie gamer I claim to be. Udina is a side character in *Negatory* that you have to go out of your way to find and meet. She's the epitome of cool, but also a total hothead who charges into situations with the best of intentions and the worst of outcomes. There's a point in the game where she accidentally burns a house down.

I need a response that will prove not only have I played the game, but also that I'm a huge fan. I'm used to having to prove my place.

Then the full meaning of his question sinks in. 'Wait, are you saying I'm like Udina?'

'Weird sense of fairness, comes up with convoluted battle schemes, overconfident, more fight than sense. I mean . . .'

When he puts it that way . . . 'Determined. Incredibly

determined. I think you forgot that. You'll regret agreeing to this when I win.'

'Did I say overconfident?'

We pause for a moment to order drinks. The menu is on a clipboard, because of course it is. It's all coffees and teas, and while I'm not interested in coffee, I'll be damned if I'm going to pay five dollars for water and a teabag. In the end I settle on a chai latte while Jay gets a Coke. The waitress takes our orders, giving our laptops a bemused look as she does so.

I've come prepared with strips of paper to write down our nominated games, and I pull those out together with an old ballpoint pen from a game jam. As soon as I put them down, Jay slides the paper over to his side and picks up the pen like it's the most natural thing in the world. I open my mouth to protest, then close it again. No point getting riled up before the competition, it's probably what he wants.

Jay doesn't seem to notice as he asks, 'First game?'

That's easy. '*Time-Twister.*'

If we're talking classics, it's the game that launched a thousand indie games. Everyone knows it, loves it, and over fifteen years down the track it still holds up. It's a good way to both establish my creds, and nominate a game I know really well.

He nods, and writes it down. 'Ooh, a classic. I'll go with a newer one, *Slo-Mo.*'

Dammit, why does this guy have such good taste? I wanted to diss him with Aneeshka afterwards for being totally basic when it comes to games. I love *Slo-Mo* because it has a really smart 'time only moves when you move' concept that allows you to stop and plan your next steps – and feel like a total badass when the sequence is played back at full speed at the end of the level.

My turn. I'll go for something that's less of an in-your-face game. It should still be a classic he'll recognise if he claims to know his indie games. And one I know I'll do just fine in, because there's no coordination required.

'*REquery*.'

His brow wrinkles. 'Is there enough gameplay in that to make it worthwhile?'

Don't tell me he's one of those snobs who only considers something a 'real' game if it's a dude bro shooter, or where death is part of the experience.

'Are you saying it doesn't count because you're not shooting people in the face?' I roll my eyes. 'Please. It's a classic that merged multimedia with gameplay in a really smart way.'

'I don't disagree. I'm simply saying you could memorise every keyword to unlock all the videos instead of actually playing it.'

'Where's the fun in that?'

To my surprise, he laughs. Shaking his head in friendly amusement instead of disdain, he writes the name down as well. After passing me the strip of paper, he looks at the list of games for a long while. Long enough that I'm certain he's plotting something.

'My next choice is *We Can't Keep Meating Like This*.'

I look down at the strip of paper I'm folding into halves so he can't see the *I am in so much trouble* expression on my face. I've never played it, because ridiculously hard games where you insta-react or die are very much not my thing. I don't play them precisely because I have no sense of timing or coordination. I'll jump when I'm good and ready, dammit, not because I have to or I'll be killed by the environment or other characters.

I can't let him know he's already hit my weakness, so I give him my most excited grin and lie through my teeth. 'Oh, I like that. Spent way too much time playing it when it came out.'

He blinks, confidence faltering a bit. 'Right. Then, what's your next choice?'

My preference would be for a good and proper puzzle game where it's brains that matter. But that might give away too much information about my game preferences and make me easy to target. I need to find a game that makes him believe I'm not avoiding any genres in particular, so he can't take advantage of me.

I glance at my prepared list of games, and there it is. The perfect choice to show I'm not scared of any game, even if I am. '*In The Shadows.*'

I only played it because the greyscale artwork was absolutely gorgeous, and even though I died a number of times I actually managed to finish it without too much swearing. Put it this way: it's doable.

He nods in grudging approval and hands me the strip with the name, so I can fold it up. 'I'll pick . . . *Superficial Giant.*'

Ugh, another kind of game I don't enjoy. Even though the art's adorable, you have to toggle between attacks, aim them from the top-down view, and avoid being hit as well.

Multitasking under pressure is not my forte. Jay watches me, waiting for my reaction, which I deny him by keeping my expression neutral.

That's it, I'm playing to my strengths and going for a purely puzzle game for my next pick.

'*Heaven's Complex*.' Let's see how he reacts to that.

'Nice choice. I enjoyed it a lot.'

I suppose it makes sense that he's played it. Or he's bluffing. 'Your turn. Game number four?'

'*Jeeper Creeper*.'

A stealth game that relies on sneaking around enemies by stringing together actions without hesitation. *Why* is he choosing all these games that rely on precise timing for your actions? I will die. I will die many times, repeatedly, and never get past the early levels.

Has he seen through me already? Surely not, I thought I kept a decent poker face.

'I'm using my veto. I don't like the violence.' That sounds believable enough, surely. Poor weak woman can't handle blood and all that nonsense.

He rolls his eyes. 'Coming from someone who chose *In The Shadows*?'

Uh. Scrabbling for an explanation, I end up with, 'The art in that is far more abstract. This is . . .'

'Pixelated gore? How terrible.'

'Yeah, but you're killing other humans, not being killed by monsters! Besides, it was your idea to give each person one veto.' I cross my arms. 'This is mine.'

'You realise I could choose something like *BrainLive*?'

At this point, I would take a zombie horror shooter like that over something requiring precise coordination. 'I don't suppose I could ask you not to?'

'I'm gonna choose . . .' He draws it out deliberately, watching me with a shit-eating grin, and I'm certain he'll choose *BrainLive* to spite me. But then he says, '*These Sandstone Walls*.' He grins at me, knowing he's got me even if I won't admit it. 'You said you liked *We Can't Keep Meating Like This*, right? So you must love its successor, too.'

Damn him. I can't even back down. 'Yeah, yeah. Good choice, much classic.'

'Back to you.'

We have one more each, so I need to be strategic about my final choice. *Oh, who am I kidding?* My strategy literally comes down to choosing puzzle-heavy games. That's it.

'*Theseus*.'

It's one of my favourites, with a smart mechanic that involves making clones of yourself. It partially inspired *Vinculum*, and although I haven't played in a long while, it still has a special place in my heart. Which is why I fully expect Jay to veto.

He doesn't. He simply writes it down. 'That's yours done.'

I frown. 'Wait, you're not using your veto?'

If I thought his grin before was shit-eating, this one's a veritable shit-feast. 'Didn't plan to. I was hoping you'd use it for an earlier pick so I could find out the kind of games you avoided.'

Thank all that is good and puzzle-y I didn't use it for *We*

Can't Keep Meating Like This. I do, however, have a reluctant respect for his strategy. 'Since you know I hate violent games, let me guess – your last pick is going to be even worse than *Jeeper Creeper*?'

'Let's see . . .' He makes a show of thinking it over.

'Pick your final game already, and let's get this started.'

He drums his fingers on the table. 'Too many games. Can't decide. I'll put in a blank paper, since you've already used your veto.'

Oh, no, he's not. 'Nice try, Jaybird. Not how drafts work. And I'm not letting you dig up weaknesses to exploit. You choose, *now*.'

'Oh, you're admitting to weaknesses?' He leans forward. 'How's this? I'll let you take out one of my games completely, if I get to put in a blank.'

I can't deny that it sounds like a very good deal, and I'm tempted. That's precisely why I'm suspicious. He wouldn't deliberately lose, so what's his angle here?

He waves the strip of paper at me. 'Chances are it might not be drawn at all. I could be giving up one of my precious picks for literally nothing. Or if it's picked today, then it doesn't make a difference either. The odds are in your favour.'

'And you'll get even more information on me, from the game I choose to remove.'

He shrugs, neither confirming nor denying. I glance at his list of games. I have no chance of winning for at least two of them, so whatever he picks can't be worse than either. 'Fine. I choose to remove *These Sandstone Walls*.'

He jumps up and pumps a fist. 'I knew it!' he crows. 'Your weakness is games that require timing and coordination!'

I shrug, pretending I'm not concerned in the least even though I hate myself for perpetuating the stereotype of women not playing 'hardcore' games. 'You gave up one of your chosen games to confirm that? You know there's no take-backs, right?' I finish folding the papers, rip *These Sandstone Walls* into confetti, then put the rest into a small velvet bag I brought along specifically for this.

'You folded them, so I choose,' he says.

I didn't spot any specific indentations on any of the papers, or other rips or tactile giveaways, so I suppose it's safe. I hold out the bag and he dips his hand in. The papers rustle as his fingers move around, sifting through the folded pieces.

I shake the bag a bit. 'You delaying your inevitable defeat?'

That gets him fired up. He pulls out a piece of paper, unfolding it slowly. I force myself to breathe, hoping against hope it's one of mine. Like a professional esports match, the first win is very important, psychologically.

Then he looks down at the strip, and smiles.

Oh, no.

CHAPTER 5

Future Devs Showcase: 27 days left

The pleased grin on Jay's face as he looks at the first game we'll be competing in is unnerving. He must have picked one of his, but which one? How badly am I going to be defeated in the first round?

'Well?' I demand. Gotta put on my confident face, so he can't sense weakness. 'What game am I about to beat you in?'

This is the moment the waitress decides to come back with my drink, and Jay deliberately waits for her to put it down and leave before passing me the slip. *I can do this.* Even if, out of all the games he chose, I've only played *Slo-Mo* before. *Please, please, let it be that one.*

It's not *Slo-Mo*.

I blink, and check to see I've read it right. It's *Time-Twister*. That's one of mine. Why's he so happy about it? Unless . . .

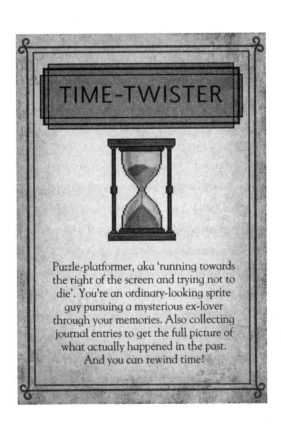

TIME-TWISTER

Puzzle-platformer, aka 'running towards the right of the screen and trying not to die'. You're an ordinary-looking sprite guy pursuing a mysterious ex-lover through your memories. Also collecting journal entries to get the full picture of what actually happened in the past. And you can rewind time!

'You're a big fan of *Time-Twister*?' I ask.

He flips his laptop around to show me he has it installed on his computer, even though the game is over a decade old. 'Huge.'

If this is meant to unsettle me, it's not going to work. He doesn't know that I spent weeks analysing every level when I was stuck on my own designs for *Vinculum*. I pulled apart everything I liked and didn't like, and I could go on all day about how well the developer used the mechanics as a metaphor for the narrative.

Time-Twister is my game, my territory. But Jay doesn't have to know that. I'm going to hustle his ass, and good.

'Oh,' I say, as though I've let the mask slip to the worry beneath. Then I give him my hammiest grin, and pick the shallowest compliment I can think of. 'Me too. I loved being able to rewind whenever I made a mistake.'

'Yeah, that was useful,' he says as he turns his laptop back around.

If I didn't know better, I'd say he sounded the slightest bit disappointed for some reason. I pull out my PS4 controller, which I've set up to work with my laptop, while he reaches into his backpack. My jaw drops when I see what he pulls out.

He brought.

A full.

Mechanical.

Keyboard.

Number pad and all. Laptop keyboards aren't the best for playing, but bringing a beast like that instead of a more portable keyboard is nothing more than the gamer equivalent of gym bros flexing their muscles. It's the kind of try-hard thing I would've done a few years ago, when I still thought I could forcibly prove to everyone that I belonged in the gaming world.

'To each their own,' Jay says with a mocking salute to my controller. 'I like the precision of arrow keys over joypads. Less wrong inputs, you know?'

I grit my teeth and swear I will leave him begging for mercy.

'We'll mark progress by the number of journal entries earned,' I say, and he nods.

We turn our laptops so both of us can see the screens – Jay's slightly awkward with the keyboard cord – and so we can see the other person's selected 'New Game'.

'Ready?' Jay asks, hands on his laptop, ready to spin it around.

I place my hands in the same position. 'Ready.'

'Go!' we both say at the same time, and then I'm jamming the nub on the controller right to move my little guy into the castle where the first memory awaits. The loud clacking from Jay's keyboard is distracting, as I can picture exactly what he's doing from his keystrokes.

I send my guy into the first world at about the same time as Jay. There's a series of tapestries on the walls that tell the story if you click into them, but today is not about story. It's not even about how beautifully the central time-rewind mechanic plays into the themes of regret and learning from your mistakes and, eventually, how some mistakes are irreversible.

As I move my little sprite through the levels past medieval weapons and nebulous balls of emotion that turn deadly and bloodthirsty, I wonder if I'll truly be able to convince my parents that giving up on the uni scholarship for a gap year isn't an irreversible mistake. If the central mechanic in the game of my future is 'having a successful game', will I be able to use it to achieve my bigger-picture goal of going straight into being an indie dev, or will I need to avoid any objections they throw my way?

It's like a puzzle game that takes the gameplay you've experienced and puts you in a situation where everything you've learned can't be used . . . until you twist your thinking and realise the level can be solved if the floor becomes the ceiling.

That's what I have to do with my parents; twist their thinking and show them that uni isn't the only path. The first challenge to overcome is Jay.

I look up to see he's completely focused on his own run, narrow brows drawn down in full concentration, soft boyish features transformed into glinting sharpness. I'm halfway through the next level when Jay hisses. I glance up, wondering if he's made a mistake. Nope. He lets out a breath and his fingers don't move from the arrows or space bar. No time rewind happening yet, meaning he's still doing well.

Disappointed, I turn back to my screen – and in my distraction I miss the timing for a very precise jumping section. It's so close, but I miss and am sent tumbling into the chasm. I hit rewind.

The clicking of Jay's keyboard fills my head, every new keypress taking him into the lead. It's hard to concentrate because I can't stop thinking about how I absolutely do not want to lose and have him dismiss me the way so many people have when it comes to gaming.

It's only a hobby.

You shouldn't be on the computer so much.

Why are you playing games all day? Go outside and play, or read a book.

Again I run and jump. This time I'm too late and the creature I'm meant to bounce off has already flown way past.

Rewind.

Repeat.

Miss.

I need to get my timing right, stat. Another attempt, another miss.

Then Jay swears, and hits the Shift key to rewind. A mistake! I try once more, and finally, *finally*, I make it and nab the journal entry I'm after.

As I go on, I fall into the flow of the game and the world, time bending around me as it does for my sprite. Level after level, world after world. I don't even notice Jay's keyboard anymore, noisy as it is. Time goes forwards, backwards, turns the world about till I can traverse it. It brings back all the quirks in the level design, the bits I ranted about to Aneeshka and the bits she ranted about to me in return. Puzzles designed to trick you the first time so you need to restart the whole level. Puzzles where the game never teaches you the rules to a particular mechanic, instead expecting you to work it out by trial and error.

I remember them all, and I fly through them. Sure, my coordination sucks, but knowing every element of the design means I'm not questioning if it's my skill that's stopping me, or if I've missed part of the solution. I should be stressed with each unnecessary rewind, except playing the game simply for the sake of playing instead of analysing brings back memories of playing it for the first time. I remember reaching the end and thinking, *I want to create something that makes people gasp in revelation with each new level.*

This is why I want to be an indie dev. My parents don't play games, so I'm not sure they'll understand what captivates me so much. I really, really hope that when I finally tell my parents what I want to do (that is, when I find the courage to tell them), they'll understand.

The big twist at the end of the game is especially satisfying. I've finally found my ex-lover, navigated everything thrown my way to reunite with them against all odds . . . then time rewinds and everything's flipped on its head. I marvel anew at how well the narrative and game mechanics were interwoven to pack a serious emotional punch. There is joy in the playing, and I'm so caught up in the moment that I sit back and sigh in satisfaction before I remember I'm in a race.

'Done!' I yell as I spin my laptop around to show Jay – a bit too loudly because the three or four other tables near us all turn towards me with expressions varying from amusement to annoyance.

Jay groans and turns his laptop around as well. He's on the screen right before mine, about ten seconds behind. He does *not* look happy.

'You spent last night reviewing walkthroughs, didn't you?' He points an accusing finger at me. 'Watching speedruns?'

I roll my eyes. 'I didn't know it'd be chosen, did I? Besides, remind me who was positively drooling over the choice of game before we started.'

He opens his mouth, shuts it, opens it again. 'Yes, but—'

'Admit it, you're not as big a fan as I am.' Arguing over who's a 'bigger' fan is incredibly meaningless, but it's ever so amusing to rile him up after all his bravado earlier. 'I can't wait for the next few weeks.'

He stills, then closes his laptop slowly. Purposefully. 'Neither can I.'

We pack away our laptops in silence, each eyeing the other cautiously. He casually takes the small black bag containing the slips of paper with our chosen games, and I grab his wrist to stop him.

'That's my bag, so I'll take it.'

His wrist is slim within my hold, oddly delicate. He twists away with a technique that forces my hand to let go, and dangles the bag in front of my face.

'All yours,' he says. 'Even though you may have won this battle, I don't need to cheat to win the war.'

'I did *not* cheat!' I snatch the bag from him. 'I analysed the level design in detail for research last year, and if you'd done the same thing you might have won.'

'Research? For what?'

I am not telling him about *Vinculum* so he can scoff at me, or worse, get all patronising about how cute it is that I'm trying to be a developer. I'm especially not telling him that I've worked on the game for over a year now and it's still not good enough and I worry it will never be.

'For nothing,' I say, searching for a change of topic. Glancing over at the counter, I see one of the wait staff wrapping leftover baked goods in cling wrap, and it gives me an idea. 'If you're so worried about cheating, let's have the staff wrap this up for us when we pay, and we'll draw on it so it can't be taken off and replaced.'

He follows my gaze, and nods. 'I hate to admit it, but that's not a bad idea.'

When we go up to the counter – that coward nudging me forwards, saying I should be the one to ask since it was my idea – the person looks at us like we've totally lost it. Despite that, they wrap the bag anyway and even lend us a red marker to write on the cling wrap. I draw the symbol of the ultimate rune from *Negatory*, while he does a cute little sketch of the main character of *Hollow Knight*.

I place the bag in the middle of the table, between us. 'Now to decide who—'

His phone rings, and he glances down at it, then back at me with an apologetic grimace. 'Hold on.' He answers it and asks, 'What's up?'

I pretend to tap through something on my own phone to give him a sense of privacy. Not that I can help hearing his side of the conversation.

'You okay? Mmhmm. Did anyone help?' A beat, then, 'Yeah, yeah, I know you don't need it. Still! You'd think *someone* would offer, at least. I'll come get you.' Jay's expression clears into a grin, and the grin is the first genuine and unguarded one I've seen from this guy. 'Shut up, I am *not* a nanny goat. I'll be there in twenty-five minutes. See you soon.'

He hangs up and shoves his phone into his pocket, slinging his bag over his shoulder as he shoves his chair backwards. He doesn't even give the bag a second glance. 'I gotta run. See you next week.'

I don't even have time to ask him what's going on before he rushes out the door.

That night, as I procrastinate on my next round of game testing by doodling new level ideas instead, I can't stop wondering why Jay left so suddenly. A dating-related emergency? A family emergency? Did something happen to someone he loves? Even if he's an arrogant ass, I wouldn't wish anything of the sort on him.

I contemplate asking my parents, but the moment they get wind that I'm asking about a boy, I'll never hear the end of it from them. Or from the aunties and uncles at church. Finding out what's going on with Jay is not worth that. I mean, I don't even know him that well.

Eventually, despite worrying he'll think me overly intrusive for asking, or that it might exacerbate whatever problems he might be having, I decide to send him a text.

Sam

Everything okay?

When I roll into bed in the wee hours of the morning, bleary from staring at the levels in my game, there's still no reply.

CHAPTER 6

Future Devs Showcase: 26 days left

The next morning, far too early for any reasonable person to be awake, my phone buzzes. It's a quick, short buzz that means a text, which sits just below phone calls in the hierarchy of important communications, so I reluctantly snake a hand out of my terry-towel blanket to grab my glasses and phone.

Jerky McJerkface

> The real question should be, are you okay . . . knowing your victory will be short-lived?

I roll my eyes. I can't believe I dragged myself out of a half-asleep state for this. Still, how can I not reply to such obvious grandstanding?

Sam

Of course it will be short-lived.
This competition will be over in
another two weeks.

Jerky McJerkface

You keep telling yourself that, Udina.
I can't wait to see how you do when
my games are drawn.

Sam

Assuming any of yours get chosen.

Jerky McJerkface

I'll have you know, tampering with the
Bag of Fate is a criminal offence.

I laugh at the name he's given the bag, thankful he doesn't
know he made me laugh again. It's a reference to the bag the hero
of *Negatory* carries around, which is said to change the destiny of
anyone who touches it. And this particular bag of games is going
to change *my* destiny by getting me to the Farrows' workshop.

I start typing a response, but before I can finish, another
message comes through.

Jerky McJerkface

Made you laugh, didn't I?
May as well admit it.

I didn't laugh, I'm a stoic.

Of course you laughed,
don't be ridiculous.

It's not until I put my phone back on my bedside table and roll over to try to fall asleep once more, that I realise how smoothly he deflected my original question.

After a late breakfast, I head to my room to work while Eva goes out to meet up with her friends. It's her last week of holidays before school starts for the year and she's making the most of it.

'I'm so jealous, you have a whole month and a half of freedom till uni starts,' she says as she heads out the door to catch her bus. 'I don't wanna wait two whole years till a long holiday.'

Back in high school, I'd enviously watch the Year Twelves leave on their final day, counting down the years till it was my turn. It was meant to be a momentous occasion, a turning point where I'd leave behind the trappings of school and walk into life as an adult. But having walked out of the assembly hall as the other grades stood for all us graduates, nothing's really changed in my life. No new city, no new lifestyle, no new friends even as my current ones are disappearing.

I'm still spending all my spare time and holidays holed up in my bedroom making games. Still struggling for the breakthrough that will prove to the world that I can stand on my own two feet.

Still scared to tell my parents what I really want to do with my life, scared that I'll disappoint them.

While I wash up the breakfast dishes, I watch a playthrough of *We Can't Keep Meating Like This* on double speed to get a feel for the game. As soon as I see the first levels, I know I'm in big trouble if the game is chosen for the competition. Not only do you have to nail the jumps on moving platforms, spinning blades are mounted on walls, fired out or swing in rotating circles. It requires split-second timing and precise control.

When I return to my computer, I immediately browse to the Steam store and buy a copy. I may not win if it's chosen, but I can at least ensure I don't make a poor showing of myself. My plan for this week involves redoing the design for three levels of *Vinculum*, which will probably take me until Saturday by the time they're properly tested. That leaves me all Saturday evening to practise.

Although I want the workshop ticket, I also want a publisher. I want to have actual professional cred when I meet the Farrows, to show them I'm more than a wannabe pushing out amateurish and subpar games.

I already spent a good three hours of my Sunday, all productive working time, playing *Time-Twister* with Jay — four hours if you count driving time to and from the cafe.

The guilt-hangover hits hard and I throw myself into testing various level designs of my game to find one that works. By evening, the frustration of nothing except failed attempts and the feeling of wasting a whole day has me picking up a pillow and flinging it at the wall with all my might.

Not long after, my mum pokes her head into my room. 'What are you doing, destroying my house?' She glances at my computer screens. 'It's just a game, no need to get so angry about it; it's bad for your liver.'

I sigh, closing my eyes so she can't see my annoyance at her words. 'It's not *just* a game, it's an important step to becoming a game developer.'

Her footsteps move across the room. Fabric rustles as she picks up the pillow that's fallen on the floor and replaces it on my bed with a poofing sound.

'Why are you so worried about that? You haven't even started university; you still have lots of time.' There's more rustling as she seats herself on my bed. 'You're smart enough to win so many awards at school and come top of your grade for your computer subject, and then get into a scholarship course. I'm sure your game will be very good, and if it isn't you can make more games with Aneeshka while you're studying. Mummy believes in you.'

I don't think she'd say the same if I told her I wanted to ditch the studying part. I avoid it completely and say instead, 'The showcase is really important for my career. All the big video game publishers and studios will be there.'

There's a bit of a pause before my mum asks, 'Why do you need a publisher? Can't you put it out yourself? You know,

Aunty Wendy's daughter also made a game and put it up so everyone can play on their mobile phones.'

I stifle another sigh. She doesn't understand the difference between creating a game for fun, and coming at it from a long-term career perspective. While it's possible to find success if your game gains traction on its own, those cases are few and far between. I've watched enough self-published games disappear into the void that is the Steam store, never to be seen again.

Video game publishers can give you serious monetary backing and visibility in an industry that's overwhelmed with hopefuls – and that can make all the difference when I need to prove myself to my parents, fast.

'They do a lot,' is all I say to my mum. 'They can be the difference between success, and getting lost in the crowd.'

My mum clucks her tongue. 'You worked so hard on your game, you're already a success. You will only fail if you give up. Aneeshka is working hard too. The two of you are so smart, you will surely do well.'

It's such an empty platitude. Working hard does not always equate to success. It certainly doesn't equate to being picked up by a publisher, or making respectable sales if you self-publish. There are market forces and trends, not to mention a good dash of luck.

All I can see when I look at my game is everything that it isn't. Everything it needs to be.

Still, I nod in response. 'I know.'

The week rushes past, a blur of designing and testing, and a lot of commiserating with Aneeshka. She's in the same boat, though on top of it all she's being dragged around Sydney by her parents to go apartment-hunting. My game should be improving except I despise eight of the thirty levels; I've trashed a ton of failed designs; made basic fixes for four levels and done nothing for the rest. It feels as though I sat down at my computer on Monday, and looked up to find it was Friday.

I still haven't got around to playing *We Can't Keep Meating Like This*. If I can integrate the latest level I redesigned into my own game by tomorrow, I can spend all Saturday evening on it. I'm excited to give it a go after watching more playthroughs. One of them even gave me the inspiration for another *Vinculum* level redesign.

I'm still in a haze of code when I sit down to dinner, enough that I don't notice my mum's unnatural silence until she places a piece of paper on the table. She's only this silent when she's unhappy, and it's usually accompanied by slamming cupboard doors and heavy knife strokes as she cooks dinner. Guess I missed that too.

I watch her apprehensively, wondering if I'm about to be roasted, and what for. Then I notice her attention is on my sister, not me.

'Khoo Yun Sun.' My mum says my sister's full Cantonese name. *She's in for it now.* 'Why do you have a ticket to a concert at a winery tomorrow night? You're too young to drink, and a night-time concert? Who knows who will be there?'

Our parents are already suss about her going out at night unless it's to a friend's place, because she's still sixteen. A concert at a winery? Good luck.

My sister drops her fork and spoon on her plate, and glares at our mum in outrage. 'You went through my things?'

Eva's still speaking in Cantonese, so I know she's not truly furious. After all, having parents up in your stuff is a basic element of living at home – of living with Asian parents, to be precise. They don't make a point of hiding anything from us either, which led to the very awkward position of digging through their bedside drawers as a kid, and finding an open pack of condoms. Nope, Eva's trying to deflect, which reminds me of Jay. The question is whether Eva will be just as successful.

My mum rolls her eyes. 'Don't make such a big fuss. I was cleaning your room like I clean every room in this house, because otherwise all of you would live in the dust. You never told me you were going to a concert at night.'

Deflection failed. Attack landed.

'Because I knew you'd react like this!' Eva pulls away from the table, back stiff. 'Wild February is coming to Australia for the first time ever, and it's an open-air concert at the winery. You know how much I like them, I bought all their CDs even though their music's on Spotify.'

'It doesn't matter, it's still a concert at night and it's dangerous there for a sixteen-year-old girl. I know you don't drink, but I read on Facebook about how the boys don't even need to put anything in your drink these days. There's a new thing where it's a patch they wear that does the same thing as the drugs, so they only have to touch you and you'll do whatever they say.'

Eva looks to our dad for support. Instead he says, 'What your mummy says is right; it's dangerous. You're still in high school, it's late at night, and if it's outside it's going to be dark. If it's the Sirromet winery, that's in the middle of the bush. How can our hearts be at peace? Who's driving you?'

'We were going to Uber,' Eva mumbles, obviously knowing it's a deathblow.

I can't *not* stand up for my sister, so I chime in with, 'If you're careful, it's fine. She'll message you through the night, and she and her friends will watch out for each other. Eva is responsible.'

She gives me a grateful smile, then turns back to our parents. 'See? If jie says it's safe, you know it's safe.'

'I'm still not happy you didn't tell me,' our mum says, though she seems slightly reassured by my words. 'Who are you going with?'

'My usual group of friends,' Eva says. 'You know, Tamara, Ethan, Linda and Liam. They've been to concerts before and know what to expect, so they'll take care of me.'

Our dad frowns. 'They also drink and get noisy.'

'One party, Daddy! You only saw them at one party at Ethan's house, and his parents were there to make sure everyone was okay. They weren't being loud because they were drunk, it's how they normally are. They're good people!'

He sighs. 'How can I trust them to watch over you if they're doing underage drinking?' He gives her a pointed look. 'Or if you are?'

Eva growls in frustration. 'Just because I had a drink *one time* at Ethan's doesn't mean I'm an alcoholic. If anything it means I know my limits and when to stop!' She gives them both the pleading eyes that always seem to work for her. 'Please, Mummy, Daddy, let me go. I don't want to miss this band and it'd mean so much to me. I'll put a tracker app on my phone, so you can see where I am all night. I'll message you every hour. I'll forward you information about the Uber so you know the licence plate. I won't get drunk or anything. I promise I'll still be fine for church on Sunday morning.'

Our mum glances at our dad, and a whole conversation passes silently between them. Then she sighs. 'Fine. But only if your jie drives you and goes with you. You can meet your friends there.'

'*What?*' We say it at the same time, in English, our outrage duplicated.

'I don't have time to go,' I say at the same time as she says, 'She's only two years older, why do you trust her and not me?'

'Because,' my mum says, 'your jie doesn't drink, and she doesn't get carried away like you do.'

I wince as Eva retorts, 'Only because she never goes out, because she's always working on her game.' She pauses as she realises she's gone too far. 'Sorry, jie,' she says, switching to English. 'I didn't mean it like that. I just meant that you're too busy to do all that. You know that I think what you do is amazing.'

She's only spoken the truth, though. How many things have I chosen not to do, because I was so focused on making this game, and making it big? Not that I felt I was missing out in any way, but it's certainly not your normal kind of high school student life. I even started skipping a lot of the social events at church this past year because I needed the extra time.

And as for gaming for the fun of it? This competition with Jay is the most I've played in months in a context that doesn't involve studying the game professionally. I can't remember what it is to have a normal social life anymore. We really *are* the sisters from *Vinculum*, making our ways through separate worlds.

The Future Devs Showcase and the chance to chat with the Farrows at the PopSplosion workshop will make all those sacrifices worth it. They have to.

'I'll be back by 1 am and not a second later,' Eva says to our parents. 'I won't stay after the band's finished their set.'

'Your jie goes with you, or you don't go,' our dad says. 'You're already lucky we're considering this.'

'But—' I protest, thinking of how I need the time to practise for the competition.

'*Please.*' Eva turns that pleading look on me. 'It's *Wild February*. They're like . . . to me, they're like what that Negagame is to you. Only difference is they're a band instead of a game. And they're making Brisbane a tour stop for the first time in five years, at a venue that'll let me in. They're not mainstream so there are still tickets available, and I swear I'll owe you forever if you do this one thing for me. I know you're busy, but one night is all I'm asking. One night, and some excellent music to sweeten the deal.'

I think back to how I was so close to the workshop pass I wanted, till Jay ripped the box from my hands. To the bitterness and disappointment and sheer frustration of thinking I'd be attending the workshop before my hopes were crushed. What else can I say?

'Fine. Just this once.'

CHAPTER 7

Future Devs Showcase: 21 days left

Aneeshka

Aneeshka

Are you enjoying the pretence of having a social life by way of your sister's friends?

Sam

I don't have time for this! How did I let my sister talk me into going out when I have a game to fix and a jerkface to destroy??? I NEED THIS SHOWCASE AND I NEED TO MEET THE FARROWS

Aneeshka

A break from working is always good, might give you new ideas for the level redesigns you're so stuck on. Or how we can rule the showcase with our games.

Aneeshka

You're going to destroy that Jerk-with-a-capital-Jay regardless.

Sam

Ooooh, I like that name for him. What, pray tell, are YOU doing tonight, hmm?

Aneeshka

I'm working on my game, but I don't even have music for it yet. Today I went to an Escher art exhibition with my parents at some fancy Sydney museum. And I actually met some of the other people in my uni course! They all seem really nice. They're going to show me some of the best bars in Sydney. Oh, and some of them make games too!

'Eva said you're big on video games?'

I look up from my chat with Aneeshka to see one of Eva's friends giving me a friendly smile. It takes me a while to remember his name: Ethan. Normally I'd excuse myself, being in the middle of a conversation, but something about Aneeshka's last message has me feeling off.

Making games was *our* thing. No one else at our school was interested in creating games, not like we were. I assumed it would stay that special thing between us, despite being in separate cities. Except, what happens to us when she makes other good friends living in the same city as her, who are also devs *and* enjoy Aneeshka-esque things like drinking and partying? Where does that leave me in the picture?

I shove my phone into my pocket, and shove down the sourness in my gut.

'Yeah, I probably play too many games,' I say, forcing out a self-deprecating grin – a good way to break the ice, I've found. If Aneeshka can make new friends, I can too. 'How about you? Are you much of a gamer?'

Seeing as Eva has very minimal interest in video games, I don't expect any of her friends to either. Ethan is well-built, not in a gym addict kind of way, more like someone who was born into a large sturdy frame.

'I probably play too many as well,' he says with a laugh. 'Mostly multiplayer, with my sisters or my friends.' He gestures at Eva and the others scattered around the picnic mat and on the grass. 'Did Eva tell you I convinced her to play the entire *Portal 2* co-op campaign with me? A forever classic.'

'Oh, so *you're* the one I have to thank for the fact she recognises the *Portal* gun in my room now.'

'You have one?' He's genuinely excited, leaning in ever so slightly as though I'm about to produce a full-size plastic model from a magic 4D pocket. 'That's so cool.'

I shrug, trying to play it casual but also relieved to have a fellow nerd for company tonight. 'It's a very good dust collector, because when am I going to run around wielding a *Portal* gun that doesn't actually shoot portals?'

During a lull in her conversation, my sister glances over at us with a knowing smile. I'm almost certain she asked Ethan to talk to me since she knew we'd have common ground, and I wouldn't feel like the sixth wheel in their group.

'What games have you been playing lately?' he asks.

Truthfully, not much thanks to the upcoming showcase. And I don't really want to explain the Jay situation either. I simply say, 'Catching up on my backlog, so nothing new unfortunately. I swear, every time I think I'm getting somewhere Steam has another sale.'

His grimace is one of shared pain. 'I gave up trying. Somehow I always find myself going back to the multiplayer ones I've been playing with friends for years. I'll just pull in whoever's available and go.'

Almost all the games I've played are single-player. The only multiplayer ones I've played are with Aneeshka, and we didn't play many because we were so busy juggling school and developing our own games. Party games requiring at least four or five people were right out.

I lean back and stare up at the stars. We're far enough away from the main parts of the city that there's so many more visible, and they're gorgeous. 'How do you find so many people to play with?'

He shrugs. 'There's always a friend or two around. And it's not as fun playing on your own, you know?'

I beg to differ. Playing on your own means you win and lose on your own skill, not anyone else's. It means you don't need to go through the added complication of lining up a time when your few gamer friends are free, and then having to wait on them before you can play the game.

Also, it helps to have more than one friend who likes games. It was hard enough trying to wrangle a group larger than me and Aneeshka to go play an escape room that required at least four players, and that was a once-off thing. Well, she has enough new friends to go play with them now.

An opening band gets onto the temporary stage and starts playing, which ends the conversation. The music is nothing that spectacular, but Eva and her friends seem to be enjoying it. One of them, the friend who I *think* is called Tamara, offers me some cheese and crackers that someone brought along.

Someone's managed to acquire a bottle of wine from the cellar door. I'm not sure how and I don't ask. But being the driver for tonight, I keep well away from it. I'm still on my provisional licence and I'd lose it immediately if even a little alcohol was detected on my breath. I've never had any interest in alcohol apart from getting to that happy tipsy phase – at home, where no one can see the ridiculous things I do and I can tumble straight into bed.

I take a sip from the metal water bottle I brought along, then focus on the electronica-guitar sounds from the current band. It helps me ignore the nagging voice that says this was not a good choice of where I spend my night, because games don't code themselves. So what if Eva really wanted to come? Isn't my future more important? *That's why you won't make it like the Farrows*, the voice whispers. *You're not focused enough, not determined enough.*

You *are not enough*.

I wonder if I'll ever feel justified in giving up the university course and job that's planned out for me; expected of me. I feel guilty enough putting aside time to game, even though making games is what I do. I don't even want to reflect on what going out tonight says about how well I'll manage in a lifestyle where you're the only one who determines your work, your schedule and your success.

I'm jerked out of my thoughts by Eva, who grabs my left wrist and tugs me upright. The tempo of the song has changed to a fast-paced, upbeat one, and the grin on her face is infectious. How much is naturally her and how much is the half glass of wine she drank is yet to be determined.

'C'mon jie, let's dance!'

None of the people around us are dancing, but Probably-Tamara and Ethan are already up, their bodies moving to the music in ways mine never could. Hips twisting, shoulders rolling, arms doing . . . something . . . that complements what's going on. Even Liam and Probably-Linda are fair dancers, and the entire scene is enough to get some other people around us dancing too.

Eva laughs and tugs at me again. The only dances I know, however, are from retro games of *DDR*. She grabs both my wrists, the rest of her body still moving.

'C'mon!' she shouts. 'It's dark, who's gonna see? Dance with me like we're alone in the living room!'

Why the hell not? I don't know where the thought comes from, but I latch on to it. Why not indeed? I shake my arms around, pumping them up and down, letting my body do whatever it wants to do. It's not dancing – far, far from it – but it's fun, and I don't care. The other four join us and we each do our thing, bumping shoulders and hips and spinning one another around on occasion. My glasses even fall off once, it gets that wild.

This could be the basis of a really fun game. Not like *Let's Dance* where you have to follow exact moves; something more like controlling a character, or a character's actions, by wild flailing movements. The faster you flail, the faster they move.

It's an idea, anyway.

I pause for a breather because I'm tired and panting from the exertion. I can't remember the last time I did this much exercise in an entire week. While I'm resting, I check my phone for any panic-texts or missed calls from our parents. They're surprisingly quiet, though there *is* a text from Jay.

Jerky McJerkface

Same time same place tomorrow? Best believe I'm gaming tonight as a warm-up so prepare to be dominated.

He wants to trash talk me, he'll find out I give as good as I get. I ask Eva to take a picture of me with the stage at my back, in a classic Asian V-sign pose. The photo is super grainy in the dim lighting, but at least the details are visible.

Sam

Already celebrating my win. Same place, same time, same victor.

He responds with a picture of a TV showing the main screen of a co-op survival game, and in front of it, a messy coffee table with two Xbox Elite controllers, a can of Fanta and a can of apple cider.

Jerky McJerkface

Enjoy your night out, Udina, 'cause I'm having a much better night in ;)

That *does* look far more fun. What's with everyone having gaming friends? Or maybe it's a date night, in which case I hope they know what they're in for given Jay's winning personality. I swipe away the messaging app and take a large gulp of water from my drink bottle.

I don't get up again because Eva and her friends, who managed to start an entire dance section around us, have filtered back to the picnic mat. They're talking and laughing about some funny incident with a teacher at school who's always been well-known for his eccentricity.

I missed most of those big events at school that the whole grade would be talking about, only finding out about them in passing days later. Aneeshka and I didn't really have a friend group, being the programming-obsessed nerds we are. And now there isn't even Aneeshka to make in-jokes with, or to go to escape rooms with 'for inspiration' during the holidays, or to feel like there's someone with me on the same grind.

I wonder, sometimes, how that'll change after she has the freedom to party, date boys, get drunk and do all the things she only talked about before. She's already building another life for herself that doesn't include me.

Before I stew for too long, the opening band leaves and Wild February comes on to absolutely massive cheers. They don't have instruments. Each of them stands in front of a soundboard as large as a keyboard. And then . . . they *play*. Hip-hop fuses with classical music and is that jazz I hear peeking through? I find myself dancing, or at least moving my body in a semblance of it. I could spend the whole night doing this, that's how deeply their music resonates in my bones and worms into my brain.

I finally understand why my sister loves them. Their music would be excellent backing for a future game. Or, perhaps, their soundboards could become the basis of a game. So many ideas. If *Vinculum* makes it big, though, then I'll have the time and freedom to explore them all, ideally down in Sydney. That's the dream.

At the end of their set, my sister drags me to the stage so she can have her CDs signed. I take a photo of her with them, and insist on having one as well, I'm so exhilarated. I don't even mind that my sister wants to stay a bit longer before we head home. She's gushing about the band with her friends, I'm gushing with them, and for a blissful half hour I feel like I'm one of them. Like I'm part of a school group. This warm and fuzzy feeling only lasts until they start talking about where they're going next weekend, and I have to tell them I won't be coming. I make noncommittal noises when it comes to anything beyond that, which is basically my way of saying no without actually saying it.

One night out is enough. I don't have time to make and keep new friends.

When we arrive home, Eva has me park outside instead of going into the garage, and I soon find out why. She pulls out a bottle of wine from her bag.

'I had my friends grab one extra for us to drink once we arrived home, since I thought it wasn't fair you couldn't enjoy yourself as well.' She also pulls out two plastic cups. 'I didn't drink much so I could drink with you now.'

I size up the bottle. Having just seen the loose silliness of Eva's friends, I wouldn't mind going for it. Maybe if I get all loose and happy, I'll stop stressing over my game for the hour or two when the alcohol's in full swing.

Hell, why not. Might as well try to live like someone with a normal social life, the way Aneeshka seems to be doing down in Sydney. I can be as sophisticated as her when it comes to alcohol. It's not like I'm going to be doing any more coding tonight, anyway.

I open my door. 'Let's do this on the front lawn. I think there's some rule about not drinking while behind the wheel, even if the car's parked.'

We spill onto the lawn, and I lay out a small blanket from the back of the car. Eva follows with the wine and cups.

I take the cup she holds out. 'Fill me up.'

She pours till it's full, then does the same with hers. 'Here's to . . . here's to an awesome sister who came with me to a concert because our parents are overprotective.'

Our plastic cups meet, and we both take a sip. It's a white wine that tastes almost like fruit juice, and is actually quite delicious.

I raise my cup again. 'Here's to an awesome sister who has excellent taste in music.'

We both take another long swig, and silently contemplate our street for a while as we sip away at the wine.

After a while, Eva says tentatively, 'You know, you're welcome to hang out with me and my friends any time, especially now Aneeshka's in Sydney.'

My cup's already empty, and I hold it out for a refill. 'Thanks for the offer – I'll take you up on it when I'm free.'

She tops us both up with a lightly trembling hand. 'When'll that be? You're always busy with your games. After the showcase? You start uni not long after, and your course is meant to be super-intense.'

I haven't told anyone else yet, but maybe I can tell Eva. *Is this what people call liquid courage?* 'I . . . I don't know if I'm gonna do it. I want to take a gap year, except . . .'

Eva nods, understanding the silence. 'Yeah. 'Cause everyone knows you're the smart kid who's gonna bring honour to our family. Honour to us all. Honour to our cow. Wait. We don't have a cow. Honour to our four-wheel drive?'

I fake-bow to the car. 'Honour, honour.'

Her laughter spills out from wine-loosened lips. 'You dork.' After it dies down, she asks, 'When's the latest you can drop out of uni without any penalties?'

'I dunno, because the scholarship course isn't like their normal ones.'

'Mmm.' Eva frowns. 'Aren't you taking up a place that could go to someone else who wants it, if you don't drop out now?'

I am, and I feel bad about it. On the other hand, the thought of actually dropping out is equally terrifying when being a scholarship student is the one big thing everyone's expecting you to do.

'Yeah, but I still don't know if it's a good idea. I mean, it'll get me a great job at some tech firm when I graduate, which is a good thing, right?'

Even *I* know that doesn't sound convincing, and Eva's no fool. 'Sure, it's good if you like that,' she says, passing me the bottle.

How is this wine-juice-yet-funner-than-juice even sweeter from the source? 'Yeah, well, you try explaining that to all the aunties and uncles and pretty much any Asian in their generation. Why don't you become a musician after high school instead of going to uni, huh?'

'Ugh.' She makes a face as she takes the bottle back. 'Nope. Not because of what they'd all think. They already look at me like, *Oh, she's so Australian, not like all the good Asian kids*, so, whatever. For me, it's that if I had to earn enough money to make a living from my music I'd end up hating it. I don't know how you're not sick to death of coding day in and day out.'

'It's not just coding. It's also art and puzzle design and even basic psychology, I'll have you know.'

'I'll leave my "career" at writing music for a future bestselling video game, thank you very much.'

I raise the now-empty bottle. 'Wait till it gets so popular I start my own company and hire you on salary to be a songwriter.'

'That's official, no take-backs!'

We talk about everything and anything for I don't know how much longer. Eva is far more hilarious than she usually is and somehow she ends up giggling helplessly, which sets me off as well and neither of us can stop. The wine kicks in hard when we finally stumble towards our front door. When did our lawn get so bumpy and full of trip hazards? It's even more hilarious when I attempt to prove to her that I am not, in fact, drunk, and can walk in a perfectly straight line. I promptly catch my toe on the mat at the front door and crash into the security gate.

'Shhhh, jie!' Eva says, but she's not being very quiet herself as she unlocks the gate with unsteady hands, followed by the inner door.

We kick off our shoes inside, not bothering to put them on the shelf, and stumble down the entry hall into the living room. Our mum is asleep on the recliner, waiting for us. Eva tiptoes over and taps her on the shoulder to wake her.

'We're home,' she whispers as our mum blinks awake.

'Have a good night?' she asks.

We nod, and I lean over the back to give her a kiss on the cheek. 'Go back to your bed, we're safe.'

Her nose wrinkles. 'Have you been drinking?'

I quickly back away. 'Only juice, I wanted something sweeter than water.'

She's not convinced. 'Khoo Sun Sun, if you were drinking and driving—'

'I swear I wasn't, you know I wouldn't risk our lives like that,' I tell her quickly. 'We were on the front lawn.'

She rolls her eyes and pushes in the footrest of the recliner with a yawn. 'Wash up and go to bed, or you won't be able to wake up for church tomorrow,' she finally says with the kind of tone that means *we'll talk more about this tomorrow*.

'Night,' we chorus, and hurry upstairs.

The world shifts askew, one way then another, and my head is not liking it. Eva has to clean off her make-up. I, on the other hand, was smart enough not to wear any. The mere idea of collapsing into bed with outdoor clothes, however, is repulsive, and I'm sweaty. So I groan and drag myself into the shower for a quick rinse, head spinning the whole time. I'm still in the shower when the contents of my stomach come back up, and spend the next five minutes washing everything down the shower drain. Eva simply laughs at my plight, heartless witch that she is.

'Your jie doesn't drink, and she doesn't get carried away,' she says in a mocking imitation of our mum.

'It was too much liquid at one time, that's all,' I say as I towel myself off. 'My body's getting rid of excess liquid because I felt bloated.'

'Suuuuure.'

I collapse into bed at long last, hair still wet. I don't care if it means I'll have headaches for the rest of my life when I'm forty, according to the Gospel of Mother. I can't stay on my feet a moment longer.

CHAPTER 8

Future Devs Showcase: 20 days left

When my alarm goes off the next morning, it's physically painful. My head still feels weird, and moving sets my stomach lurching in all kinds of unpleasant directions. I thought I'd slept it off last night, but it seems I'm still being haunted.

Eva stumbles into the bathroom as I'm brushing my teeth, way too bright and ordinary for someone who drank as much as I did last night.

She takes one look at me and asks, 'Didn't you drink any water last night?'

'No,' I mumble around the toothbrush and foam filling my mouth. The words come out as fuzzy as my head feels. 'Should I have?'

I spit, rinse and groan softly at the world as I straighten up.

'Yep,' my sister says. 'Because now you have a hangover.'

This can't be. I have to compete with Jay in a few hours with a hangover?

Send help.

I get to the cafe almost ten minutes late. Although I'm flustered, I force myself to slow down when I'm outside and stroll in as though it was planned and not because I forgot to pack my controller and mouse, and had to race home after church to pick them up.

At least I'm feeling a bit better. My stomach's settled and the motion sickness feeling has receded somewhat. There's still a slight disorientation that lingers and twists at my insides, but it's nothing I can't manage. I'm ready to defeat Jay for a second week running.

As I step inside, the wooden ceiling fans beat a steady thuck-thuck, a muted version of the bass last night that I'd rather forget in my hungover state. I spot Jay in the back corner, with the same over-the-top laptop and keyboard set-up as last time. This week he's copied me and brought a controller as well. One of the Xbox Elites I saw last night. He means business.

Good, because so do I.

Strangely, the tables around him are empty, even though the cafe is rather busy. The reason becomes clear as I get closer. Even from a distance, the odour of artificially-scented body spray assaults my senses. Not only assaults – it grabs them in a chokehold, performs a vicious body slam, and pins them for the three-count.

If I wasn't hungover, it would merely be another irritating tactic from Jay the Jerk. But today it sets my stomach churning. I take slow shallow breaths and fix my face in an 'I'm so cool that I'm sauntering in late' expression of unconcern. He looks up at the sound of my sneakers against the wooden floor.

'Thought you were too scared to show, Udina,' he says, lifting a greasy burger from a plate beside him and taking a huge bite.

The smell of the burger and chips doesn't mix well with the already-overwhelming body spray, and the loud sound of him chewing can only be deliberate.

I plonk myself down on the chair, determined not to show him just how sick I'm feeling. He won't have the satisfaction of winning this first unspoken battle. 'I'm early in Asian Standard Time, thank you very much.'

He takes another big bite from the burger, watching me casually as he does so. 'Extrapolating from the picture you sent last night, I'm guessing you're simply late.' Another bite. 'Possibly at the tail end of a hangover, since you were at the Sirromet winery.'

I roll my eyes as I pull out my laptop and boot it up. 'Who's to say making you sit here and sweat isn't part of my strategy?'

'Sure, Udina. If it helps you feel better, go right ahead and pretend I believe you.' He pushes a full glass over. 'The internet says hydration is key, so I went ahead and got you an orange juice just in case.'

I push the glass back at him. 'I'm sure your sudden obsession with burgers and body spray has nothing to do with putting me off my game right before this round.'

He shrugs, sighs and takes back the glass. 'Your loss. I can't help it if I did some exercise before this and decided to spray up so I wouldn't offend your senses.' He reaches into his bag and before I can stop him, pulls out a can of deodorant and sprays himself liberally. 'Better, right?'

I choke down a retch. It's fine. I can manage. 'You're an ass. Are you here to actually compete, or do you have nothing better to do than attempt to torment someone you suspect has a hangover?'

'I'm not the one who was late.' He finishes his burger at last, cleans his oily fingers on a napkin, then pulls out a small pack of wet wipes from his bag and cleans off his fingers more thoroughly. 'Besides, you have the Bag of Fate.'

Oh, right. I find the small black bag and place it between us. Time to forget about the growing headache from his disgusting spray, and force my stomach to settle. 'Ready for Round Two?'

As he picks up the bag and examines it carefully, especially his drawing, I wave the waitress over. Her nose wrinkles as she approaches – it's not only me! – though she's completely professional as she asks me what I'd like. I order a green tea. It goes against my 'no purchasing teabags' policy, but I've seen Eva drinking it the morning after she's gone out with her friends so I hold some hope it'll help.

As she leaves, Jay nods to himself and tears the cling wrap open.

'I'll draw the game again,' he says, 'since you had the Bag of Fate all week. Then we'll trade next week. Fair?'

I don't care at this point. All that matters right now is finding the focus I need to win this round. 'Sure. Take your pick.'

He reaches in, and I hold my breath. Please don't let it be *We Can't Keep Meating Like This*. He pulls out a folded square. Opens one fold. Glances at me with a *Well?* look. Opens the second fold. Pauses again.

I stab a finger at the table. 'Put it down where we can both see and finish unfolding the damn thing already!'

'Where's your sense of the dramatic?' he asks, but does as I say and opens it.

Heaven's Complex.

Oh, thank all that is good and holy. The Bag of Fate is on my side again. It recognises the true hero and villain in this story. This guy thinks he can cheat to win? He'll get what's coming.

Jay glares at the paper slip. 'Your game again? Come *on*!'

He empties out the bag and unfolds the other slips quickly and efficiently. As I could have told him, they're the exact same slips he wrote on last week.

'You were the one who picked the game from the bag.' I can't stop the smirk as I connect my mouse to my laptop and adjust its settings so it moves across the screen at a zippy speed.

The movement is fast enough to make the cursor blur a little. That, combined with the lingering smell I can't erase from the back of my nose and throat, sets off a ripple in my stomach. Nothing I can't handle, though.

I take a sip of the green tea the waitress has just placed beside my laptop to stabilise my stomach before we start. 'Ready, or are you going to sulk for a few more minutes?'

HEAVEN'S COMPLEX

Puzzler (brains over brawn!). You're a
spirit who's awoken in a mysterious
complex where a booming voice in the
sky is talking at you. Collect orbs,
access additional worlds and work out
why you're being talked at. You get to
play with force fields, pew-pew lasers
and bouncy platforms that send
you flying!

He unceremoniously dumps the paper back into the bag, still looking at it as though it's personally offended him. Then he stands and stretches as though he's an athlete about to compete in a tournament and not a guy about to play a video game for a few hours.

'Yeah, yeah,' he says as he stretches one arm across his chest, then the other. 'Let's get started.'

As before, we turn our laptops so we can watch each other select a new game. I put my phone in the middle of the table and set the timer to three hours. There's a chance one of us will finish the game within that timeframe, but it's unlikely unless he's using glitchy speedrun tricks. From the way he reacted to the game being drawn, I suspect we'll both be solving the game normally.

'The person with the most orbs at the end of three hours wins,' I say, finger hovering over the timer on my phone.

He nods, eyes fixed on the screen. 'Ready? Go!'

I start the timer, then spin my laptop around and impatiently tap the space bar as the game goes through the opening sequence. The view shakes a bit as I turn my character with my mouse, since I set it to be super sensitive. Unfortunately, it also shakes my stomach at the same time. *Oh, no.* Now I remember how I got motion sickness when I played this game for too long. With my brain still refusing to process inputs normally and Jay deliberately making everything worse, this will kill me.

What have I done?

It would be so easy to blame everything on the troll across from me. Deep down, though, I know exactly whose fault it is.

He merely took advantage of my state. I'm furious at myself as I ignore my dangerously churning stomach to grab the orbs in the starting area.

The initial four are easy. The problem is the final orb. It requires quick movement to avoid two wandering wolf sentinels. Normally this wouldn't be an issue. Today, however, every time I jerk the mouse for a quick change of direction, my stomach follows suit. My head is spinning from all the movement.

How will I last three hours? I'm not even ten minutes in and I'm already close to spewing. I take a gulp of the green tea, burn my mouth, suck in disgustingly scented air with a hiss and keep going. I will get through this even if it kills me.

I have to lower the sensitivity on my mouse so the character doesn't turn as quickly . . . but that also means the character doesn't turn as quickly. The game has motion sickness options, which I already turned on for my previous playthroughs. There is one that slows down your character except I refuse to use it. Not this early on. Jay is guaranteed to be playing at full speed and he doesn't deserve a single advantage, no matter what it does to me.

Curse the game designers for making each area so large that I have to run between the various puzzles. I appreciated it when I first played, though what I wouldn't give for them to automatically transport me from one puzzle area to another right now. At least I can hope it will slow Jay down, if he can't remember where to go next.

Eventually I resort to closing my eyes when I know I have to run in a straight line, peeking on occasion to confirm I haven't overshot. Despite my best efforts, bile slowly rises in my throat, and I'm glad I didn't eat anything for lunch today. Swallowing hard, I push on. There's no time to be sick. Mind over matter.

I keep the character running, refusing to slow down even though my head is pounding more heavily. After completing the current area, I get to an area that involves a lot more jumping. Jumping means jerky shifts of my character's view and it's not a particularly pleasant experience.

Mind over matter, mind over matter. I keep repeating the words, a mantra to keep everything together and, more importantly, to keep everything down. At one point, Jay reaches for his body spray, and I've had enough.

I slam a palm down on the table and rise from my chair so I'm towering over him. 'Touch that can and you'll learn exactly what it means to be sprayed in the face at point-blank range.'

He laughs, moving his hand back to his mouse while his left hand continues to tap away at the keyboard. That's when I realise I've been played. I snatch the spray can from him, place it by my chair leg with a glare and keep going.

I complete the entire first world about fifty minutes in and move on to the next world. Which introduces bouncers. Bouncers are platforms that toss objects through the air. Objects, and you. It's when I'm tumbling through the air the second or third time that my matter decides it will no longer mind me.

The taste of green tea mixed with remnants of breakfast floods my mouth, and my glasses fog up from my watering eyes. I glance up quickly at Jay and thankfully he's staring down at his screen, too tied up in the game to notice. So I stare out the windows at the front of the cafe, into the distance, and force myself to swallow. It's so, so, *so* gross and I never want to do anything like that again. But desperate times call for desperate measures. The green tea washes down the lingering sourness, though after today, I don't think I'll be able to drink it again for a good long while.

I can't give up, not when Jay's brow is stitched into a frown and I know he's struggling with his current puzzle. I'll take it slow. Dial down the character speed to the lowest possible setting. No more running, only walking. Careful mouse movements. Close eyes when thrown through air, wait, open only when I'm certain I'm back on the ground.

It's frustrating, and more than once I have to shove down the anger, the blame: *How irresponsible are you, getting drunk when you had an important competition the next day? So much for being the reliable older sister. This is meant to be* your *game and you're blowing it. Do you want to be that person who fails when push comes to shove?*

I have never been more relieved to hear the alarm on my phone. I cannot hit the escape button fast enough to bring me to the menu, as I swivel my laptop around. Jay swivels his around too, though he's still in the game. Same area as me, I realise. It all comes down to how many puzzles we've solved here.

'Go back to the menu,' I tell him, but he pauses at the warning that all unsaved progress will be lost. So I add, 'It saves every time you collect an orb, which is what we're counting.'

'I know,' he says, though he still clicks on it with great reluctance. 'I was so close to finishing that puzzle, though. Now I'll have to remember how to do it all over again.'

He copies me as I choose the *View Progress* option from

the menu. This screen conveniently shows the number of orbs you've collected. I check mine – seventy-seven orbs. I glance over at Jay's.

He has seventy-seven orbs as well.

Jay doesn't look pleased at the tie. 'We can't stop here. We need to decide on a winner. I propose the first person to get one more orb wins.'

It's a reasonable suggestion, and much as I want to object, I can't find a good reason to. 'You have an advantage because you were close to finishing that puzzle.'

He crosses his arms. 'Except I lost all my progress when *you* made me quit to the main menu.'

'Fine.' Thankfully that was the easiest way to compare the number of orbs collected. If I can solve the next puzzle fast enough, I might still win this. 'Let's finish this.'

'Ready?' he asks. 'Load from the latest backup.'

'Go!' I say, and we spin our computers back around.

I waste valuable time realising my movement speed is still set to slow, and changing it back to the fastest one. I'll deal with the motion sickness later. I don't run to the nearest puzzle, but one slightly further off that's less labyrinthine. *C'mon level design knowledge, don't fail me.*

I keep my entire focus on the screen, doing my best to ignore the world spinning queasily around it. *One more, just one more.* I've got the last laser in place and the final barrier is down, the orb in sight.

'YES!'

Jay's yell echoes through the cafe as he spins his laptop

around in time for me to see the orb he collected zip up to the top corner.

I . . . lost.

I would've beaten him handily if I didn't have to slow down my movement.

If he had nothing on me to take advantage of.

If I hadn't been trailing a hangover.

If I hadn't relaxed and enjoyed the wine-fuelled chat with Eva last night.

If I hadn't gone out at all.

If I hadn't lost focus on the *one* goal I've been working towards for years.

Slumping into the chair, I tilt my head back to stare up at the ceiling where the fans lazily spin around and around in unending circles.

'Congratulations,' I manage to croak out.

Then I race to the toilet, and throw up.

When I emerge from the bathroom, I avoid Jay's gaze even though I can feel it on me as I pack my laptop. It's humiliating as hell to keep my head down, as though I'm bowing before the winner, but it would be even worse if he noticed my puffy eyes. The last thing I want is for him to think I was actually crying – the tears from my intense upchucking did all the work. Knowing him, he'd take it as an even more comprehensive defeat and I will *not* give him that satisfaction.

I throw his can of body spray back at him and go to the counter to pay the bill and have the Bag of Fate cling-wrapped for next week. I stare at the server's hands as he wraps it, frustration twisting my insides. The Bag handed me a big opportunity, and I wasted it.

Although it's infuriating to lose to Jay after all my trash talk, the worst part is how the loss is no one's fault but my own. This cannot – will not – happen again. No more distractions like nights out or watching random sitcom episodes or reading webtoons. Definitely no more social media, either, aside from chatting with Aneeshka since she's in Sydney. I don't need more friends. I need a hugely successful game.

The server's also kind enough to lend me a marker, and I draw the logo I created for my one-person 'studio' as a reminder of the only thing that matters. Two stylised suns, overlapping. Let Jay puzzle over that if he's so inclined; he won't find any information about my studio without a name.

I dump the cling-wrapped bag and marker on the table as I pass and snatch up the cash he's left there for his drink and burger, pausing only to issue a challenge and show him I'm not done yet. 'Same time next week. I won't play dirty like you, but don't expect any mercy.'

His hand closes tight around the bag. 'Udina—'

'What do you want?' I keep my face turned away from his, my voice clipped and formal. 'Is there something else to discuss?'

There's a long pause. At first I think he's deliberately waiting for me to look at him before he'll deign to answer and nearly leave, till I notice his fingers clenching and unclenching around the bag. He takes a breath and seems about to say something once, then twice, but nothing.

I'm not sure why I'm waiting around. If it's an apology, I don't want it. I know I turned up in sub-par condition even if I'll never admit it to him, and anything he offers up now will do nothing except twist that sword in deeper.

All he says is, 'You're on, Udina. Get ready to be defeated again next week.'

You know what, who cares if my eyes are puffy? That claim will not go unanswered.

I face him straight on. 'Dream on, jerkface. Next week, you're through.'

Then I march out to my car. When I get home, I'm going to throw myself straight into *Vinculum*. I'll push through the lingering nausea because I don't have time to be sick. I'll keep playing through the levels and find ways to break the game, then break it more till I've dug out all the flaws.

This coming week, every moment I'm not sleeping, eating or maintaining some semblance of family relations will be spent working on my game. Every night I'll put aside an hour or so to play the games Jay selected for the competition, and get a feel of the controls.

I might not be a natural when it comes to making and playing games. That's fine. I'll simply be the one who works the hardest.

CHAPTER 9

Future Devs Showcase: 18 days left

I stay on schedule Monday, feeling proud of myself. This is the discipline I need.

The pride of succeeding gets me through a tougher Tuesday, where every little thing threatens to blow up into a distraction. Especially when Aneeshka sends through a text that makes me wonder if she's coping with the stress.

Aneeshka

> I was talking with some of my new friends, the ones who'll be in my course and make games

Aneeshka

Aaaaaaand ... I may have been inspired to make a new game that I want to bring to the Future Devs Showcase instead

Sam

YOU *WHAT*?

Aneeshka

It was also inspired by the art exhibition I went to. I know it's the one, and I can have a proof of concept ready in three weeks if I do nothing else

Sam

You've been working on *MetaVision* since Year Eleven!

Aneeshka

I know, I know. I think it's a risky gamble too. But my gut says this one'll be good and I want to take a chance on it.

Sam

You were chosen for the showcase because of *MetaVision*, though! Will they let you bring a substitute?

I'll bring it too, though I'll make this new game the focus. I think that kinda gets me around the rules :P

Sam

Are you sure this isn't last-minute 'I will now sabotage myself' nerves? Because it's sure looking that way.

Sam

And when do I get to know more about this new game of yours?

Aneeshka

I want to surprise you with it at the showcase. I promise, it'll be worth it – I'll test it with everyone in Sydney first so you get to see the awesome version!

Sam

It better be amazing, 'cause I'm not letting you throw away your big chance if it isn't!

I don't know if I trust Aneeshka's so-called 'friends' in Sydney, talking her into these wild ideas. At the very least, they don't seem to have the first clue about actual game development, and it shows.

While everyone is doubling down on getting their games for the showcase polished, she's starting on something completely different and hoping it'll work out. Some pretty awesome stuff comes out of game jams that are only two to three days long, but this is a showcase of what they're calling 'up-and-coming talent' to pre-vetted Big Deal Publishers. They're looking for games that are far enough along to not be high-risk.

Well, that's her and her new friends' problem. I've already raised my issues with it and I don't want to sound like that nagging mum who won't shut up. When it comes to showcase time and this new game is a disaster, I'll be there to help her pick up the pieces and make sure *MetaVision* is good to go. She'll realise that maybe, just maybe, her new friends aren't all they're cracked up to be.

Not that I'm feeling left out or anything.

At dinner that night, Eva wolfs down her rice like she's been starving for days.

'Eat slower,' our mum tells her. 'How was your second day of Year Eleven?'

Eva shrugs but doesn't stop shovelling. 'Same as yesterday. I need to run in five minutes because I've got a video chat with Tamara and Linda. They want to make sure we're the planning team for our grade's semi-formal.'

Our mum frowns. 'This year and next year are most important for your schooling, why are you taking up even more things? Are you still going to do Choir and Strings and Bible study and leading the youth at your other church on weekends?'

'It's not that much more,' Eva says between bites, 'and I want to do it with them. We already missed so many bits and pieces of school life thanks to the lockdowns at the start of high school, so I want to spend more time with my friends in person.'

'Your cousins, they're only in Year Eight and Nine but they have so much homework every night, your dai gu jie said they stopped doing drama after school this year because they're so busy.'

Eva's shovelling finally slows down. 'Gu jie sends them to extra tuition classes and they want to be top of their grade, of course they don't have time. I'd rather have more life experiences and learn by doing. Isn't that what you and Daddy always say is important?'

Our oldest aunt on my dad's side is a lot stricter on our cousins than our parents have ever been on us, and the difference shows in our academic results. My parents must have felt vindicated in their parenting choices after I won the scholarship, because they stopped with the subtle comparisons after that.

Our mum's stopped eating. 'Balance is also important. You don't need to get straight A's like your jie, but you should at least be trying for B's and not settling for C's like your gwei lo friends. With better grades you have more options in life, and can choose what experiences you want. Maybe they have parents who think they're adults and can do whatever they want. You're still sixteen and don't know enough of the world yet. You don't want to regret this in the future.' She sighs. 'Do you know how hard your jie had to work in Year Eleven and Twelve? It's not as easy as Year Ten, you know.'

'Ugh.' Eva stops eating as well and leans back in the dining chair, eyes raised to the ceiling as though she's asking for patience. 'Fine, I'm just like a gwei lo, okay? A fake-Asian with white friends who does activities instead of studying or whatever.' She deliberately looks away from me as she continues, 'And I'm not the kid who's gonna stay home in front of my computer all day and get academic awards and a big-deal uni scholarship. C'mon, jie isn't even—'

She stops herself before I fling my plate at her to shut her up. Even though I'm furious I can't explain why to my parents, so I have to swallow it down.

Eva changes tack. 'Jie didn't even study that hard. You know she spent most of her time in her room making her games instead.'

I drop my fork and spoon onto the melamine plate with a clatter, droplets of black gravy splattering onto the table. She stopped herself before blabbering my secret, fine. Except what came after was even worse.

I thought Eva, at least, would understand how important creating games is to me.

Bitterness twists my heart, my tongue, my words. 'I have a goal I'm working towards. How about you? Go waste your time on unproductive hobbies that won't take you anywhere.'

I want to take back those words as soon as I say them, but it's too late. They're already out there, gleaming sharp like a finely honed weapon, dripping with blood. We know each other too well; know each other's weaknesses so we can land critical hits if we're not careful.

Eva and I stare at each other for a long moment, both knowing we've messed up, neither sure how to broach it or wanting to be the one to start. In the end, I push my chair back and stand up.

'Thank you for the meal, it was delicious,' I tell our mum automatically. 'I'm full.'

I go straight to my room, hating myself for running away like a coward. Across the hall, I hear Eva's bedroom door slam shut not long after. I lie on the carpet, staring up at a ceiling as blank as the so-called career I want to have, surrounded by walls full of video game art I can never hope to emulate.

Who knows how long later, my phone buzzes with two texts. I groan and pull myself upright to check. Because what if it's Eva, texting to apologise?

Jerky McJerkface

Just raced through *We Can't Keep Meating Like This* as a light warm-up, as you do

His next message is a photo of the two main characters framed in a sausage heart, happily mincing meat and making pies together for the rest of their lives, I assume.

107

> Be afraid. Be very afraid.
> My superior skills in every aspect
> will leave you crying for mercy.

After the crap he pulled on Sunday, he has the nerve to act as though nothing happened? But I happen to be upset and in need of a punching bag right now, so lucky him.

Sam

> You're certainly superior when it comes to
> screwing people over. Congratulations.

Even though I see those three bouncing dots on his side of the conversation, his reply takes a while to come back.

Jerky McJerkface

> I must've missed it; which of the agreed
> rules did I break? Did I mess with your
> laptop or interrupt your game somehow
> while you were playing? C'mon, I didn't
> even know if you'd turn up hungover,
> but you did, unless you're going to
> blame me for that too.

He.
Did.
Not.
Say.
That.

> Wait wait wait wait. Are you saying that what you did is my fault because I had a few drinks, and my fault for having a hangover?

How dare that sack of breathing garbage turn his choices into my problem? We had classes on emotional manipulation at school. I can already see Aneeshka yelling at me in all-caps to CLOCK HIM IN THE FACE GOOD. If she were here, that is.

Jerky McJerkface

> What? No! It'd be *my* fault for not anticipating an opponent's potential weakness and exploiting it for victory. That's not screwing someone over. It's more like fighting enemies with elemental weaknesses.

While it's still a jerk move, him trying to justify his actions is a thousand times better than trying to blame them on me. Which is, admittedly, a very low bar. I'm about to respond when I see the three dots again. Very well, let him dig himself into a deeper hole with his rationalisations before I blast them – and him – apart.

To my surprise, my phone starts buzzing with a call from a certain Jerky McJerkface instead. I reject the call. Five seconds later, it rings again and I reject it again. Another five seconds, and the guy's still trying. I'll give him some credit for persistence. With a sigh, I give in and pick up before it rings at full blast and my family wonders who's calling me at this time of night.

Jay's voice is boisterous and unconcerned as always. This guy has the thickest skin I've ever seen. 'You finally picked up, Udina! I figured I'd call you because it'd take forever to type this out and I didn't want to leave you with the wrong idea.'

I don't mind yelling at him over the phone instead of through text. It's more satisfying anyway. 'Go ahead, then.'

'I'm never going to say this again so listen well.' He sighs. 'After the first round I knew I had to take every single advantage I could get. You're incredibly good when it comes to puzzle games, and I'd be a fool to underestimate you when it comes to your game picks. I mean, I did a refresher on the game last week, and we still ended up tied at seventy-seven orbs each. I'd have gifted you the round if I'd treated you as an easy opponent instead of a boss fight.'

Oh. Somehow he's managed to de-arm and de-fang me with a single statement. He didn't look down on me. He didn't think I was a nothing who couldn't accomplish anything. Instead he had me pegged as a serious threat, and saw himself as the underdog. I can almost forgive him for what he did. Almost.

My voice is flat as I reply, 'Still a low blow, Jaybird. All your nice-sounding words don't change it.'

'I'll embrace it. Because remind me, who won Round Two? On a game that wasn't theirs? It's the results that matter in the end, Udina. That's all the world sees.'

The audacity of this guy. 'Did you just pull the *I'm not here to make friends, I'm here to win* line on me?'

'I'm not gonna be the fool who gives his opponents openings "because honour" or whatever. We're not in a shounen anime.'

That makes me laugh for the first time tonight. I know the intended audience for shounen is young boys, but sometimes I just want the power of friendship to triumph, mmkay?

'Too bad we aren't, because then you'd be the minor villain the heroes teach a lesson to.'

'I don't even rate as the main villain?' He pauses, then adds in mock outrage, 'Wait, why am I even accepting the villain role? I call a miscast!'

'"Respected rival" requires giving your opponent openings "because honour". Not tormenting them until they throw up.'

'So you *did* throw up!'

What the hell did he think happened? 'Yeah, hence the hasty exit stage left after the game. If I so much as get a whiff of that disgusting body spray again I will ensure the next mess gets emptied all over your fancy laptop.'

His laughter is starting to feel warm, like friends sharing a joke, instead of disparaging. 'We both know the only way you'll win on my games is to destroy my gear. You have no chance otherwise.'

It's weird how it feels okay to talk about it now, because I know he's not looking down on me. He fears me as his opponent. Respects me. So what if I threw up? It simply means I need to outmanoeuvre him next time.

There's something about Jay's insults and taunts that stokes the competitive fire in me. It's exactly the kind of line that fires me up enough to smash past the blame I've heaped on myself, so I can focus on next week's competition. If I was inclined to give him the benefit of the doubt, I'd wonder if he's using this kind of competitive trash talk to coax me back into some semblance of normal, as a kind of apology.

It gives me the confidence to ask him a question that's been bugging me since this started. 'How come you're so desperate to attend the workshop, anyway?'

'Uh, because I'm a huge *Negatory* fan like you.'

He states it as a matter of fact, instead of questioning me on every tiny factoid about the game to prove I'm a 'real' fan. Boy, it feels good.

'But for the record,' he continues, 'the ticket is not for me. It's for my brother.' There's a subtle hesitation in his voice I wouldn't have picked up if I hadn't just heard him talk so confidently. 'Last year was rough for him, and he's probably a bigger fan of *Negatory* than either of us. Won't stop talking about it.'

'You're not spinning me some sob story so I'll go easy on you, are you?' There's not much suspicion in my tone, because I do believe him, but I'll tease him if I get the chance.

Thankfully, he laughs. 'And what if I am?'

'Seeing my awesome skills scared you into coming up with some fresh dirty tactics, hey?'

This back-and-forth is relaxed; I don't need to worry about being too much for him because he'll give as good as he gets. Perhaps he feels the same.

'Wait till one of my games comes up. This is my week, I can feel it. Don't cry when I soundly defeat you, Udina.'

'You wait and see; I'll make you eat your words. They'll be bitter to swallow, I guarantee it.'

'I am a master bitter melon eater, I'll have you know. Where others run from it, I embrace it.'

I roll my eyes even though he can't see it. 'Is that really something you're boasting about?'

'Wait till you're at dinner with aunties and uncles you want to impress. They love that there are still people in our generation who like eating that thing.'

'Oh, so you only eat it because you want to show off. Sounds about Jay.'

'I enjoy it too, thank you very much. Fried with sambal belacan, it adds an extra layer to the flavour. Or with salted egg, yum.'

Aaaaand now he has me drooling over the thought of sambal belacan, because even though the spicy shrimp paste stinks up the house whenever my mum cooks with it, it's delicious. The fact that we can relate over these foods that most other people would have no clue about? Also delicious, in that comforting homemade food way.

Because whether it's food or gaming, I don't need to code-switch the way I do to make my Malaysian-ness more palatable to others at school – or, more importantly, to make gaming more palatable to my parents.

I can just be Sam, foodie and gamer and overall nerd.

'I'd better go, Jaybird, but get ready for an ass-whooping this weekend.'

'Right back at you, Udina.'

When we hang up, I pull up a chat with Eva. So what if she underestimates me? My family have yet to see career success come from my games. All I need to do is work harder and prove myself to them, the way I did with Jay in the earlier rounds of our competition.

Sam

I'm sorry

Eva

Me too. Wanna come to my room to talk?

Sam

Sure thing, coming now

CHAPTER 10

Future Devs Showcase: 17 days left

Tonight is the first inaugural family game night, as thought up by Eva and pitched by me. After vague apologies on both sides last night, we decided to find a way to explain to our parents how all her non-academic activities are equally important learning experiences.

After talking to her friends at school today, Eva ended up convinced that chatting while playing games together would be a lot less awkward than trying to sit them down for a serious talk.

'You suggest it, jie,' she said to me when she got home from school, 'because if it's me they'll go on about how I should be using that time to study because of all my other activities. But if it's you, since you don't go out as much and you're the one they hold up as an example, then they'll agree for sure.'

I wanted to protest, but the 'since you don't go out as much' aside, it was probably true that they were more likely to agree if the suggestion came from me. And I wanted to be a good big sister to Eva, so despite it destroying my carefully scheduled week, I did it to help her out.

Which is why my parents are seated at the dining table as I clear the dinner plates, while Eva brings out the games we'll be playing. I catch a glimpse of Uno and Rummikub as she enters the dining room – good choices, as our parents know how to play them. Best to start with something familiar before working them up to the *good* classic board games like Ticket to Ride or Hanabi.

Eva's eager to start, so I leave the dishes in the sink and wipe down the table, insisting our parents remain seated all the while. The moment they get up to do anything else, we'll lose them.

We start with Rummikub, plastic tiles clattering on the glass top of the dining table as we spread them out facedown and mix them. I swear my dad takes a peek at one tile, but I decide not to kick up a fuss before the game's even begun. Eight hands reach out and grab at tiles until we all have fourteen on our rack. Mine's sorted by colour, in ascending order. We each pick one more tile to see who starts – our mum gets the highest number, so she goes first.

She takes one look at her rack, determines she doesn't have a high enough combination to start play and draws a tile.

'Finished your homework today?' she asks Eva, as our dad contemplates his rack then draws a tile.

Eva shuffles the tiles around on her rack, rearranging them carefully. 'We don't have much yet, since school just started.' She switches back to English. 'But I'm already studying some pieces that we'll be covering in Music this year. I got interested in making arrangements because of Choir and Strings. Like the simplified pop song I did for your piano student over the holidays.'

Our mum smiles at her. 'I forgot to tell you, they were very excited about the score! It was the first time I've seen them eager to go home and practise.'

'I can do a few more if you want,' Eva offers. 'It won't take me long. I can also do any other songs you want for your students.'

She places a four-tile combination on the table. With a sum of over thirty, it means she's officially 'entered' the game.

'I'll ask them this week,' our mum replies. 'You're great at arrangements; you should do some for church.'

It's my turn, and I don't have a big enough combo to enter the game, so I draw a tile. 'Yeah, Eva's got a really wide range of skills. I'm envious.'

Am I a supportive big sister, or am I a supportive big sister?

It never fails to amaze me how diverse Eva's talents are. She sings, plays the piano and cello and guitar, does arrangements our piano-teacher mum admires, can climb the most difficult courses at the indoor rock-climbing facility she frequents, gets into the top division school netball team every year, leads a group of youth at the other church she attends on Sundays (all of whom love her to bits). She's done so much. Everyone can see her brilliance. If she wanted to take a gap year after school to work on her music, no one would object.

'Hey, don't put yourself down,' Eva says with a grin that never leads to anything good. 'You make excellent instant noodles.'

I grab a tile from the mix and throw it at her. 'I could cook if I wanted to. I choose to make instant noodles because of efficiency. Fast, easy and delicious.'

'And bad for you if you eat too much,' our mum chips in with a meaningful glance at me. 'I'll make more for dinner and put the leftovers in containers, so I don't have to find you staring at the pantry every day trying to find something instant.'

She doesn't get what true efficiency is. 'I have to heat up the leftovers and wash all the containers and my plate! If I make instant noodles I only have to wash the pot.'

'It's not proper food,' she says as she puts down her opening combo, a run of seven to ten of the same colour. 'There's no nutrition.'

'*Anyway.*' I hastily change the topic. 'I'll cook more after the showcase is over and I have more time. Life is about more than what you learn in school and university, especially as an adult.'

I'm pretty proud of this comment. Not only does Eva see me bringing up the idea she wanted to talk about and I earn good-sister points with her, it's also a good way to feel my parents out on the whole 'taking a gap year' thing.

'It's true that most of what you learn, you learn on the job,' our dad says as he draws yet another tile. 'But your degree is what opens those doors for you. You think your ma and I would have been able to migrate here without degrees?'

'There's more options these days,' I counter. 'With the internet, you can learn what you need, gain an audience, find other ways to make a living.'

'Sun Sun.' Our dad gestures at Eva to indicate it's her turn. 'You're a good big sister, looking out for your mui, but you shouldn't encourage her to take on an impossible dream of becoming a musician after high school. Life is hard, and a career like that is even harder.'

Our mum nods in agreement, turning to Eva. 'You need a backup plan, Yun Yun.' She uses Eva's pet name, so she's not angry or anything. Just firm. 'With the scholarship course, your jie can easily get a job at any company while working on her games. You should follow her example.'

I pretend to sort my tiles, unable to look at them or at Eva. How can I tell them what I want to do now? I won't have any cred if I can't get a publisher at the showcase.

'Don't worry,' Eva says. She starts placing her tiles on the table, combo after combo. 'I'm still planning on becoming an occupational therapist. I'm not as serious about my music as jie is about making games.'

I try to sound nonchalant as I say, 'Sometimes if you find success, you have to pursue it no matter where it takes you, don't you think?'

Our dad laughs. 'If either of you does that well, then of course you should.'

'You should still have that backup plan,' our mum adds quickly. Her side-eye game is on point. 'Careers like that can change quickly. One success doesn't mean a lifetime of success, and you want to make sure you can always find work.'

To my surprise, Eva nods in agreement. 'One of my friends at the other church decided to pursue acting, and even though they're earning enough to live on their own, it's really stressful because they have to do whatever it takes to get jobs, or take on other part-time work. I definitely don't want to do that, I'd rather enjoy music.'

'But would your friend want any other kind of lifestyle?' I ask as she ponders over her remaining tiles. 'Would they be happier if they'd gone to university and got a non-acting job?'

Eva knows where I'm headed with this. 'No, I don't think they'd be happier. They're the type who doesn't mind extra stress and working all hours if they're chasing their dream.'

I nod, and she continues, 'Except that's not me. I'd rather take it slow, enjoy life as it happens. I don't like focusing on academics only when there are so many fun things to try. As long as I can get into the course I want and later, find a job where I can go home and turn off, what's wrong with that?'

Our parents exchange glances, and finally it's our mum who speaks. 'As long as you can support yourself, that's all we want for you, Yun Yun.'

That's the baseline I have to meet.

'I'll be fine; I know how to manage my time,' Eva says. At least it's not in her irritated tone. 'So you trust me too, okay?'

'We'll see how your grades go,' is all our mum says. That counts as concession on behalf of both of our parents.

'I know, I know,' Eva says with a roll of her eyes. 'Jie, your turn.'

I glance at the tiles on the table, then my own. Mine are

nothing special, but I can probably get rid of half of them from the combinations already on the table. Time to start rearranging.

Over the click-click of plastic on glass, Eva says, 'By the way, Tamara's family is holding a heroes and villains themed party at their house on the Friday three weeks from now, and they want to invite all of you. I thought we could do a group costume as a family, and dress up as the characters from *Journey to the West*.'

'You could do that with your friends,' our mum replies, to absolutely no one's surprise. 'I don't know Tamara's parents, and I'm too old for these costume things.'

'Linda's whole family is going. You've talked to her mum before,' Eva counters. 'And they're all dressing up as well; they're going as The Avengers. That's how I got the idea for our family. You'll have the chance to meet them, and see they're good parents too.'

Guess I'd better back her up. 'It could be fun. And I'll—' Suddenly the date sinks in. 'Wait, that's when I'm in Sydney for my showcase. I'm sorry, Eva.'

Her face falls. 'Oh.' She glances at our parents. 'Mummy, Daddy, you'll come, right? It'll be a lot of fun, and you said you wanted us to spend more time together.'

Neither of them looks convinced.

'You know me and your ma aren't party people,' our dad speaks up while our mum busies herself with putting out tiles. 'This seems more like an event for you young people to enjoy.'

'Yeah, I should've known,' Eva says. Her shoulders are slumped, but there's real frustration in her voice. 'Forget I asked.'

'Why don't you ask your friends over for dinner?' our mum offers. 'I can make food for you all. You said they liked my chow mein when you brought it to school yesterday.'

'That's not the point.' Eva controls her disappointment well, and I feel guilty that I can't make it so she'll have at least one family member there. 'Don't worry about it.'

Eva's mood remains low for the rest of the game, which our mum wins. I don't think anyone's up for another round, so I throw my hands in the air. 'You trashed us, Mummy. I'm ready to surrender!'

Also, I *really* need to get back to work on *Vinculum*.

'You think you can beat your mummy so easily?' she says with a laugh. She collects the tiles and returns them to the box. 'Remember who taught you everything growing up. I still lose most games of Rummy to your Poh-Poh, so of course you'll lose to me.'

As we all leave the table, I glance over at the dishes in the sink. I should really offer to do the washing-up so my parents don't have to, since they were both working today. But I've already lost almost an hour playing Rummikub, and with all the pots and pans, it'll take me another twenty minutes at least.

Then Eva rolls up her sleeves. 'Thanks for making time for the games night,' she says to me. 'I'll do the washing-up. You go work on your game so you can make it big at the showcase and show Mummy and Daddy you can make it on your own. Make it worth missing the best party in Brisbane.'

I nudge her. 'We'll find some way to convince them to go.'

'Nah. There's no point if they don't want to come. I should've known it'd be too "childish" for them.' She even makes the air quotes. 'They're more understanding than a lot of Asian parents, but they'd never mix with my Australian friends' parents. Now go! Get to work!'

I give her a one-armed squeeze. 'Thanks. Love you, Eva.'

She flicks water at me. 'Love doesn't bring home the big bucks, so you better not forget your promise to hire me on salary when you hit the big time.'

'Soon,' I promise her. 'Really soon.'

I don't dive straight into my game when I reach my room, because my schedule has an hour-long practise session blocked out for *We Can't Keep Meating Like This*. I feel really guilty sticking my sister with the chores so I can play a game (as opposed to working on *Vinculum*), but remind myself that getting to the Farrows' workshop at PopSplosion and pitching to them is also part of my grand career plan.

The opening of the game is cute, although the story makes no sense. But I guess it doesn't have to. While it starts off adorably cartoon-y, the menu screen has an eighties arcade game aesthetic, which already gives me a sinking feeling about my chances.

The first few levels are simple introductions to the movement. The game designer in me notes how satisfying the sound effects are – they give the movement a solid, visceral feel. I make a note to add footstep sounds to *Vinculum*.

Then I get to the slaughterhouse levels with exposed spinning saws to avoid. The initial one is easy. One jump, and

WE CAN'T KEEP MEATING LIKE THIS

Platformer set in a slaughterhouse, chock-full of instruments of death. Get your buff, cleaver-wielding butcher to the end of each level of a deadly labyrinth, while chasing an angry bull who escaped mincing and has now kidnapped your girlfriend. Try not to die. Die repeatedly. Yell.

I'm over. The other two, however, are in close succession. Unsurprisingly, I die on my first attempt. The second attempt sees me jump too early, attempt to recover, then mash the jump button in a panic until I end up hitting a saw for instant death.

And this is one of the early levels.

I groan and bury my head in my hands. The other two games Jay and I played were manageable, but this? I'm so hopeless.

Stubborn determination makes me pick up the controller once more. I nearly die again, then manage to make a save with a frantic jump backwards onto safe ground. Once more. This time, I get to the end of the level.

On and on I go, bloodstains that mark each death splattered all over the levels like the grotesque aftermath of paintball. There are walls that crumble after one bounce, blades that move, platforms full of spiky death. There's a lot of swearing under my breath, and a lot more contemplation of how hard I can throw my controller through the screen.

Oddly enough, the game turns out to be rather addictive. Perhaps it's sheer bloody-mindedness, but despite my internal screaming I find myself set on completing each level. When my alarm rings to let me know an hour is up, I set it for one more hour. After all, I need the practice, don't I?

When it goes off again an hour later, I'm still being killed, repeatedly, in the first boss battle. I'm not sure if I'm grateful for the reprieve, or annoyed that I won't get the chance to try again because next time, dammit, is going to be the one where I defeat the boss!

Closing the game, I open my latest build of *Vinculum*. I'm back to working out why this level or that level feels too much like trial and error, or if a series of levels introduces a new mechanic naturally enough. Why am I not more confident and assured and most importantly, why don't I have more perfect ideas to implement?

I'm good enough. I have to be. Everyone's said so since I got serious about creating games at the start of high school. I've won awards for my short games – hell, I'm on scholarship level. I've always known what I wanted, always known that becoming an indie game dev is the only goal I'm aiming for. So why am I doubting myself now?

My contemplation is interrupted by a text from Jay.

Jerky McJerkface

Hey Udina, practising hard so you don't get totally destroyed this week?

I'm learning that this is what passes as a greeting from Jay. The guy's too awkward to even say hi normally.

Sam

Yeah, I was doing visualisation practice . . .

Sam

Visualising your face when I trash you

Oh, so you were thinking of me?
How sweet

Sam

gagging-face.gif

Sam

What's up?

When my phone starts buzzing, I pick it up. After all, having an actual conversation with Jay last time wasn't so bad.

'Too lazy to type,' Jay explains. 'I'm not up to much, just keeping tabs on my opponent because I got bored compiling the textbook list for next semester's courses.'

That's right; my dad mentioned he was doing a degree in chemical engineering. It makes me wonder, if he's so into games then why isn't he getting into a game design or software engineering field? It feels weird asking him outright, as though we're good friends, so I take our usual approach.

'Doing chemical engineering shows you don't have enough dedication to games, Jaybird. Your gamer card has been revoked. Hand over that special ticket to the future software engineer.'

'Nice try, Udina, but every time you try to scam me out of the ticket I read it as you chickening out of facing me.'

'Chemical engineering of all things? Really?'

'Chemistry is amazing and I'll fight anyone who says otherwise, you included. It's like a game, where you can work out the outcome based on the inputs. Uh, how to explain it?' He thinks for a moment. 'Results can be predicted, and they're consistent, and you can control everything that happens if you have enough information. If something goes wrong, you can work out what went wrong and then fix it, and it stays fixed.'

I was *not* expecting a whole spiel about how great chemistry is, but here we are. It's getting harder to think of him as nothing more than an opponent I have to defeat. There's something about actually talking, not trading barbs, not merely texting, which makes him feel more . . . *real*. Like someone I could be proper friends with.

He continues: 'Not to mention, jobs in the field, especially biomed, pay pretty well so I can support my family. And Brisbane is one of the leading cities for biotech, so I can stay here. Gotta be the complete gwai zai package, you know?'

At least he's self-aware enough to poke fun at himself, even as he makes me feel like a terrible daughter.

'You never thought about going into gaming?'

His answer is instantaneous: 'Nope. Not with all the horror stories about crunch in the industry. I'd also probably have to go overseas if I wanted to work on any big projects.'

'That's true. You could make your own games, though.' Like what I'm doing. 'That doesn't interest you?'

'Eh,' he says. 'Games are great, but not as my life. I prefer doing things in the physical world. Kinda like, I could go around an open-world game in camera mode and take pictures of sights that aren't possible in the real world. Even then, it can't compare to a real camera and a scene I've set up with my own hands. Different levels of satisfaction and all.'

A smile spreads across my face as he talks about something he's so clearly passionate about, yet I still feel the urge to tease him. 'Get out of here, normie.'

His laughter rolls through the phone, warm and hearty. 'Tell you what. Let's meet at the Dovewing cafe in Cleveland this week. It's near one of my favourite photography spots. I'll ease you gently into 3D life so you can stop cuddling your anime man-pillow to sleep every night.'

'If this was a video chat, you'd see me giving you the finger.'

More laughter. 'You can give it to me in person before all the aunties and uncles.'

'Now who's the one trying to eliminate their opponent before the competition's over?'

'Oh, I can wait until after it's over. I'm more than ready for whatever you have to throw at me, Udina.'

'That's my line, Jaybird.'

We end the call not long after that, and I return to staring at my game. It stares back. That's all it does, really. Stare. I make an executive decision: If I'm not making any progress on the game, I might as well use my time to continue practising *We Can't Keep Meating Like This*. It's research. Surely more gaming and analysis is what I need to refill my design tank? I'll finish the boss fight, then get back to *Vinculum* after.

I told Jay I'd be prepared for anything and he didn't question that. So I won't let him down.

By three in the morning I've decided that after I conquer this game to prove I can, I will never, ever touch another game like it again. I don't understand why Jay willingly plays these anger-generators. Then again, he *does* seem like the kind of guy who'd get enjoyment out of proving he can do hard, painful things that others can't.

I think about my still-imperfect game. I guess I'm one of those people, too.

CHAPTER 11

Future Devs Showcase: 13 days left

The cafe Jay chose for this week's showdown isn't that different to the other cafe. It has the brick and recycled wood look happening, vintage lightbulbs dangling from a high open ceiling, and fake greenery adorning the walls. I've arrived early, earlier than Jay for the first time, so I can set up in a leisurely fashion.

· It's good to feel relaxed and ready for a change, and I'm already sipping on my chai latte when he arrives. When he smiles and waves, I start to return it before I remember that I need to be in competition mode, and change it to a nod of acknowledgement instead. Rivals before an important match and all that. After all, he was the reason I threw up last week, even if we had some (really) nice conversations later in the week. Competition first, friendship after.

He seats himself across from me and pulls out his own

laptop. 'If I said you're cute when you're in fight mode, would you then get out of fight mode just to spite me?'

Is he . . . calling me cute? If it was any other guy I'd accept the compliment with grace, but it's Jaysen Chua the Ruthless we're talking about, so instead I'm wondering if he's already started with the mind games.

Two can play at that. I give him what I hope is a coy grin but is probably more of a 'don't-panic' grimace.

'Are you saying you think I'm cute, Jaybird?'

He shakes his head with a barely hidden trace of franticness, which is amusing. 'No. Can't blame a guy for trying to find loopholes to change the situation from hard mode to easy mode, right?'

I don't plan on letting him go to easy mode till after we've finished today's round. 'So you're saying I'm not cute, then.'

'No! I—' He stops, mouth open, then shuts it firmly and waves a waitress over. 'A flat white double shot, please and thank you.'

I tap a finger on my chin. 'Does extra caffeine put you into the category of "drug cheat" for the competition?'

He seems relieved that I've moved on from the previous topic. 'You could get the same; see how you handle the caffeine.'

If he thinks he's getting off so easily . . . nope. 'I wouldn't want you to lose because you think I'm even cuter as a manic not-pixie dream girl.'

'I didn't say you were cute!' He flushes, and I silently chalk it up as a win. 'And I didn't say you weren't. I was trying to gross you out of being so serious!'

'So I'm Schrödinger's cute girl?' Let's see if he gets this reference.

'You're still observable, so no.'

I don't love that he got it and even topped it, not at all. It's definitely not an even bigger distraction from competition mode.

'You're neutral,' Jay continues. 'Neither cute nor not-cute. Unless you want to do something that will raise your cuteness level?'

Today I can give him the finger for real.

He snorts. 'Wow, cuteness level +10.'

It's harder to fight the smile on my face than it is to fight him. 'In which case, mistakes were made.'

'What?' He raises his eyebrows in fake shock, but he's also grinning. 'Did the great Samantha Khoo admit to making a mistake?'

'The great Sam Khoo overlooked the fact that you were a masochist.'

He laughs as he pulls out the Bag of Fate and offers it to me for examination. It might only be the third time we've done this, but it already feels routine.

It's my turn to pick the game this week. I reach in and grab the first slip I touch. After all, feeling around isn't going to make much of a difference – the odds remain the same no matter what. I unfold the paper.

We Can't Keep Meating Like This.

This truly is my Bag of Fate. I should be dreading this. But I've practised so hard all week; I'm excited to see how I measure up.

'Easy win for me, then,' Jay says, flexing his fingers over his keyboard.

'Are you going pull out that spray because you're scared of me?'

He narrows his eyes. 'I didn't say I was *scared* of you.'

'Hmm, what was it you said?' I imitate his baritone. 'I knew I had to take every single—'

He goes red. 'You don't need to repeat my words! That's being prepared, not scared.' He pulls out his phone and scrolls to the picture he sent me of the game's ending. 'Like I said, I understand if you hate me after the stomping that's about to happen.'

I pull out my PlayStation controller, and plug it in. 'Keep thinking that, Jaybird. It'll make my come-from-behind victory that much sweeter.'

Music blares from both our computers, indicating the game's loaded.

'Ready?' he asks.

I've never been more ready.

'Go!'

The controls are just as I remember them from my sessions all week. I fly through the first few levels feeling great. In fact, the entire first stage of the labyrinth with slaughterhouse-themed levels feels as natural as any puzzle game, something I wouldn't have expected at the start of the week. Maybe I have a chance at winning this after all.

Then I get to one of the levels in the processing factory stage that uses conveyor belts. I conquered this level yesterday.

Today, however, I simply can't get the timing and controls right. I die over and over. Five minutes pass, then ten. Jay is pulling further and further ahead, while I'm stuck in this damned area with an aggravating buff butcher I've killed enough times to be charged with mass murder. Why won't it work? I practised! I made it through levels more complex than this. What is my problem?

Somehow – I'm not sure how – I finally make it through. After which I immediately end up stuck on the next level. What was all that practice for, if it doesn't help me when it counts? Everything's off, and all I want to do is put down the controller and walk away from this game for good. But not only would that guarantee defeat, it would also mean utter humiliation in front of Jay. So I try the level again.

Again.

Again.

Againagainagainagainagainagainagainagain arghargharghargh this is the WORST.

I claw my way through one level, and one more. They took me five minutes before, now it's easily twenty to thirty. My thumbs are sore from manipulating the joystick and mashing at the buttons. And I'm getting worse and worse.

Simple things I did in the earlier levels are a challenge today. I'm running straight into blades, missing jumps for time-crucial elements. I can't remember why I was so hooked by this game. When the round is over, I'm deleting it and removing it from my Steam library. I wish I had a physical copy so I could burn the damn thing to ashes.

Across from me, Jay wears an intense look. There are flashes of frustration, but not the 'I'm going to smash my controller' kind. More like 'Damn you, you won't get the better of me'. At one point he even gets up, does those pre-exercise style stretches of his, then returns to the game.

I turn my attention back to my own game and keep going. Except no matter how hard I try, I can't recapture the flow of when I played the game at home. More than anything, I want this challenge to be over because I hate how much time I wasted on this game in the past week, which I'll never get back. Make that, which *Vinculum* will never get back.

After far, far too long, he yells, 'Done!' and spins his computer around. I place my controller on the table – maybe a little harder than usual, but give me some credit for self-control – and shrug, palms up.

'Guess you won again,' I say with a calm I definitely don't feel, and offer him a resigned smile when really, I just want to scream in his face.

'Where did you get up to?' he asks, and comes over to take a look before I can stop him.

Which means he sees I'm still in the early slaughterhouse levels, and my humiliation is complete. I brace myself for the teasing, the glib *Well you got far*, the gloating. Or the *I knew girls couldn't play real games* comment I've heard so many times. Though I've learned to take them in my stride, the phrases never stop hurting. Or, worst of all: *Turns out you were nothing to be scared of.*

Then he says, 'The game's super brutal when you're having an off day, huh?'

I'm ready to absorb brash and cocky, and fling it back under the guise of our usual trash talk. But understanding? My emotions don't know how to cope. To my horror, the potent mix of frustration and confusion kicks my body into its default response: my eyes tear up. Then they drip, pooling on the bottom edge of my glasses' plastic frame. I am *leaking* in front of my frenemy, one who felt so sorry for my miserable performance he was nice about his win.

I was wrong, last round – *this* is the definition of complete humiliation. It's impossible to wipe away my tears discreetly, so I lift my glasses up and settle for an angry swipe with the back of my hand.

'You should've seen me play it for the first time,' Jay says as though nothing's happened and I haven't broken down before his eyes. 'I broke a controller when I threw it at the couch cushions with all my strength and it bounced onto the coffee table. Which, being glass, also broke. Then I had to explain it to my parents. I was banned from the game for a good month. I only play the damn thing with a keyboard these days. They take more effort to throw.'

Despite myself, I laugh. It comes out nasally and slightly bubbly, but it's still a laugh.

'It's especially frustrating because I spent so much time playing it this week,' I admit. 'I was confident on these levels, dammit. Now . . . this game can go to hell.'

Jay pauses in the middle of packing his gear. 'Those are definitely the words of someone about to break a controller and a table. Just remember, a PlayStation controller costs seventy to eighty bucks new. Unless it's on sale. Cheapest I've seen is forty to fifty, which is still a lot.' He gestures at the table. 'And have you seen the price of recycled wood furniture? You'll be washing dishes for months to pay them back.'

I let him go to the counter to get the Bag of Fate wrapped up, leaning back and closing my eyes with a sigh. It's not as though I went into this game expecting to win, except I didn't think I'd be trashed this badly either.

'Udina!' Jay slaps something down on the table. 'I found something even better than introducing you to photography spots. Check this out!'

I open my eyes to see a bright flyer. 'It's . . . advertising an escape room?'

'The place is just around the corner!' His eyes are bright. 'They're so much fun. Have you been to one before?'

I stare at the flyer, which has a moody-looking image of an Egyptian figurine. It's one I wanted to play with Aneeshka. To our dismay it only opened after she moved to Sydney and I didn't have anyone else who was interested to drag along with me.

'Of course I have,' I tell him. 'It's totally my thing. Well, mine and my best friend's, though she's in Sydney now. I can see how it'd be your thing too, since it's like video games – just in the physical world.'

'Yeah, I played one for the first time a month ago with my cousins. It was exactly that! Oh, and we escaped with a lot of time left because we're awesome.'

He says it with an edge of challenge, but it isn't harsh. If anything, there's almost a feeling of waiting for me to come back at him with a retort. Anticipation, perhaps?

I have one ready and waiting. 'My best friend and I set a record or two, no big deal.'

'Well then, Ms Big Shot, want to see if we can set a record too?'

There's no way we'll set a record, but I'm in desperate need of *something* to make me feel good about myself again. Something I'm skilled in and can show off to Jay. 'I'm in, even if current company leaves something to be desired.'

'Oh good, the feeling's mutual,' he says, his grin mirroring mine. 'Let's do this.'

There's something else in his voice. Is it relief? A sense of *thank goodness I sorted out the issue*, as though I'm one of his chemistry experiments gone wrong.

'If you're offering just to make me feel better, don't.' Despite my best efforts, the words come out sharply. 'I'm not a video game character whose problems you can solve by completing a quest or choosing the right dialogue option.'

He seems taken aback by my words, and goes silent for a long while as though he's actually contemplating them. Digesting them. Which raises him quite a few notches in my estimation.

'I *did* want to make you feel better,' he finally admits. 'But I swear, Udina, I want to play an escape room because it's my thing, as you said before. And why not with someone who's good at puzzles?' He huffs out a laugh. 'I only wish I could fix things for everyone that easily in real life. I mean, isn't that why you play games, so you can pretend it's possible?'

Even though it's not why I play, everyone has their own reasons and I can respect that. I can also understand that feeling of doing everything you can to make the people around you happy. Too well, in fact.

I regard him for a few moments longer with narrowed eyes, then nod. 'Okay, okay. Give them a call and see if you can book it in.'

He gave my words serious consideration, so I'll give him the benefit of the doubt. Besides, not only do I want to play this new escape room, I also wouldn't mind showing Aneeshka I have a life of my own. She has new friends in Sydney; I have someone else to play escape rooms with in Brisbane.

I wait through Jay's 'Mm-hmm's and 'Please do's, till he finally reaches the climax of 'See you soon!'

'Your quest was successful?' I ask.

'The girl said they have an open session if we can get there right now.' He passes me the Bag of Fate and slings his messenger bag over his shoulder. 'Let's go.'

CHAPTER 12

Future Devs Showcase: 13 days left

The escape room is in a lowset brick building that looks like it warped straight out of the seventies. The windows are blacked out, and I eye it suspiciously.

'The ones I've been to looked a little more like actual public places. You sure this isn't a way to lure us in and then we'll never be seen again?'

Jay gives me a too-bright grin. 'I'm not, but what's life without a little adventure, right? The best quests start by telling you that it's dangerous if you go alone.'

I trail behind him as he pushes the front door open. 'Yeah, but no one's given me a sword and told me to take it.'

To my relief, the lobby is reminiscent of a waiting lounge at the doctor's, with fluorescent lighting and simple decor. There are a few couches around a low coffee table, and at one end is a long desk with the company's name and logo on the wall behind. A girl around our age jumps up from behind the desk, a firecracker bursting to life. I can't tell if she's genuinely excited that we're here, or if she's at the end of a long day and is at the point where exhaustion can only be masked by an excess of energy.

'Welcome to Locked and Coded! I'll be your games master today!' She is way too perky for a Sunday evening. 'Have a seat,' she continues, gesturing at the couches as she hands each of us a small tablet. 'First thing you'll need to do is fill out this waiver form. It's got all the standard stuff about agreeing not to sue us if you are horribly maimed and/or die, as well as agreeing not to break our props . . . or each other, for that matter.'

'Maiming or death, eh? Trying to off the competition?' I mutter to Jay as I fill out the waiver.

'Yup,' he says, calmly tapping away at the on-screen keyboard. 'I intend to use you as my human shield when everything goes to hell.'

I use my finger to sign the last part of the waiver and hand it back to the girl. 'I'd ask what happened to chivalry, but that makes the assumption you're a gentleman.'

He hands off his tablet too. 'Chivalry died the moment you tried to grab my game.'

'You mean, the moment *you* tried to grab *mine*.'

There's the sound of a gentle cough, and we look up to see our games master watching us with a bemused smile. 'I'll go through the briefing, shall I?'

Oops. I'd forgotten she was here. 'Yes, please do.'

She launches into the stock-standard spiel they give everywhere, like 'Don't climb on the furniture' and 'Don't stick stuff into power points' and 'Don't write on anything except the pad of paper we give you, and definitely don't draw genitalia on the walls'. I wonder if she added the last part in for the laughs till she follows it up with a short aside about how another staff member had to go on a genitalia hunt through one of their games, armed with nothing save for an eraser and sheer grit.

Then there's the actually important stuff like how locks work and how certain marked ones are for staff only, to reset the room. That's more for Jay's reference, since I'm clearly the escape room expert between the two of us.

'Any questions?' she says at the end.

'One,' Jay says. 'What's the record for the game?'

'Forty-two minutes and twenty-eight seconds,' she says. Her recall is impressive. 'We're still a new company, so I expect it'll be beaten sooner or later.'

Although Jay said one question, he's not done yet. 'How big was the group who made the record?'

Now she frowns. 'Hmm, four people, I think.'

'And did they get any hints?'

'No hints,' our games master says. 'A single hint will disqualify you from the record.'

'How linear is your game?' The look in Jay's eyes is the same as the one he gets when we're about to start a game. Serious business. I feel sorry for our games master.

She frowns. 'Linear, as in?'

'Can only one puzzle be solved at a time, leading you to the next? Or are there multiple puzzles that can be worked on at any one time?'

'Oh, right!' She taps her fingers on one arm, squinting at the far wall for a moment. 'I'd say . . . mostly linear, but there are one or two parts where you could work on different puzzles.'

Jay nods and turns to me. 'We'll get the record.'

His unfounded confidence is staggering. 'We're half the size of the team that set the current one and you've only played one or two escape rooms. Are you kidding me?'

'You're saying you have no confidence in the very puzzling skills you're challenging me with?' There's no trace of teasing in his tone. 'Weren't you the one who claimed she'd set records before?'

'Yeah, with an experienced partner I've known for years and played a ton of rooms with. Not a relative noob.' I say this with zero sarcasm or disdain; I simply state the facts.

'Wait and see, Udina,' he replies. 'You'll see the true power of the Jay.'

Rolling my eyes at him gets no response. To one side, I spot our games master giving us a surreptitious look that means 'these two are going to be trouble'. But when we turn back to face her it's her customer service smile.

She asks, 'Ready?' We nod, and follow her to a nearby door as she explains the story behind this escape room. 'The two of you are adventurers who have stumbled across an ancient tomb. You decide to explore deeper—' She gestures at the plain white corridor we're walking down, '——when you see a door with strange markings.' She points at the door, which is painted with glyphs that resemble dwarfish runes from *The Lord of the Rings*. 'You decide to go inside . . .'

She pulls the door open for us to enter. Jay steps aside to let me go first. It seems to be a polite gesture, but when I check if he's following, it turns out he's using the extra time to survey the room. Which areas offer the most possibilities for exploration? Are there any markers that we should investigate? Any strangely shaped areas that conceal secrets?

It's all very tactical and I'd admire it if our games master wasn't waiting for us to get in so she can close the door behind us. At this point in time it's downright embarrassing and I'm second-guessing my decision to play an escape room with him. Where's my Best Partner Aneeshka when she's needed?

'Tick-tock, Jaybird,' I tell him. 'Or are you scared you can't back up your boast?'

He gives me a dirty look. *Why aren't you being a team player?*

I jerk my thumb over my shoulder in response. *Get your butt inside now.*

He huffs out an exasperated sigh. *Can't you see I'm giving us an advantage?*

My gaze cuts over to the games master. *Our GM is waiting, stop being a stubborn jerk.*

His gaze follows mine and he nods with some reluctance. *Fine, but I still think you're making a big deal of this.*

'Once you're inside the chamber,' our games master continues, 'the door slowly swings shut behind you.' Her voice grows fainter as the door closes. 'A ghostly voice echoes in the cave, and it says, "If you can't escape in sixty minutes, you'll be lost in my tomb . . . forever!"'

She shuts the door, and above it, a red LED timer starts counting down from sixty minutes. Jay's already exploring the room, searching every nook and cranny. He passes me a gold-ish statuette of an Egyptian-esque cat. I immediately know what to do with it before he says anything, placing it in the depression of a 'marble' plinth near me, one of four around the room. Nothing happens, of course, since we'll need to put the other statues in as well.

He knows I know what I'm doing, and immediately turns back to searching for more items while I examine the plinth itself. I can't see any markings to indicate which statue goes where. Perhaps it doesn't matter, as long as they're on a plinth. Then I hear something, so quiet I almost miss it. It sounds like . . . a monkey?

I hurry over to another pedestal. This one has the sound of a warbling bird. Glancing down at my statuette, the pieces of the puzzle fall into place and there's that familiar rush of adrenaline I live for. The one that got me and Aneeshka hooked on escape rooms in the first place. The feeling I try to evoke with every level of *Vinculum*.

'Jaybird!' He glances over, two statuettes in hand. 'Got one of those with your namesake?'

He rushes over. 'It goes here?'

'Yeah, the pedestals play animal sounds.' I point at the previous plinth. 'That's a monkey.'

'I haven't found that one yet,' he says, handing me a small bird statuette, 'but I'll keep searching.'

By the time I've put the two in their place, Jay's placed another statuette, got the monkey, and fast-walks to the remaining plinth. He puts it on. There's the sound of crumbling rock – from hidden speakers? – and suddenly, one part of the wall that seemed perfectly ordinary lights up with four symbols.

That's what I love about escape rooms, the sheer magic of them. It's seeing the video games I love come to life, with a kind of physicality that VR games can't emulate. The good escape rooms, anyway. The bad ones are just things locked in boxes with puzzles that make no sense and have no relation to the narrative whatsoever.

I pause for a moment to examine the nearest statue. The entire base seems smooth with no obvious seams, nothing to give away the secret behind the magic. I'll have to ask the games master later – while I can make this happen in a game in ten minutes with a few lines of code in the framework, making it happen in real life is infinitely more complex.

'Udina!' I turn to see Jay's expression, which combines amusement and exasperation in equal measure. 'Don't be distracted by side quests, you can ask them how they do it later! We have a record to break.'

'Fiiiiiiiiiine.' I stick my tongue out at him. Childish, for sure, but it feels good.

Stepping back, I squint at the symbols. 'You know, they each have some really strange markings . . .'

We've spent the past forty-one minutes solving puzzle after puzzle with what I'd say is considerable efficiency. Jay's excellent at finding things and, as much as I hate to admit this, his spatial awareness outclasses mine by . . . a lot. But I'm the one who's making most of the connections between seemingly unrelated objects. The discarded blanket that he thought was an atmospheric prop, for example, had a series of different stitches on the edges that led us to the combination for a lock.

Jay grumbled that it made no sense narratively and why would any explorer hide a code with stitches anyway? He simply didn't want to admit I was better at those 'ah-hah!' moments than he was. I conveniently neglected to mention that experience with escape rooms helps a lot when it comes to making those connections.

Now, there's a minute left before we miss the record. I'm staring at a screen mounted in a faux-stone plinth with a cryptic image, while he's in another room with a stone that needs to be placed on the pedestals there in the right order. We could work it out together then run the stone over, but we have a record to break, people!

There are five lines on the screen, and the fourth one is a different colour to the others.

'Second pedestal from the right!' I yell at Jay. 'Put it there!'

'Now what?' he demands from the other room.

I squint at the screen, where the image has changed to an array of symbols. I remember seeing them around the room because Jay pointed them out earlier – I would have missed them otherwise.

'Work faster!' he shouts. 'Forty seconds left!'

'Shut up, I'm thinking!' *Wait, I don't remember seeing that one . . .* 'Okay, put it on the one engraved with a picture that's like an upside down Macca's symbol.'

'And then?' When I take more than a second to answer he makes a strangled noise and adds, 'I should've been the one in there.'

'You'd lose us the record; you're way slower than me at general puzzling.' I squint at the colours onscreen. 'Whichever one is blinking red-yellow-red!'

'Twenty-five seconds, Udina! Go, go, go!'

'You're not helping!' *How many more are there, dammit? Do we have a chance? Surely this is the last one, because it's more complicated than all the rest.* 'Is there one that looks like limestone?'

'How should I know what that looks like?'

He needs to brush up on his general knowledge, dammit. 'Yellowish brown!'

'Then no! FIFTEEN SECONDS, WHAT ARE YOU DOING?'

I see my mistake. 'THE ONE WITH THE BRICKS, DO THE ONE WITH THE BRICKS!'

Everything falls silent. The sound of rumbling stops. All we can hear is our panting.

'Did the timer stop?' I demand as I race out to join Jay.

He's staring up at the clock and he turns to me with the most shit-eating grin I've ever seen.

'We beat the record!' he shouts, and we're high-fiving and

I'm pumping my fists and he's got both of his hands thrown in the air.

A ghostly voice says something, presumably to tell us we've escaped and *I'll have my revenge!* Both of us no longer care. The door opens to reveal our games master on the other side, laughing at us or with us it doesn't matter because WE ARE THE CHAMPIONS!

'Congratulations!' she says. 'I wasn't sure you'd make it, except you pulled through at the last minute!'

I turn to Jay when we stop to catch our breath. 'What was I doing, you ask? I was getting us the record, SUCKER!'

He laughs, slinging an arm around my shoulders. 'Excuse me, who got all their lefts and rights mixed up when giving me instructions on how to move the magnet in the maze? And who had to let me swap places with them?'

I give him my most innocent look. 'No idea what you're talking about.'

'You were holding up your hands to see which one made the "L" shape for left!'

'Doesn't everyone?'

He shakes his head, grinning. 'I can't argue with you, can I?'

'Of course you can, if you don't mind losing every time.'

'Awww,' our games master says as she steps into the room. 'You two are such a cute couple!'

'We're not together.' We both say it at the same time with equal intensity, and hastily step away from one another so we're not touching.

'He's a sore loser,' I say right as he says, 'She's an arrogant punk.'

I swipe at him, and he dodges and retaliates, which I avoid as well.

The games master smirks. 'Whatever you say.'

Jay nudges me. 'Didn't you want to know about the mechanics of the room?'

That's right, I did. I nearly forgot in the excitement of the moment, not that I'll admit it to him.

'I thought it would be fitting to celebrate first, but since you insist . . .' I turn to the games master. 'The first puzzle with the statues, how did they do that? And the bit where you touched spots on the walls and the coin dropped, the walls were totally smooth and I couldn't feel anything there. What did you do there? Also the puzzle with the runes; the design was so elegant. How did you develop that into a puzzle? And—'

She holds up her hands. 'I just work here; you'd have to ask the owners about that. All I know is that when you solve the puzzles, certain things happen.' She must see my face fall, because she quickly adds, 'How about we do a debrief of the room and we can go through each of the puzzles? You're the last group of the evening, anyway.'

Be still, my game-designer heart. 'Yes please!'

She takes us through puzzle by puzzle, offering stories of other groups and how they approached them, as well as common misconceptions that we apparently managed to avoid quite deftly. It's a fascinating insight into how different people view various situations and make connections, and I'm taking notes on my phone as we go. Aneeshka used to collect her own notes whenever we played escape rooms together so we could compare them, but now it's up to me alone.

'Any questions?' the games master asks when we get to the end, as though I haven't been peppering her with them the whole time.

I take a final look back at the rooms, but I can't think of anything else. I probably will the moment I leave this place, though.

'Planning to start your own escape room?' Jay asks as he glances at my phone screen full of text. 'I don't think the owners would take very well to you copying their rooms.'

I'd never even thought of that. Everything I do is in pursuit of becoming a better video game creator, after all. If I want to drop everything and disappoint my family in order to create indie games, then I have to give it my all. I can't afford distractions of any sort. Not from other hobbies, and certainly not from some boy.

Vinculum is everything.

'It's for the game I'm making,' I say immediately, then realise too late I wasn't meant to tell him about it.

I want to take it all back, swallow the words up whole. What if he thinks the concept is ridiculous? Or the narrative? What if he laughs at me for even attempting such a thing, because I have nothing on the Farrows or Toby Fox or any of the devs that created amazing games?

But his eyes light up and there's genuine respect in his look.

'You're creating an indie game? What's it about?' Before I can answer, he says, 'Wait, I'm going to guess it's a puzzler with a core mechanic that's expanded on in each level. Am I right?'

'Got it in one,' I say grudgingly, but also oddly pleased that he already knows me this well.

As we follow our games master back to the lobby, he asks, 'So how do I get my hands on this game, then? If you need beta testers, that is. I'm more than willing to sign up to your earlier-than-early-access program.'

I eye him suspiciously. 'So you can make fun of it?'

'You wound me, Udina.' He places an overly dramatic hand on his heart. 'I'd never make fun of something you'd poured your soul into.'

It gets me thinking that maybe, just maybe, the part of me that thought he was coaxing me back to fighting form after the second round of our competition was onto something. Maybe the Jay who would casually comfort me after being trashed by the game and would take me to an escape room to cheer me up is the Jay I've been trying to convince myself doesn't exist.

If he can trust me enough to ramble on about chemistry and photography, maybe I can trust him with this secret, fragile part of me I've been longing to show.

'I'll . . . I'll bring you a copy of the latest build next Sunday.'

I immediately regret the offer, except it's already there, hanging between the two of us.

And it becomes less scary, the way his face shines. 'I'd love to see it.'

Back in the lobby, we sift through an assortment of signs for the victors' photo. Jay goes for one that says 'MVP', while I grab one with a pointing hand that says 'Didn't help at all' and ensure it points at him.

'Hey!' he exclaims when he sees it. After a minor tussle where he's snatching at it and I'm fending him off he finally concedes, letting me hold it proudly while the games master takes our photo.

'Congrats again, both of you,' she says as we head to the lockers. 'That was impressive.'

We fetch our bags. The first thing Jay does is pull out his phone, crocheted rune-charm dangling from it, and I remember that it's normally part of a rune combo.

I point at the charm. 'Whoever you're with doesn't mind you playing an escape room with a female friend?'

'What?' His eyes go wide, and there's genuine surprise there. 'Is this a way of seeing if I'm single or something? No, I don't have anyone.'

A warm flush rises in my cheeks as I realise how that came across. There's also an element of relief, which I pretend doesn't exist because I'm not about boys, I'm about game development and making sure my ass doesn't end up at uni. I'm not losing my reason.

'Oh *hell* no. Don't go getting inflated ideas about yourself, Jaybird.' Tapping the rune, I say, 'The "Reflect/Reinforce" rune combo is such a core of the game, I assumed there'd be another half to this.'

He flicks it and sets it spinning. 'Doesn't mean "Reflect" is useless without "Reinforce" – they're best together, but also really strong on their own. Especially for boss battles like the Dark Serpent.' Turning on his phone, he glances at the screen and his face turns chalk-white. 'Oh, no, no, no, no, were we talking for that long? I can't believe she called five times.'

He quickly dials a number, foot tapping nervously. I glance at our games master who's hovering somewhat awkwardly to one side. 'Go ahead and reset or whatever else you need to do,' I tell her, 'don't worry about us. We'll let ourselves out. Thank you so much for everything!'

'My pleasure,' she says. 'And if you loved us, please give us a review – we rely on them to survive!'

'We will,' I assure her, and she disappears down the hall to the game rooms.

When I turn back, Jay's in the middle of a conversation in Cantonese.

'I know,' he's saying. 'I said I'm sorry, I lost track of time. You know he's able to deal with stuff like this these days, you don't need to keep calling me.' His brow is furrowed; lips pinched tight as he releases a sigh through his nose. 'Fine! Put him on, then. Geez.'

He pauses, then his tone changes to a much calmer one as he switches to English. 'Yeah, I know they're panicking over nothing. Do whatever you need to make yourself feel comfortable, don't worry if they think you're not coping. I'll be back in half an hour and we can get on to our games night. Yeah, put me back to Ma, I'll talk to her.'

A pause, then, 'I told you he's fine and it was nothing. This is all normal. See you soon.'

He doesn't wait for a reply before hanging up and shoving his phone into his pocket.

I'm not sure what to say in the silence that follows. 'Everything . . . everything all right?'

He shakes his head as he pushes the door open. 'One night, one damned night where I act like an ordinary uni student and don't keep a close eye on the time. My parents keep getting worked up over the smallest things and then it's good old Jay who needs to sort things out and reassure them, because he's the only one who—' He stops himself. 'Sorry you had to hear all that.'

'Hey, what happens in the escape room stays in the escape room.' I give him what I hope is a non-pushy smile. I've heard similar complaints from Aneeshka for years, and all she really wanted was a listening ear. 'Need excuses to get out of trouble? I have lots.'

He laughs. 'So do I.' Shaking his head, he mutters in an embarrassed kind of way, 'It's just parents throwing their responsibilities onto me 'cause I'm the big brother. As though my younger brother can't handle things himself. I really shouldn't have lost my temper with my mum.'

'Nah.' It feels sacrilegious to say this, but I do anyway: 'Sometimes they expect so much of us simply because we're the oldest and it's overwhelming and you don't want to do anything anymore.'

Like the scholarship. Like the expectation I'll get a uni degree and a steady job. Like I'm the responsible one who should keep an eye on Eva when she goes out with her friends even though I have my own plans and she doesn't even need me there.

'Yeah,' Jay replies with a wry smile. 'Though you do it anyway because if something actually does go wrong you'd feel guilty, you know?'

I return the smile to show I understand, then poke him in the side. 'And it's nice being the gwai zai everyone praises?'

'It has its benefits.' He wriggles his eyebrows at me. 'So irresistible you wanted to find out if I was seeing someone.'

'Cringe. I am literally saying this, cringe.' I reach out and tentatively pat his shoulder. 'Seriously, Jaybird. It's okay to be a bit selfish and take time for yourself. I've spent days – weeks, even – holed up in my room working on my game and the world didn't fall apart. At least, that's what I tell myself when I feel bad for not acting the way an older sister should when I'm in the middle of a marathon coding session.'

He finally laughs, looking a bit better for the first time after the call. 'Thanks, Udina.'

I give him a gentle shove towards his car. 'Go do what you need to. Or better yet, don't. I'll see you same time next week for the long-overdue ass-kicking I owe you.'

'I told you that you were an arrogant punk,' he says, but his words have no trace of hostility. 'Don't chicken out of bringing your game, either. I want to see what came from this eldest kid guilt.'

I can't wipe the smile off my face as I drive home.

CHAPTER 13

Future Devs Showcase: 13 days left

After returning from the escape room, I receive a text from Aneeshka later that night.

Aneeshka

Did you kick Jerky McJerkface's ass into next week?

Sam

Um.

Aneeshka

Oh nooooo, what happened??? You were practising so hard!

Sam

I ended up stuck and frustrated and it made me play worse so I became even more frustrated . . .

Aneeshka

THE SPIRAL OF DOOOOOOOOM

Sam

He felt bad for me, I was playing that terribly, and we somehow ended up at an escape room after?

Aneeshka

WAIT *WHAT*
I want all the details about this escape room partner in crime who's replaced me!

Aneeshka

Is there something happening between you and Jerky McJerkface I should know about?

Sam

No! I mean it was fun and we broke the record but there's nothing happening between the two of us

Sam

My head is in the game and nothing else. In more important matters, how is your new game going?

Aneeshka

You aren't changing topics on me that easily, we're coming back to this

Aneeshka

Since you ask, I think I'll have something ready for the showcase that I might actually be proud of :)

Aneeshka

I got some really awesome feedback and advice from my friends here, and they've been saying it's great. You have no idea how excited I am to surprise you with it!

Aneeshka

I can't wait till you come down here and meet them. Deciding to go to Sydney for uni was the best decision ever. I even got a red dye streak in my hair that my parents are mad about but they can't do anything about since I'm in another city :D

Sam

I can't wait to play your game

Sam

Oh, and I'm so happy for you!

I really am. At least, I can convince myself I am, as that's what best friends should do. I shouldn't be jealous of her new friends and so I won't be, because I'm a better person than that.

When she ends up video calling to chat after, I am, as always, the perfect friend.

On Monday night, our extended family gathers for an understated Lunar New Year dinner at a Chinese restaurant that's our designated favourite-for-the-next-three-years. It's a poky little place in the suburbs with decor out of the nineties. Padded vinyl chairs, tables draped with cloth underneath soft plastic, faux Chinese brush paintings on the walls. Even the plastic chopsticks come in paper packaging with instructions on how to use them.

But the owners know us, and they cook us proper food, in that it gets the grandparent stamp of approval. I'm not sure us kids could say for sure what's 'genuine' and what's not.

Our family's the first to arrive. We're super-early in Asian Standard Time – that is, punctual. My Yi Gu Jie and Yi Gu

Jiong turn up with my cousins in tow ten minutes later, by which time Eva and I have already demolished most of the prawn crackers set out in the middle of the kids' table. You snooze, you lose.

'Congratulations on the scholarship, Sun Sun,' my Yi Gu Jie says as she gives me an ang bao, then Eva. 'We're all so proud of you.'

The way she looks at me, the way they *all* look at me, it's easy to see this achievement means so much to them. I know how many people I'll be disappointing with my choices, how much I have to give up in return for following my dream.

'Gong hei fatt choi, Gu Jie,' I respond as I receive the red packet full of sweet, sweet cash, and restrain myself from checking how much immediately.

'Thanks to you, we all have High Standards to live up to now,' my cousin Harrison says as he accepts an ang bao from my parents. I can even hear the capitalisation in his words. But the face he makes in my direction tells me he's kidding. 'Gotta top it by getting into first year med, since that's more prestigious than being a software engineer. Oh, gong hei fatt choi, Ai Yi!'

His younger sister Steffi giggles, and my Yi Gu Jie shakes her head at them both. 'I'm only saying, see what you can achieve if you work hard like Sun Sun?'

'Yeah, yeah,' Harrison says as he plops down in the seat next to me and nabs one of the last prawn crackers. 'We get it, Sam's the pride and joy of the whole family and we should all be like her.'

'Hey!' I nudge him, and change the topic as quickly as possible. 'You're the first out of us to be gainfully employed, and at a bubble tea place, no less. Where's our freebies?'

He points at my ang bao. 'Pay for them yourself, you cheapskate.'

'I still can't believe you talked them into it.' There's some envy in Eva's tone. 'When I turned fifteen I tried to convince my parents but they said no.'

We all do the sneaky check of our ang bao to see how much everyone got. It turns out to be the exact same amount for everyone. There is definitely collusion happening on a grand scale.

Our Dai Gu Jie and Dai Gu Jiong arrive with the grandparents and our final cousin on my dad's side, Kris. He's also into games so we talk a lot, though he prefers strategy and exploration ones. My Dai Gu Jie follows him over to the kids' table and distributes the ang bao. When she gets to me, she comes to a complete stop with a strange look on her face that cannot mean anything good.

'Sun Sun!' she says as she gives me a hug.

She's always been a loud, huggy, social type, in stark contrast to the rest of our family. I brace myself for the inevitable 'We're so proud of you for your scholarship', 'Don't forget your Gu Jie when you're rich' and all the other phrases that are meant to be encouraging but make me squirm uncomfortably on the inside. I even wish they weren't so proud, that what I've achieved wasn't such a big deal to all of them.

What comes out of her mouth instead is, 'Why didn't you tell us you were dating the Chuas' oldest son?'

Every head at both tables swivels my way.

I blink. 'I'm sorry, I'm doing *what?*'

She gives me a sly grin. 'Aiya, don't lie to your Gu Jie. I saw that photo of you both at the . . . escape thing. The game you children play. You even won a record so your picture was big on their Facebook page. Aunty Deonna's daughter saw it and Aunty Deonna asked me about it. I told her of course not, Sam is a gwai lui, she wouldn't not tell us about a boyfriend. And then she sent me the picture, so maybe you're not so gwai after all?'

Everyone has this image of me as the 'good girl', but also, that *damned* escape room record. Eva wriggles her eyebrows at me with a 'what is this new thing I can tease her about?' expression. I know everyone at the adult table heard because my Yi Gu Jie is nudging my mum and I hear a snippet of, *You're so lucky you'll have him as a son-in-law!*

'I'm not dating him,' I say loudly enough for everyone to hear. 'We're friends, that's all.'

'Friends don't sneak around like that,' Eva says with a smirk, and I want to strangle my sister. I wonder if I can get away with it before they pull me off her corpse.

I throw my hands in the air. 'It's because I knew everyone would react like this!' I stare at each person on the adults' table in turn as I speak each word. 'We're. Not. Dating. We're. Rivals.'

'Who play an escape room together?' Steffi raises an eyebrow, a look I *know* she's been practising for months now.

'I hope you don't hide the wedding from us as well,' my Dai Gu Jie says with a wink, and I'm left to the stares of everyone at the kids' table, while knowing that my so-called 'relationship' with Jay is all the adults will talk about all night. In whispers to give me privacy, as though it makes any difference.

'You can date at university, but wait until you're both graduated to marry, okay?' my Yi Gu Jie adds, and I can't tell if she's serious or joking.

At this point, I'd much rather go back to having them praise me for my scholarship, thanks.

Eva's already on her phone, searching for the incriminating picture. Since she's not paying attention, I manage to snatch it from her hand.

'Hey!' She tries to grab it back and I keep it out of reach.

'Nope. Don't even.'

'Jie, give me back my phone!'

'So you can look up that photo? No way.'

Eva turns to Steffi. 'Look it up on yours.'

Steffi's on the other side of the table, so I can't reach her from here. When I try to stand up, however, Eva plonks herself firmly on my lap. She knows she's heavy enough that I can't move her. So I tickle her. She squeals, and clamps her arms tightly to her sides.

'Hurry, Steffi!' she says.

'Which escape room?' Steffi demands, scrolling and tapping.

Eva tries to grab at my hands, but it's easy to avoid her since she refuses to remove her upper arms from her sides.

'Sun Sun! Yun Sun! This is not our house, behave!' our mum finally snaps from the other table.

'Tell Eva not to poke into my private life,' I grumble.

'Tell jie to give back my phone,' she retorts.

Our mum fixes us with a stern 'stop it now *or else*' glare, so I shove Eva back on to her chair and she lets me.

'I found it!' Steffi says, and holds up her phone.

Everyone crowds around to see. Even the adults. I mean, come *on*.

'Yep, you definitely seem like rivals,' Eva says with enough sarcasm that every single adult picks up on it.

'He's pretty good-looking,' Harrison adds.

'And Aunty Deonna said he studies engineering like you're going to,' my Dai Gu Jie says in a way that's meant just as much for my parents as it is for me. 'Goes to church every week, is one of their youth group leaders.'

'They look so good together!' my Yi Gu Jie exclaims. 'Sam, you keep this one.'

I throw my hands in the air. 'I never had him in the first place!'

Even my grandparents add to the running commentary when Steffi's phone is passed to them.

'You should be so proud of Sam,' my Dai Gu Jie tells them. 'Not only is she smart, she's found the perfect boy to settle down with.'

'After Sam goes to university and graduates,' my mum hastens to add, with a meaningful glance my way, even though she's beaming. 'Don't worry, she won't sacrifice her future for a boy.'

I bury my head in my hands and groan. If I tell them now that I'm taking a gap year, it'll be blamed on Jay, and they won't take my determination to become a game developer seriously. It'll be all about a boy I'm *not even dating*, and I cannot stress how much that sucks.

When all the adults finally return to their seats, Harrison leans in from two seats around. 'Come on, then – how'd you meet this Jay?'

I sigh. There's no way anyone will let me avoid what they expect to be a juicy story. 'I wouldn't so much say we *met* as we clashed.'

They're enthralled as I tell them about the limited edition of *Negatory* – 'I knew you'd be gunning for it,' Kris says – but I don't mention Jay's blatant theft, as agreed with him. Instead I say that we respectfully (hah!) came to an agreement to compete for the ticket to the Farrows' exclusive workshop at PopSplosion. It's odd to be recounting the incident, because it feels like Jay and I have come so far since then, even though we've only met in person three times since I issued the challenge.

Steffi pretends to swoon. 'What a catch, Sam, finding a guy who's willing to do things fairly.'

If only they knew the truth. If only I hadn't agreed to keep it a secret. Dammit!

'Hey!' Harrison protests to his sister. 'What are you saying about me as a guy, huh?'

'No one would trust you,' Steffi retorts immediately. 'I still remember you cheating in Cluedo when we were kids by peeking at the murderer cards when I wasn't watching.'

'You have no proof,' Harrison says, but his grin gives it away.

'Back on topic, why *did* Jay agree to a fair fight?' From the way Eva looks at me, it's clear she means this as a rhetorical question. 'Maybe he, oh, had some feelings towards the person asking?'

It's not that at all. I know now that Jay would've agreed to the challenge no matter who asked, because he's super competitive and can't pass up the opportunity to prove he's the best. I happened to hit the right buttons, and lucked into the whole thing.

My phone buzzes with a text message, then two, then three.

Jerky McJerkface

Heads up, all the aunties and uncles think we're dating

Jerky McJerkface

Just got grilled by my parents

Jerky McJerkface

Don't say I didn't warn you

Sam

Too late, already got ambushed. Hope you're suffering as much as I am.

'Texting your boyfriend?' Eva asks, craning over to peer at my screen as I angle it away.

Thankfully the rice arrives, as well as the first dishes of Beijing pork ribs and tofu clay pot, so I have every excuse to shove my phone back in my pocket.

Kris takes charge of the rice bucket, filling each of our bowls to the top. 'How's the competition going? That's what I want to know. How many rounds have you played and who's in the lead?'

I really didn't want to talk about that, but I don't think I can avoid it either. 'Two for him, one for me. And don't give me that disapproving frown, you try playing *We Can't Keep Meating Like This* under pressure.'

Kris isn't impressed. '*He* clearly did.'

'Shut up. Can we please move on to talking about something else?'

Steffi swipes the mushroom I was angling for in the clay pot. 'Like the impending meet-the-future-in-laws event our parents are all talking about at their table?'

Thankfully, Harrison takes pity on me. 'How's your game going? You've got the Future Devs Showcase soon, right?'

I love my cousin. And I think he's genuinely interested, too. 'Yep. Not this weekend, the next. *Vinculum*'s close, except I always feel like there's more I can do, you know? I mean, industry professionals are going to be playing my demo and making snap judgements based on that alone.'

'Sounds terrifying. Glad it's you and not me.' Turning to Eva, he asks, 'How are you finding Year Eleven so far? All my teachers are talking about is preparing for the external exams even though they're almost two years away.'

As the conversation drifts away from JaySam gossip (Eva's term, not mine), I check my phone to see Jay's replied.

Jerky McJerkface

Pretty sure I got you beat in the suffering stakes, my mum's asking how far we've gone and reminding me that there'll be hell to pay if I knock you up

Jerky McJerkface

This is the last conversation I wanted to have with her, ever

Sam

Well, I was surprised with the fake news that we're dating in front of all my extended family

Jerky McJerkface

Nope. Doesn't even reach my level of cringe. She started talking about condoms. CONDOMS. After a lecture on abstinence and the responsibility of kids.

Sam

A FULL COMPLEMENT OF COUSINS AND AUNTS AND UNCLES AND GRANDPARENTS TALKING ABOUT GRANDCHILDREN

> And how I absolutely shouldn't be doing any funny business but I should make sure I was protected if I did because diseases can be passed around. My mother. Was talking. To me. ABOUT STDs.

I haven't even *considered* anything of the sort before. Ever. I don't even want to think about sex with a boy I'm not dating, or – thank you religious and Asian conservatism – married to. My mum's never had the birds and bees talk with me and I've never understood how people can want to have sex with someone based on their looks alone, despite Aneeshka's attempts to explain it to me in the past. I've never had that fluttery feeling because someone's got a great face or body (whatever that even means, apart from 'not unpleasant'), and I'm happy to remain blissfully ignorant.

Sam

> I'll gladly concede you win this round :|

Happy Chinese New Year to everyone.

When we get home after dinner, my mum pulls me aside. Eva leaves us with a knowing look, and what is most definitely a smug grin on her face. Brat. She's enjoying it since the attention's turned to me.

We sit side by side on the living room couch, my mum turned slightly to face me.

'You know I don't oppose you going out with Jaysen, right?' she says. 'I was worried you'd get so obsessed over making your games, you would never find a boy.'

To her, my biggest dream in life is nothing more than a hobby. She doesn't understand that this is all I've wanted, all I've dreamed of, since I made my first (terrible) game at the start of high school. It's not a boyfriend I'm scared of never finding. It's a game publisher.

It's joining Aneeshka in Sydney on my own terms before our orbits become completely out of sync. Not stuck going to uni because I moved there for it. It's being there because I'm ready to grow my career as an indie dev.

'If Jay and I were really going out, I'd tell you.' I should be exasperated, even though I can feel in my bones that she wants me to be happy. 'We're only friends. Right now, my focus is on my game. And I . . .'

I trail off, wavering on whether I should simply tell her that I want to take a gap year. 'I'm thinking . . . well, not *just* thinking . . . I don't know . . .'

I try to find the right way to break the news. Using Cantonese, no less. I'm starting to think this is a very bad impulse and I need to prepare a proper speech and everything.

My mum pats my hand. 'You don't have to hide anything from me. You can talk to your mummy about anything, you know?'

'I know.' I look down at where her hand rests on mine. Should I tell her? *I want to give up my scholarship and take a gap year so I can build games and make a career and never go back to uni.* The words are right there in my mind, but I can't force them out.

Before I can find somewhere to begin, she continues, 'Whatever is going on with Jaysen, it's okay. I just don't want you to lose your head when you start dating. Aunty Cecelia's daughter Katie, she dropped out of school to follow her boyfriend to Melbourne. He left her and now she's a single mother living at home with Aunty Cecelia.'

My tongue is filled with ash, remnants of sentiment thankfully unspoken. I manage to choke out, 'Poor Katie.'

'That's why, even if you're certain Jaysen won't leave you, having your own qualifications and career is so important. That way, no matter what happens, you can always take care of yourself.'

'I promise I will never lose my head over a boy.' That much I'm certain of. 'No matter what I choose to do, it will be because of what I myself want, not because of a boy. Especially not Jay.'

My mum frowns. 'What's wrong with Jaysen? He's studying hard as an engineer, which is a steady career. And his parents aren't very traditional, so they would understand someone like you who is more . . . Australian.'

I pull my hand away. 'It's not about Jay; it's about dating in general. I have my own career to think about and my own dreams to pursue. My five-year plan doesn't include dating and marriage.'

It also doesn't include university.

'I'll make my own success,' I add firmly. 'I don't need a boyfriend to be someone.'

I'll show my family at the Future Devs Showcase. I know my game is good, and if I can get just one publisher interested, that's all I need to prove to myself to everyone. In the future, whenever anyone sees the name Samantha Khoo, they'll immediately associate it with video games. And then, only then, will I consider other distractions like boys.

CHAPTER 14

Future Devs Showcase: 10 days left

As it turns out, my mum's talk about not being carried away by a boy turns out to be the best pep talk she could've given. It seems I'm a creature driven by spite and the desire to prove people wrong – and believe me, I intend to prove her *very* wrong, when it comes to what I'll devote my life to. I attack bugs and level design changes with increased intensity, add more layers with sound effects (thank you for something, *We Can't Keep Meating Like This*), and polish the background and character art.

I put it all on pause on Wednesday for our second family games night. Because the first one went *so* well. But Eva's determined to make this work, since it's what her friends' families do and everyone loves it. Even if it kills us all in the process. I insist on picking the games this time, because if we're going to suffer together it might as well be over good games.

Our parents eye the tall stack on the dining table suspiciously.

'You know I'm not very good with complicated rules,' our mum says, stretching out in her at-home clothes of a light batik dress. 'I get confused easily.'

'Rummikub was fun, wasn't it?' our dad adds. His comfort-wear of choice is a ratty polo shirt and shorts. 'Or we could play Monopoly.'

I take out one of the smallest boxes, Love Letter. 'We're not playing Monopoly. Do you want us to still be a family by the end of the night?'

Eva takes the slim deck of cards and starts shuffling. 'Good choice, jie.'

'It's a simple game,' I tell our parents, who still don't seem convinced. I give them instructions in English, because it's more natural that way. 'Every card has a number from one to eight. You want to end the game with the highest number in your hand.' Our parents' eyes are already glazing over. 'You know what, let's just play, and you can learn as we go. Eva and I will start.'

'It would be easier if you explained in Cantonese,' our mum says to me. 'You should speak more or you'll forget a lot, like your mui.'

She's already starting on the comparisons between me and Eva. This is going to be a fun night.

'Why don't you invite Jaysen over next time?' my dad asks. 'He likes all these game things, doesn't he?'

'No,' I say immediately. 'We're not close or anything like that. He's too obsessed with winning, so I don't have those kinds of feelings towards him. I like my boys kinder.' This wouldn't have been a lie before this past week so it's a . . . temporal truth?

'You need to give that boy a chance,' our mum says. 'Spend more time with him. You might grow feelings for him.'

'I can find him on Facebook and invite him next week,' Eva says with a grin. 'Jie would love it even if she doesn't want to admit it.'

I throw one of the small wooden cubes used to mark wins at her for a perfect bullseye on her forehead. She simply smirks at me.

'Deal the cards already,' I tell her.

She hands each of us a card briskly. 'Don't show it to anyone. Jie, you go first.'

I check my card, and see I have a Baron, which is a number three. Then I draw a card from the deck. A Guard, number one. Eva explains what I'm doing to our parents as I place the guard in the discard pile.

'She can't hold both cards, she has to put down one,' she says in halting Cantonese interspersed with English, obviously trying to make a point to our mum. 'That card says that she needs to guess what someone else's card is. If she gets it right, then you're out of the game.'

Turning to our dad, I ask him in English, 'Do you have a . . . Prince? Don't tell me what card you have, just tell me yes or no.'

'Sun Sun, listen to your ma and speak in Cantonese,' he says as he checks his card. Then, 'Do I have to tell you the truth?'

'Yes!' Eva and I chorus – in English. 'No cheating!'

'Is that so?' He puts his card down again. 'I don't have a Prince.'

Eva laughs. 'Jie does, though. A cute, video-gamer prince.'

I mock-glower at her. 'You're begging for me to run all the hot water in the house next time you have a shower, you know that?'

'Sun Sun, don't you dare waste water like that,' our mum immediately says. 'Do you know how expensive it is?'

'Yeah, jie, don't waste water.'

That girl better lock her bedroom door tonight if she knows what's good for her.

I give her my most pointed stare. 'Eva, your turn.'

She draws a card and puts it down immediately. It's a Priest, a number two, which allows her to take a look at anyone else's card.

'Daddy, show me your card.' She stretches out her hand.

He holds on to it. 'Isn't that cheating, looking at other people's cards?'

'But that's the action of this card, so I can.' The resemblance between Eva's grin and his leaves no doubt she's his daughter. 'Come on, Daddy, hand it over.'

He sighs and passes it to her.

'Hey!' She puts it down on the table, face-up. 'You had a Prince!'

'Ah, I got mixed up,' he says, face contorted into false innocence.

'You're out,' she declares. 'Because jie actually guessed right.'

I turn to our mum. 'Your turn.'

She takes a card, and squints at the text on it.

'Mummy . . .' Eva's tone is probing.

Our mum's somewhat distracted from reading the card, since English isn't her native language. 'Mmm?'

'Tamara's parents booked a holiday house in the Bunya Mountains, and invited us all along. It's during the Easter holidays so I wouldn't be doing much anyway.' Eva says this with the casualness of someone trying too hard to disguise her eagerness. 'I can go, right?'

No wonder she wanted to have another games night. She wanted to use it to try to slip this trip through.

Too bad for her, that immediately gets our mum's attention. 'Where's that? Isn't it far away from the city and everyone else? Doesn't Tamara have an older brother? Will he be there? Are those male friends of yours going too?'

Eva tries to dismiss it. 'Their family goes there every year. I can show you a picture of the place they rent. There are a lot of bedrooms. I'd share with Tamara and Linda; we wouldn't be sharing with boys. Everyone else is going. Their parents don't mind.'

Our mum's completely forgotten about her cards at this point.

'I don't know Tamara's family,' she starts, before Eva cuts her off.

'Then meet them! There's the party they're hosting coming up, I already asked you both to go and you said you wouldn't!'

'And,' our mum continues, 'you shouldn't be sharing a place with boys. You never know what they're really like until it's too late.'

Eva's growl is badly suppressed. 'Oh, so we shouldn't let Kris and Harrison sleep over, then?'

'That's different,' our dad says. 'They're family.'

Eva rolls her eyes. 'Like that changes anything. These are my best friends, and my best friends' families. You know I'll be fine.'

'The Bunya Mountains are very remote,' he says. 'If anything happens no one else will be around.'

'There's a lot of other holiday houses there,' Eva retorts. 'And even then, *nothing will happen*. All my other friends' parents said yes straightaway.'

'They're gwei lo,' our mum says, as though that explains everything.

'So what?' Eva's pushed her chair back from the table. She stands, leaning forwards over the table. 'Nothing will happen to them because they're Australian?'

'Yun Sun, don't yell at your mother,' our dad says sternly. He hasn't used her last name so Eva's not in deep trouble . . . yet. 'Your jie never went on trips with her friend's family, and she didn't complain about it.'

'Well, I'm not her, am I? I can't help it if Aneeshka's family never asked her to go anywhere. It's not fair you're saying I should miss out because she didn't go!' She straightens and decisively turns away from the table, and them. 'Forget it. I'm going to my room.'

I chase after her as she storms off. 'Wait, Eva!'

She doesn't acknowledge me, though she doesn't chase me away either when I follow her into her bedroom.

'I know it's not your fault,' she says stiffly after shutting the door behind me. 'But I really hate how Mummy and Daddy keep comparing us like I'm not . . . Asian enough.' Eva's shoulders slump. 'I want normal parents like my friends, where going on trips with your friends' families isn't this big deal, where they can have fun games nights and proper adult conversations. I want parents who don't think it's weird going to parties with my friends' families, who treat their kids like – like – *adults*!'

I keep forgetting that most of her friends are Australian, thereby becoming the standard she compares everything to. As for me . . . there's Aneeshka, who's Bengali-Australian, and do developers you've met in online communities count as good friends?

It's true that the people I click with tend to be other third-culture kids, so I suppose that makes a difference. Or at least, I never took enough notice of what was normal in an Australian family.

'We're a normal Asian family, is what we are,' I tell her. 'There's a clear line between generations, you know? Mummy and Daddy care for us in a different way, which errs on the side of overprotective. As for the parties, they wouldn't even know what to talk about with our friends and their families anyway.'

'You mean *my* friends and their families,' Eva says bitterly. 'Because I'm the Australian sheep of the family.'

'Please.' I huff out a laugh. 'I'm the one who wants to give up a prestigious scholarship to chase a precarious career making my own video games. Meanwhile, you're already planning to be an occupational therapist, which is close enough to a doctor. If we're having a "who's less Asian" competition, I think we know who wins that one.'

Eva grimaces in sympathy at my plight. 'So . . . when are you planning to tell Mummy and Daddy?'

'When . . . when I know for sure, I guess.'

Even thinking about it scares me. I can deal with anger. I can deal with yelling and resistance and frustration. What I can't deal with is disappointment. I can't deal with becoming *that* kid all the other parents warn their own kids about. Unlike Eva, who's long been on her own path by way of her friends, I was always the model Asian kid. What am I, if not that?

'When will you know?' Eva asks.

I swallow. 'After the showcase, probably.'

She pats my shoulder. 'You know, jie, you can do what you want to do without justifying it. Remember Ethan from the concert? He's really smart and could get into any university course, but he's gonna go for a carpentry apprenticeship after school because he loves working with wood.'

My mum's words from earlier echo in my mind. *They're gwei lo.*

They don't have parents who've migrated entire continents and struggled with a different lifestyle and culture, hoping to provide a life with more opportunities for their kids. They don't have an entire community looking to them as an example of what can be achieved with hard work.

In order to break the mould, I have to be even more successful than all the gwei lo.

Of course, I don't say any of this to Eva. Instead, I simply say, 'Thanks. I'm glad to have a little sister like you.'

She nudges me with her shoulder. 'Right back at'cha. If you

want backup when you talk to Mummy and Daddy, just let me know.'

I give her a Look. 'The same kind of backup you gave me with the whole Jay not-a-boyfriend drama?'

She cracks a small smile. 'That's my job as a little sister too, isn't it? Besides, the soup's already out of the xiao long bao, so it's not like they'd fuss less.'

'You achieved peak Asian with that phrase,' I say, shaking my head. 'But really, we're not dating.'

'I know.' Eva plonks herself down on the music stool in one corner of her room. 'You've always been completely focused on making games, which I think is really cool.'

My baby sister is proud of me. It's the kind of encouragement that makes me feel like I can do anything.

Then she adds, 'So of course you wouldn't be distracted by a boy, or by anything else.'

Of course I wouldn't be constantly thinking of how well we worked together in the escape room, or the way his grin lit up his face when we broke the record, or how excited he was to hear about my game.

Eva continues, 'I've always looked up to your determination and how you know what you want, and never hesitate to go for it no matter the sacrifice. So screw your courage to the sticking place, or whatever that line in *Macbeth* was.'

I go over and hug her silently, one foot in each culture, both of us trying hopelessly to bridge what seems like an impossible gap between worlds.

CHAPTER 15

Future Devs Showcase: 7 days left

Eva and my parents spend the rest of the week pretending-to-but-not-really ignoring everything that happened on Wednesday night. Except there's still a distance between them, a kind of dissonance like when a movie's soundtrack is slightly out of sync with the action on screen. It's a false truce neither of them is willing to discuss.

Meanwhile, I'm completely wrapped up in polishing *Vinculum*. By Saturday night, my game feels ready. Though it still needs work for the showcase, it's ready to be shared with the wider world. Probably.

Ready to be shared with a boy who could crush my hopes with a few words.

Much as I hate to admit it, I trust Jay's opinion. We have similar sensibilities, minus the 'I love torturing myself with platformers and other insta-react games' part. I create a build of *Vinculum*, copying it onto one of my treasured Star Wars USBs since I know he'll appreciate it. Not that it means anything. This isn't some special gesture for a boy I like. I'd do the same for Aneeshka, for example. I'm still fully focused on my game and nothing else, because that's what's admirable about me – and it's also the first time Eva's explicitly said anything like that.

The *Persona 5* boss theme blasts through my room, and I jump. It's my ringtone, though I don't know of anyone besides my family who'd call me out of the blue at ten-thirty at night, and that's only if I'm out. I check the screen, and it says *Jerky McJerkface*.

What's he calling about this time? I find I'm looking forward to the conversation with him, whatever it might be. First, though, I check my door is firmly shut before picking up. Now that our family knows we meet up and do things together, the last thing I need is any of them walking in on us chatting, and getting the wrong idea. Again.

'What's going on, Jaybird?'

'Figured you'd still be awake, Udina. Tell me I guessed right and you won't blame a lack of beauty sleep for your inevitable loss of the entire competition tomorrow.'

Weeks ago, I'd have pegged this as arrogant trash talk and nothing more. After getting to know him better, I can see that beneath that, he's genuinely concerned he woke me up. He's simply too Jay to admit it.

I eject the USB from my computer. 'Still awake. Still working on my game. Did you call to try to throw me off my game with trash talk? Not gonna work.'

'Are you sure?' he asks, though I can hear the smile in his voice. 'Maybe my words are already taking root in your subconscious, waiting for you to go to sleep so they can spread deep into the cracks of your mind.'

'Please. If you could actually do that, you would've already won this competition.'

'I was showing you pity, so you wouldn't go out with a big fat zero to your name.'

'Hello, are we talking about the same Jay here? The guy who said he'll do whatever it takes to win?'

There's a long pause, which is weird because Jay is normally the kind of person who has an instant comeback.

Then he says, no trace of joking in his voice, 'Because the only way you can change the world is by being a winner. Otherwise, the world at best ignores you, or at worst destroys you.'

'Because no one will take you seriously if you're not successful,' I whisper, unsure whether it's to him or to myself.

'Yeah,' Jay says firmly, almost bitterly. 'No one wants to listen till you're good enough to win decisively and cause a stir. Till you've sorted things out yourself.' Then he catches himself and quickly adds, 'And winning is fun, obviously.'

It's a pathetic deflection, and even though every byte of my being wants to ask about the story behind that, it's clear he doesn't want to talk about it. Neither do I, because I'm not here for a deep and meaningful with a guy I'm not interested in. A point which I should make very clear to him.

So instead I say, 'Getting the record was fun . . . right up until every aunty and uncle in Brisbane started shipping us together.'

He laughs. 'It took me all week to convince my parents we aren't going out, and when I finally got through, my mum acted like I was a traitor to our entire family line.'

'Ouch.' I consider telling him my mum thinks I'm going to lose my mind over him, then decide against it. 'I'm now the golden child for the entire family – scholarship kid *and* supposedly dating a guy who's really good at faking the whole gwai zai thing. They want to believe the dating thing so badly they're probably making up their own fanfics.'

The sound from the phone is somewhere between a laugh and a groan. 'Why can I picture that being passed around the entire Asian Gossip Network as canon? Just as long as it isn't smut, because I might as well say goodbye to my family jewels in that case.'

I snatch my pillow from my bed and laugh into it, glasses pressing hard into my face, so I can't be heard through the walls of my room. 'No. No, no, no, no, no. I did *not* need to picture my aunts and uncles writing smut about us, thank you very much. Stop talking and wash out those cursed words with soap.'

This time Jay's laugh is more unrestrained, more relaxed. More . . . Jay. 'They may have more source material after what I'm about to ask you.'

Why is my heart pounding? Surely he wouldn't. 'What is it?'

'I was—' He stops mid-sentence. 'Oh, shit, I just realised what that sounded like and it came out all wrong. It's nothing to do with asking you out.'

While I'm relieved because I don't want to make that decision at this point in time, there's also a hint of disappointment. Mostly relief, though.

'I get it, I get it. What was the question?'

Another pause. 'Did that come out weird as well? Are you unhappy because I accidentally led you on? I don't *not* like you or anything, but it's not like we've known each other long and we didn't exactly start on the right foot, I'm just—'

He really is a rambler, and it comes out when he's nervous.

'I'm not angry,' I say, 'I think we both made it pretty clear where we stand.' Hopefully he can hear the amusement in my voice. 'Spit out your question, Jaybird, before we're ninety.'

He takes a few deep breaths. 'Wow. I made a total fool of myself. The question. Right. Tomorrow's contest. Can we have it at my place?'

'And give your mum false hope, right after you set her straight?'

'Nah, my parents won't be there. That's why I need to change the location. A distant aunty of mine fell and hurt herself pretty badly, so they're going to see her.'

I'm still not following his reasoning. 'Wait, are you trying to gain a home ground advantage? Is that it?'

'I need to keep an eye on my younger brother.'

That's a relief. It means he wasn't thinking of anything more.

'He'd be fine on his own,' Jay continues, 'but . . . *parents*.'

'If you're busy, should we cancel?'

'Nah. He already said he's cool with you coming over for the competition.'

Huh. Okay, then. 'Should I be worried about him thinking that we're dating? Because my younger sister definitely would, and she'd give us so much crap we'd never live it down.'

Jay laughs. 'He asked me in full seriousness if I was planning to marry you one day, if that counts.'

'Please tell me that misunderstanding was cleared up.' I manage to keep my tone dry despite the most inconvenient corkscrew twisting my vocal cords when I think of being together with Jay. 'He won't be calling me "sister-in-law" tomorrow, right?'

'Yes!' Jay's voice is also a barely-controlled squawk. 'I mean, no! I mean, yes it's very much cleared up, and no, he won't be calling you that!'

I search for something, anything, to move on from this particular topic, and it's Eva who gets thrown under the bus. 'I'm glad you have a sibling who gives *you* as much crap as my sister gives me about, uh, this.'

I nearly say 'us', but that's too close to acknowledging there might be something there, and I'm not ready for that. Not till I've made good on all I owe my parents and sister for their support. Not till my name's big enough to prop me up as my own person.

Jay lets out a breath so loud I can hear it clearly from my end. 'I think you'll get along with him really well. He's pretty funny and just as nerdy as I am.'

'You do set a pretty low bar when it comes to "People I'd get along with".'

'At least I set a bar, unlike you.'

'Eh, average comeback. You can do better.'

'Yeah, I regretted it the moment I said it.'

How does talking to him feel so comfortable, as though I've known him for far longer than I actually have?

Gotta get my head out of the clouds. 'I'm looking forward to establishing my dominance before an actual witness tomorrow.'

'Excuse me, the Chua brothers are going to stand triumphant when all's said and done.'

'Hey! No double-teaming allowed! Then again, you already showed you're capable of jerk-worthy actions . . .'

He groans. 'I'll never live that down, will I? But my brother has a really strong sense of fairness, so in all seriousness, it's not something you need to worry about. Though he might pull you aside to tell you all about the history of video game art, current trends and all that.'

Oh, now he has my interest. 'Video game art, you say?'

'Yup. Ansen's always loved creating art. That's how I got him into games, by showing him *Negatory*'s artwork. That's what hooked him on gaming. Then I showed him other gorgeous games like *Gorogoa* and *Hollow Knight* and he never looked back.'

'Oh, *that's* how you found yourself a gaming companion. Maybe I should try it on my sister with video game music . . . oh wait, I tried and failed. She's an utter disappointment.'

Jay laughs. Somehow, every time I hear that contagious laugh of his, the butterflies inside go afluttering.

'Hey, don't try to steal my gaming partner from me,' he says. 'Consider yourself warned.'

'No guarantees, Jaybird. So that means I'll meet him tomorrow?'

'Yep. He's excited to meet an actual developer. He'll probably ask you about the inspiration for your art too. That's why being able to attend the Farrows' workshop would mean so much to him. You know, being called *Art* of Game Design and all.'

'Pity will not sway me, Jaybird. Even if your brother is super cool.'

Laughter again. 'It was worth a try. Gotta throw out every card in my hand. I'll text you our address. Don't forget to bring your game!'

'Already packed.'

'See you tomorrow, then.'

Is that nervous excitement in his voice? My breath catches, and I try to sound calm despite how I can feel my heartbeat thudding through my body.

Remember my goals. Remember how much I'll owe my family if I don't accept the scholarship. Remember that I can't afford to be distracted until I've found success, if I've learned anything from the debacle with the hangover.

'Tomorrow.'

CHAPTER 16

Future Devs Showcase: 6 days left

Jay's place is in Runcorn, one of the suburbs in Brisbane that falls within the heartland of Asian territory. It's nerve-racking driving my car there, wondering how many people will recognise it – or worse, how many people will know that it's parked outside Jay's house.

In the passenger seat, I've got two red dragon fruits from our garden. There's also a small bag of calamansi limes and a pack of dried plums to make kat chai suen mui, one of my favourite Malaysian drinks. Just in case, I added more common stuff like chips and lemon iced tea from Coles. My mum taught me to never show up to anyone's house empty-handed.

The house itself is an old place, a two-storey brick building with arched windows and flat white metal bars on the outside of the windows in a wide rectangle pattern. Very nineties Asian chic. I drive right up the stone-tiled driveway and park on one side of the garage door.

Round Four, all or nothing. Pulling the keys from the ignition, I take a deep breath, mentally reviewing *Superficial Giant*, *Slo-Mo*, *Theseus* and *REquery*. I can handle any of those games. If Jay's wildcard comes up, though, I'll be in trouble. He already knows my weaknesses and like he said last night, he'll do whatever it takes to win.

So will I. Time to execute my come-from-behind victory.

Backpack on one shoulder, huge recyclable grocery bag in the other hand, I ring his doorbell. The *bing-bong* of the chimes echo inside the house, and Jay's voice shouts, 'I've got it, Ans.'

Footsteps hasten down the hall, and the door opens to a Jay who is very much dressed to go out despite being at home. Neat black jeans, a slim-cut shirt with an image of the main character from *Negatory* and hair that's subtly spiked with gel. The only thing out of place are the Snoopy house slippers he's wearing.

'Hey Udina!' Okay, he's far too overexcited not to be finding this as awkward as I am. It's so much weirder being at his house instead of a neutral cafe somewhere. 'Come on in. Grab a pair of slippers because the tiled floor's pretty cold, even in the middle of summer.'

I slip into one of the pairs lined up just inside and follow him down the hall. Framed drawings line one wall, gorgeous pencil sketches of instantly recognisable game characters and environments, all in different styles. You get the feel of the various games at a glance. These must be by Jay's brother.

The other wall, meanwhile, has lots of photographs of toy figurines mid-action. A Miles Morales Spider-Man is caught mid-swing around a drainpipe, the main character from *Negatory* casts a glowing rune, Sephiroth 'falls' against a backdrop of water with his longsword extended purposefully downwards.

Now I get what Jay meant when he said he was into photography. It's not the landscapes or still poses I was thinking of. These pictures make the figurines feel like they're alive, as though I'm looking through a window frozen in time instead of a photo frame.

Jay catches me staring and seems almost embarrassed. 'That's what I wanted to show you that time, except I figured you weren't in the mood after *We Can't Keep Meating Like This* and then things got out of hand with our families and all . . .'

I point at one with a Chinese zombie caught mid-bounce against a moody backdrop. 'I recognise the other characters, but where's this from?'

Normally I wouldn't bother asking, so that my geek cred won't be called into question, but with Jay I don't feel on edge at all.

'Oh, that one isn't from any media,' he replies. 'It's made by this really awesome Singaporean artist called Daniel Yu. His toys tend to have elements of Lovecraftian and Asian inspiration, which I thought was a cool merging of cultures.' He looks over without his usual confidence. 'I can show you my toy collection after, if you want.'

'Yes! Please. How did you even get into this?'

The way his eyes light up, I would agree to many things just to see that expression again. 'I was given a lot of figurines as a kid; I guess people figured they were easy gifts for a boy. And I loved that you could pose them and they'd remain exactly how you wanted them to. My interest in photography came later. Then I figured, why not combine the two? Create the perfect moment and capture it in an image where it'll stay that way forever. Also, they're bad-ass.' He pauses, and looks away from me to the pictures. 'Sorry, I become rambly when it's my favourite topic. C'mon, Ans is looking forward to meeting you.'

I don't even have the chance to tell him I want to know more, to hear him speak about things he loves with such obvious passion, before he's already gone ahead. At the end of the short hallway is a living room that's divided from the kitchen by a high counter. Seated on one of the stools is a boy who seems around Eva's age, or a little younger. This must be Jay's brother. They have the same prominent cheekbones and rounded noses, and something else I can't define, like a *feel*, except his is less edged than Jay's.

His grin is eager, his wave excited, and he's practically vibrating in his seat as the words tumble out of his mouth. 'Hi, Sam. I'm Ansen, Jaysen's brother. Jay said you make games? That's so awesome. You're way too cool for Jay, you know. Oh, and he told me about the competition you guys are having, it sounds so fun!'

I can't help tweaking Jay's nose, metaphorically speaking. 'Did he tell you why we ended up competing?'

'You can put the bag down on the counter,' Jay says hurriedly, and I allow myself a mental grin for getting to him. 'You didn't have to bring anything, it's too much!'

Ansen doesn't take the hint, though. 'He did, the other day.'

'To clear up the confusion we were talking about,' Jay says meaningfully to me, 'I came clean.'

Ansen nods sternly. 'I want to apologise for him because I know he won't. If I'd known what he'd done I would have told him to give you the workshop ticket, but you've both made an agreement with the competition already. If it helps, he said he felt bad about—'

'*Okay, Ansen, she gets it.*' Jay's cheeks are bright red and he can't look at me, choosing to riffle through the bag instead. 'Hey, you brought dragon fruit! Check it out, Ans, isn't that great?'

Ansen glances at Jay, then me, then back at Jay. I get the impression he knows he's said something he shouldn't have . . . and also a hint of mischief after, that feels very much like, 'Oh well, let him squirm'.

'Hold up a moment,' I say. 'Is the real reason you agreed to the competition because if I spread the word that you'd snatched the game off me, Ansen would've made you give it to me?'

Jay's silence speaks volumes.

It's Ansen who says, 'Of course I would have. I like this idea better, though, because it means you're both competing fair and square for it. Jay will win anyway, but it's a proper fight so there are no bad feelings. Like how the hero in *Negatory* wins over Udina and convinces her to help with the quest.'

'You, at least, are honourable,' I tell him, then turn to Jay. 'I wish I'd known your little brother had you wrapped around his finger!'

I can't completely hide my dismay. The workshop ticket could've been mine already. On the other hand, I wouldn't have got to know Jay the way I do now.

Jay says firmly, 'I don't do everything Ans asks, okay?'

Ansen breaks into a grin. 'Just most things.'

If this isn't the epitome of a sibling who's doted upon, I don't know what is. Unlike Jay, I'm not wrapped around Eva's finger, no siree. I would never sacrifice something important to me like a whole productive evening, just because she asked.

Okay, he's a guy who cares a lot about his family. Cool cool cool cool cool cool cool. I'm cool.

Jay makes a face at me so I declare, 'For the record, I'm already liking your brother more than you.'

Ansen beams at me. 'Jay said that you made a video game and did the art yourself, so you know lots about video game art.' When I nod, though with some reservation because what do I know compared to an artist, he continues, 'What do you think about the cutscene art in *Negatory*? Aren't they amazing? It's the way they use the lines with varying thickness for emphasis, but also how they frame the characters and shade the scene.'

'I didn't notice to that level,' I admit, 'but they gave me serious feels the first time I saw them. What did you notice in the cutscene where the hero realises the Bag of Fate can't actually help them?'

We spin off into an entire conversation about *Negatory*'s art and comparisons to other games. Ansen even pulls up various screenshots on his phone to point out specifics. It's fascinating to have an artist's insight into what makes various elements work, and I realise how shallow my own thought process around *Vinculum*'s art style was.

The more we talk, the more I find myself grateful that Jay and I are competing for the workshop ticket, because Ansen would get so much out of attending it too. Ansen was right. A competition like this means there's no bad feelings, no guilt, no wondering who deserves it more. It's clean. In a few months, either Ansen or I will attend the Farrows' workshop and it will be what it will be.

Our conversation comes to an abrupt halt when Jay, getting distracted, pokes around in the bag I brought over. He pulls out the two baggies, shaking them in front of Ansen's face.

'Hey, you brought lime and suen mui,' Ansen says delightedly when he sees the calamansi limes and dried plums. 'We need to make drinks!'

'Our mum's always talking about how she misses good kat chai suen mui!' Jay grins at me. 'I can't believe you found the small round limes. I always have to make do with the normal ones from Coles or Woolies and they don't taste the same.'

'Homegrown,' I say, and revel in their envious looks.

While most of my friends are Asian, most of them aren't Malaysian. To find two people who know exactly what I have in mind, purely from the ingredients, makes this place feel like somewhere I belong.

Jay points meaningfully at his laptop, already set up on the counter, and the Bag of Fate next to it. 'Let's start the competition before it gets too late, and make drinks after to celebrate my win.'

'You seem a little confused there, Jaybird. I think you mean *my* win.' I make a show of examining the cling wrap even though I know Jay better than that by now.

'Jaysen wouldn't play dirty with you, not anymore,' Ansen says.

'Wait,' I say as I open the cling wrap. 'Do you mean he'd play dirty against other people?'

'Yes,' Ansen says without any hesitation. 'Depends who, though. If they deserve it, he would. He always says that they won't hold back so you should win in a way where they won't come at you again in the future.'

I glance up to see Jay standing behind Ansen, wincing. 'You ruthless vigilante, you.'

'Can we focus on the competition, please?' It should be a demand, but plaintiveness tinges his words.

I take pity on him and reach into the bag, feeling around. *Please don't let it be the blank. Please.* I withdraw the small slip of paper and unfold it with far more confidence than I feel. Here goes nothing.

Theseus.

'This bag is cursed!' Jay pokes at it suspiciously. 'How are we constantly getting your games?'

'Fate cannot be denied,' I intone, a line taken straight from *Negatory*.

'She's got you there, Jaysen,' Ansen says with a grin.

THESEUS

Philosophical puzzler. You're a space colonist left behind in an abandoned colony, using a blaster to make clones of yourself that move as you move, and mass-murdering them to access new areas. Or ... are you really the same colonist if you're one of the clones? Will do your head in.

Jay seats himself in front of his laptop, Ansen standing behind him like a great guardian gazing down at his screen. 'Fine, let's do this.'

I take the other seat at the counter, far enough that if we both angle our computers slightly we can't see what the other is doing. We both go to 'New Game' in the menu, fingers hovering over the Enter key.

'I'll count you down,' Ansen says. 'Three . . . two . . . one . . . GO!'

We're off. I blast through the initial tutorial text, not even stopping to admire the art – which was made, by the way, out of clay and found objects to create the gritty, earthy feel of the space colony. Together with the dim lighting it creates an eerie, claustrophobic atmosphere full of different textures.

I make a mental note to bring this up with Ansen after, and pick his brain on art design. In the meantime, I grab the altered blaster that allows me to make clones of myself and get going.

The first time I played this game, I spent ages looking up its inspirations, including discussions about the Ship of Theseus. If you were a clone, functionally identical in all ways, with the same memories, were you still the same as the original? Especially if the original was destroyed. Does the perception of continuity mean that so long as the clone has a copy of the original's soul, it is what the original would have been, had it continued on instead of the clone?

Did it mean that even though I wasn't Malaysian in the same way my parents were, as long as I kept that spirit and worked hard and achieved all the things my parents (the 'true'

Malaysians) expected, I would also be Malaysian in my own way? I could still be the 'good Malaysian kid', the pride of the community.

There's no time for philosophising today, though. I'm so focused on the puzzles, I only vaguely notice Ansen coming around behind me to watch for a while, then next thing I know he's behind Jay again.

'Ooooh, she's got more passes than you,' he says, and I allow myself a grin. 'You better hurry up.'

'I. Know,' Jay says through gritted teeth.

Another thirty passes later, I hear Ansen say, 'No, not like that, you need to make a clone over there like Sam did.'

'Pause,' Jay calls, and I hold my hands clearly away from the keys so he can see I'm not playing. I have, however, taken a page from his playbook, and use the time to stare at the puzzle and work out my next moves.

He turns to Ansen. 'Remember, Ans, this isn't one of our usual gaming sessions. You can't help me in the middle of a competition.'

Surprisingly fair play, coming from Jay. Though I understand the feeling of wanting to win fair and square, without accusations of help.

'Yeah. Sorry. Got too focused on your game. I won't say a thing.' Ansen nods, more to himself than us, and picks up a slim black pen from the counter. He pops the cap off and then presses it back on again with practised movements, over and over. The clicking sound as it snaps back on is strangely rhythmic and satisfying.

Noticing this, Jay says, 'Why don't you join the competition? If you set up your laptop, I'll give you my latest save file so you're not starting from behind.'

Ansen frowns. 'But I don't want to start from the middle, and it wouldn't be fair if you started again because you're at different points.'

Jay glances at me. There's an odd stiffness to his posture that makes me feel like I'm on probation and one wrong answer will see me out the door. *Insult my brother, and you insult me* is the vibe. Defensive, ready to spring at a touch. Ansen doesn't seem concerned, though.

I decide to ignore Jay and talk to Ansen instead because it seems easier. 'We'll take a record of how many passes each of us has, and Ansen, you start from the beginning. At the end we'll count the passes each person gets from this point. Sound fair?'

A quick glance over at Jay, and he seems to have relaxed a bit.

'It's a good idea, even if I don't want to see how many passes you have right now,' Jay says.

'Ansen, you look at each of our screens and write it down.' I pull out a notebook and pen from my bag, and offer them to him. 'I don't want to know how many Jay has either, by the way.'

'Make sure you only write it,' Jay tells him. 'Don't say it out loud.'

Ansen writes down Jay's number first. I avert my eyes as he comes over so I don't accidentally catch a glimpse of what's on the paper.

'Done,' he tells me, folding it up and placing it on the table. 'I'll bring my laptop down, just wait.'

He hurries out of the living room, his footsteps fading as they go up the stairs.

I look at Jay. Jay looks at me. This isn't awkward at all.

'Sooooo . . .' I search for something to say that's not about him, or me, or whatever's between us. 'You have some serious "protective big brother" vibes going on. I thought I was bad with my sister Eva, but you . . .'

He glares at me. 'People have been assholes in the past. You have a problem with that?'

'Whoa.' I raise my hands in the air. 'Okay, Jay gor, lower those hackles. Learn some chill from your brother. I don't think "beating up Sam" was on the cards for today.'

He relaxes a bit, enough for the Jay I've known till now to peek through. 'Not beating up, only beating.'

I take a page out of Jay's book on how to relax the tension. 'Yeah, *me* beating *you*. And possibly Ansen, if I can pull off a double-kill on the Chua brothers.'

It works. 'Keep dreaming, Udina. I guarantee that if I don't kick your ass – which I will – then Ans has got it.'

'And if you try to hurt either of us, my gor will kick *your* ass,' Ansen says as he comes back down the stairs, laptop in his arms. He has the whole 'respect the older family members' Asian vibe going. 'Gor's been doing Krav Maga for years and he's dangerous.'

I'm not, Jay mouths at me. We're back to normal again, and it's all I can do not to laugh.

'The physicality of it, hey?' I ask, recalling one of our previous conversations.

He immediately knows what I'm talking about because he gives me a head-tilt of acknowledgement, and it's like we already have our own private references and in-jokes.

'What?' he says even though I've not so much as raised an eyebrow. 'It's useful, efficient and it feels good to know your body can move like that.'

'He also watched a lot of Jackie Chan movies on SBS as a kid, but he said he wanted it to be brutal when he destroyed the boys who were beating me up, not funny,' Ansen adds. 'I still thought it was funny when he threw a "diu lei ma" at them at the end, and they looked at him all confused because they didn't understand Cantonese.'

That's the Jay I know, and I can't help laughing. 'Sounds like they got what they deserved.'

Ansen appears exasperated. 'Yeah, but I didn't ask him to.'

Jay turns his head away and mutters, 'Those boys were the worst, so I had to do *something* about it. If it wasn't you it would've been someone else.'

He nudges his brother. 'Come on, boot up the game. We need to finish the competition before it gets too late, or it'll eat into the time for our games night.'

I attempt Steffi's eyebrow raise at Jay, but I'm pretty sure both my eyebrows have gone up. 'Deflection skills not maxed out yet.'

I go to poke his shoulder to make my point. He uses one hand to block my wrist and comes in for the low attack with the other, finger hitting the ticklish spot on my side. Jay has a smug expression as I squeal in surprise, while Ansen nods with what I'm going to guess is approval.

'See?' Ansen says. 'He's dangerous.'

'How do you rate my deflection skills now?' Jay says, a cocky tilt to his head.

'Major humour points deducted for not swearing at me in Canto to cap it off. Otherwise, you get a pass.'

'Yeah, but you'd understand it, which gives you potential blackmail material with parents finding out.' He stretches and focuses on his laptop once more. 'Ready, Ans?'

Ansen spins his own laptop to show his start screen. 'Ready.'

Jay pulls his laptop back in front of him, and I do the same. He glances at me and the tension is back. This game will decide if I lose the competition or not.

He looks at me and his brother, and counts down. 'Unpause in three . . . two . . . one!'

CHAPTER 17

Future Devs Showcase: 6 days left

I'm so close to the end of *Theseus*. I've grabbed the final pass, and I'm now racing for the exit where I'll make my final choice. The first time I played, I agonised over whether to leave my final clone behind and get off the colony, or remain abandoned with 'myself' for the rest of our lives. If you choose to leave your clone behind, the game does this cool thing at the end where it switches to the perspective of the clone so 'you' are then the one left behind.

Today, however, I simply stand there and spin my laptop around as the spaceship lifts off without me.

'Finished!'

Jay groans, leaning back in his stool as he shoves his laptop away in resignation. 'Dammit, I was three passes off finishing.' He glares down at his screen. 'Those two cursed levels in the last section – I thought I remembered how they were done and that screwed me up so much.'

I smirk. 'That's why you do it not only by memory but also by understanding, Jaybird.'

He glances over at Ansen, who's completely focused on his screen. 'Ans! Hey, Ans!'

Ansen looks up, irritated. 'What?'

'Competition's over. Udina – uh, Sam – just finished.' He points at me with a thumb, looking thoroughly unimpressed.

It's weird hearing him call me by my name, instead of *Udina*. 'Can't help it if some of us are better endowed in the brainpower department.'

Ansen laughs. 'She got you again, Jaysen.'

'Hey, I thought my own flesh and blood would be on my side,' Jay says. 'Isn't that something you should do as my gaming partner?'

I *tsk* at Jay. 'You fundamentally misunderstand a younger sibling's job. Biggest part is giving their older sibling as much crap as possible, at least according to my sister Eva.'

Jay shakes his head. 'My own brother's allied against me. What is this world coming to?'

'You can't trust anyone, gor,' Ansen says with mock seriousness.

'How many passes did you get, Ans?' Jay asks, peering over at his laptop screen. 'Hey, you got eighty-three! That's impressive!'

It really is. I think he would have thrashed us both if we'd all started at the same time.

Jay picks up the paper where Ansen noted our orbs and continues, 'Sam was at thirty-eight when we paused, and I was at . . . whatever, I had fewer than her.'

'Oi!' I grab at the paper but he whips it out of my reach. 'You can't not announce your number!' I turn to Ansen. 'How many did he have when we started?'

'Don't tell her, Ans!' Jay says as I come around and continue my attempts to grab the paper. *How on earth does he move so quickly?*

Ansen says without hesitation, 'Thirty-one. He had thirty-one.' He shrugs in the face of Jay's pout. 'Can't lie to a special guest.'

I snatch the paper away from Jay and take a look. Sure enough, it says '31' against Jay's name in neat handwriting.

'And Udi – uh, Sam, was worried it would be a double-team against *her*.' Jay shrugs. 'Well, we both lost to Ansen in the end, so Sam, you are *still* a loser.'

He dodges Ansen's swat. 'Don't be mean to her, gor.'

Confirmed, Ansen is the better sibling. 'Yeah, don't be mean to me, Jaysen.'

He backs away in surrender. 'Can we make drinks now instead of beat up on me? Please?'

'Do you even know how to make kat chai suen mui?' I ask as I head to the kitchen side of the counter and pour out the small round limes from the freezer bag. I only know because my dad went through one of his phases and made it for us regularly till he got sick of it. 'I'll make it if you get me a small chopping board, knife, and jug. Oh, and sugar.'

He fetches everything, though he doesn't relinquish the knife. 'I'll chop the limes and you can squeeze them and mix the drink,' he suggests. 'Anything else we need?'

'Hot water to steep the plums and melt the sugar,' I tell them.

Jay glances at Ansen, and without anything more being said Ansen's already grabbing the kettle. The two of them work together so well. I wonder if Eva and I would coordinate as smoothly, or if we need to play more games together?

We fall into a rhythm, Jay chopping, me squeezing and, later, Ansen sieving the juice. I fill three cups a quarter of the way with freshly boiled water and mix in the dried plums and a teaspoon of sugar.

'Normally you'd also blend the lime skin with some water and pour it in through a sieve at the end,' I tell them, 'except I'm too lazy to do the washing-up.'

'Same,' Jay says emphatically.

'I'll wash up,' Ansen offers. 'I want to make the drink properly.'

Jay rolls his eyes at his brother. 'Fine. But you better keep your promise to wash everything.'

'I wouldn't lie,' he says indignantly, as Jay opens the oven and retrieves a blender, base and lid.

'We don't use the oven much, so our mum treats it as an extra cupboard,' Jay explains when I let out a surprised laugh.

Makes sense. 'My sister loves baking, so ours only has cooling racks and baking trays. We're very Western thanks to her.'

We blend the lime skin with water, pour some lime juice and the blended lime into the cups with soaked plums and sugar, and stir them well. Add a few ice cubes to each glass as the final touch. I take a sip, add a bit more of the lime juice to all three glasses, and it's just like my dad's. Jay's eyes flutter shut in pure bliss as he takes a sip, while Ansen drinks his slowly and purposefully as though savouring every drop.

I feel very accomplished.

When Jay finally returns to us, he glances over at me. 'Now we have drinks, time for the second main event. Did you bring your game, Udina?'

'You call her Udina?' Ansen asks. He turns and studies me seriously. 'I can see that.'

'I'll . . . take that as a compliment.'

'It was.'

Jay waves his hand in front of my face. 'Game, Udina, game. I've been waiting for this all week.'

I've never had anyone excited for my game before. Aneeshka, perhaps. The difference is, she's almost obligated to be since we're best friends. A more petty part of me is also thinking this is my chance to step away from Aneeshka and make new friends of my own. Though I haven't known him for long, Jay surely counts as a friend at this point, right? I mean, we've only met four times so far yet we've had some solid chats, played an escape room and my entire extended family is already shipping us together.

And, okay, he's funny, can be nice and he's made it clear he doesn't underestimate me.

I pull out the USB from my backpack to the approving nods of both brothers when they see the R2D2 colours and pattern on it.

'Pop it on my computer,' Jay says.

'Mine next,' Ansen adds.

My hands are shaking a bit as I plug in the USB to Jay's computer. Will they like it? Hate it? Think it's terrible but be too polite to say so? What if they say it's bad and needs a lot of work?

'Everything okay?' Jay places his hand on my shoulder, a gentle touch.

I want him to squeeze it, to give the silent reassurance that even if it's not okay he'll be there. I catch myself in time. Since when have I needed, hell, *wanted*, a guy to make everything right? That's ridiculous, and backwards, and everything I've fought against since Aneeshka and I went to our first game jam and some guy with his head up his ass told us we'd never be able to make good games because we were *girls*.

Jay must sense my hesitation, because his hand withdraws and he adds, 'If you don't want to, you don't have to show us.'

Ignoring my disappointment, I wave it off as though it's nothing. 'Oh, no, it's fine.'

Better to know now than find out at the showcase and embarrass myself. I get on with installing it on his computer, then do the same with Ansen's as Jay fires it up.

'Double Sun presents,' he says, reading the title card out loud. 'Hey, that's a cute name and logo.'

That's a good start. 'Thanks.'

The strains of a piano fill the air as the game's main menu loads. It was composed by Eva and played by my mum, so it means a lot to me even without the game. There are two intertwining parts, one high and soft for the younger sister, and a low alto for the older sister. I wanted it to be as emotionally charged as *Spiritfarer*'s soundtrack, and Eva delivered.

Jay sits on the menu screen, eyes shut as the music plays. He only opens them once it loops, by which time I've finished installing *Vinculum* on Ansen's computer. Ansen eagerly takes it back and loads it up as well.

Echo-y sound effects accompany the white text on the black screen, dialogue between the two sisters. It may only be text, but how it's animated contains a lot of subtlety when it comes to conveying emotion. Note to self: get feedback from Ansen on the animation later.

Then the first level loads, and I hold my breath. Here, at last, is the meat. My mechanic. One joystick, two icons onscreen that move. These first few levels, the music is sweet and reassuring.

'The art's gorgeous,' Jay says, and my heart swells ten sizes because it's one of the elements I created myself.

Then, 'Oh, that's how it works.'

I glance over at Ansen, and see he's already on the third level. He's not taking it slow to enjoy like Jay. Instead he's focused on solving the puzzles one after the other. The only thing he lingers on is the text between levels, the new fragments of memories collected by both sisters. Does it mean he isn't interested in the gameplay? That it's boring and all he wants to do is progress the story? He hasn't said anything about the art, either.

Jay's still on the first level. It's meant to be an easy tutorial level – walk both characters down the hall, side by side, till they reach the door at the end. I mean, it's a straight line! Except he's trying to walk characters into walls, spin them in circles, get them out of sync by having one character walk into a wall where the other character isn't facing one.

Which is all well and good but none of that can happen in this level because it's so simple. I consider making a snarky comment, and eventually decide against it. Better to observe how he plays and what catches his attention.

He *finally* decides he's had enough and goes on to the next level, where he tries everything again. This is going to take a while. Ansen, meanwhile, is powering through the game. He thinks like someone experienced in the ways of puzzlers. No wonder he beat us both in *Theseus*. When he hits a dead end, where it's clear one character or the other won't make it to the memory fragment, he doesn't even waste time trying to backtrack. He simply restarts the level, repeats his actions to a certain point of divergence, and tries another path. It's fun watching him play.

Jay really needs to learn from his brother, because he's slow as hell. At least he's making decent progress now. I can't tell if he actually likes the game, or if he's forcing himself to play out of politeness.

'If you don't like it,' I tell him thirty or so minutes in, 'you don't have to keep playing.'

'Oh, I always take time exploring when I play a new game,' Jay says.

'He does,' Ansen adds, looking up briefly. 'It's very annoying and I don't like playing new games with him because of that.'

That's a relief. Jay must sense how nervous I am, because he adds, 'I like how you play with the core mechanic of moving both characters at the same time. It works with the narrative of the sisters finding their way home after a terrible event, how they're separated in different dimensions, yet still connected. That really hits home.'

'Yeah, like how Jay's mind works in weird ways sometimes and it makes no sense, but he's still my brother,' Ansen adds. 'It feels like that.'

'However,' Jay continues, 'I think you spend too long on similar puzzles before changing up how the mechanic can be used or introducing new elements. They go on for one or two levels too long. I could help you work through the mechanic itself. We could find a way to change it up so it can be expanded beyond the initial "both move at the same time" effect and even flesh out the story more to explore the family beyond the two sisters to support that, or you could also—'

'Jaybird.' He stops mid-sentence and looks at me with a kind of puppy-dog eagerness. 'Those are huge changes that would impact the core of the game, what it is and the story it's trying to tell.'

'Okay, then how about—'

I press a finger to his lips the way I'd do with Aneeshka when her ideas run away with her and she loses track of what she was trying to say in the first place. The movement is instinctive, and it takes a few seconds to realise that I have just done this to Jay friggin' Chua.

'Shhh, Jaybird.' If a finger is pressed to someone's lips but no one acknowledges it, it never happened, right? 'This isn't your game to fix.'

'I'm only trying to help.'

Although the words are a bit muffled, the important point is that his lips are *moving* against my finger. I'm panicking, except I refuse to show it because he seems calm as well. Instead I draw back and hope he didn't feel my pounding pulse.

'I know, but I only asked for your thoughts. Not for you to solve what you think are my problems when you haven't even asked what I was trying to do with the game or what my goals were. Or even if I wanted your help.'

Was that too harsh? Will he turn on me and go full defensive? Even though I know he's not one of those guys who disparages my skills due to my gender, I've encountered misguided people with the best intentions so many times that I'm no longer willing to stay silent.

He freezes, mouth slightly ajar. Blinks. Blinks again. 'Oh.'

'Whoa.' Ansen's staring at me. 'You managed to shut him up. Teach me how.'

That snaps Jay out of his daze. 'Because *she* made a good point.'

Ansen gives him that knowing sibling look before returning his attention to the game. 'Sure.'

'Uh. Sorry.' Jay watches me nervously, waiting for my reaction before saying anything else.

It's a genuine apology, and he didn't try to make excuses. 'Don't worry about it, Jaybird. The Fix-It mode is an occupational hazard that comes with being an older sibling.'

Jay glances at my game, then back at me, and something in his eyes softens. Which must be exponentially contagious because in that moment it feels like my entire body has gone soft enough to melt.

'You put so much of yourself into the game,' he finally says. 'Not only in the story, with the sisters, but in the level of polish on absolutely everything. I love — I like how passionate you are about the project. While I enjoy photography, it's not on this level.'

I don't tell him that while it started that way, much of my dedication now springs from desperation. I've known for years that this is *the* path for me and I need to make it work, so I'll back myself and do whatever it takes. I want to tell him that even though this single-minded dedication isn't all it's cracked up to be, it's also okay to lose yourself in something you love and let your family fend for themselves every now and again, because his talent in photography is so self-evident.

What my brain manages to get out is a squawked, 'Thank you.'

Before I can kick it functional again, Jay reaches into his pocket and pulls out a keychain with a crocheted rune from *Negatory*. It's the 'Reinforce' rune, which boosts your stats and can turn a battle around. He hands it to me. 'A power-up for your showcase.'

He doesn't mention that it's a pair to the charm on his phone, so I don't either. Maybe he honestly means it as a support spell cast on me in preparation for the biggest boss battle of my life. After all, he was pretty clear at the escape room that he thought the runes worked just fine on their own, a sentiment I admire.

Instead of getting too caught up in wondering, I attach it to my backpack zip. 'I love it! Where'd you get it from?'

He seems embarrassed. 'I, uh—'

'You didn't steal it from someone else, did you?'

'He didn't,' Ansen says shortly, his focus still on the game. 'He made it.'

I laugh in delight and examine it again. 'You crochet?'

'It gives my hands something to do when I'm waiting around.' His fingers fidget as though backing up his words. 'I picked it up after my grandma started it.'

'I love this so much! Do you do commissions?' The words shoot out, each faster than the last, as my excitement takes the reins. 'Can you make the sisters from *Vinculum*?'

'Whoa!' He holds up his hands with a grin. 'Slow down! I've never made anything for anyone besides myself—'

'And me and Ma,' Ansen adds, not bothering to look up.

'And Ansen and our mum,' Jay concedes, 'but only if I can find a pattern for it online. Meaning no, I can't make your characters specifically, because no one would've made a pattern for them. So all you've gotta do is make it big with your game and I'll be able to.'

He reaches over and closes my hand around the rune. His

hands are larger than mine, long fingers stretching over my own and resting gently on the base of my palm. It sends tingles down my arm, and there's a warmth there that spreads all the way to my chest, to my heart.

Normally I wouldn't be comfortable with a guy holding my hand out of the blue. In this moment, though, the contact feels right. A natural extension after seeing parts of who he is that he chose to reveal to me, and not to others. After I chose to do the same in return, and want to continue doing so. For the first time I understand the butterflies, shortness of breath and strange physical reactions that Aneeshka claims to get when looking at 'hot' boys.

We remain this way, unmoving, neither wanting to be the first to break away but also unsure of what to do next.

Then the phone rings, and instinct has us yanking apart. Ansen's next to the receiver, so he pauses the game, turns the laptop carefully to one side and picks it up.

'Hello?' he says. Then switching to Cantonese, he continues, 'We're fine. No problems. Gor is with me, and—' He stops. Beside me, Jay is waving at him to hand over the phone. It doesn't seem to register. 'We're playing a game. He's playing on his laptop and I'm playing on mine.' He's breathing heavily now, eyes darting between Jay and me. Jay's gesturing becomes more urgent. 'Yes, it was a good afternoon. We . . . we . . . we played. A game. Just gor. And me. Only us. And we made drinks. Our drinks. From our limes and our plums. Yes.'

Jay wraps a hand around Ansen's wrist, his middle finger tapping the underside rhythmically. Ansen falls silent, blinks a few times, and something unspoken passes between the two of them before he hands the phone to Jay and pads out of the kitchen. Footsteps sound on the stairs while Jay continues the conversation as though nothing's happened.

'He's fine, we're fine, I'll check in on him after and we'll see you at dinner and yes pick up takeaway for us on the way home, bye.'

He hangs up without waiting for a reply. 'Don't worry about Ans,' he says to me. 'He knew he was getting anxious, so he decided to leave the situation and go somewhere quiet to stim. It wasn't absolutely necessary at that point, but it makes him feel more comfortable and why force himself not to when he can?'

I wait for the big brother hackles to come up again, for the wary gaze. They don't come. Instead he gives me a casual shrug like it's no big deal. 'I should've taken the phone from him at the start so he didn't have to lie. He told me that he finds lying really stressful because he wants to get everything perfect and tries to account for every possibility. Except there are so many things to consider and adapt to on the spot that it can become overwhelming.'

'It's . . . good to know he's inherently honest, then?'

'I think it annoys him a lot, truthfully.' Jay leans back in the stool and stares up at the ceiling. 'He hates not being able to hide things from our parents when they ask. They can be a little overbearing sometimes, and it's easier for both of us if they don't know every detail of what we're up to.'

'Oh.' I hadn't thought of that. Imagine struggling to

lie to your parents. That would be the *worst*. 'Should I leave? Will I cause more trouble if he has to cover up more of the day? If you have to tell them I was here, then it's okay. We'll deal with the fanfics.'

'Don't worry about my parents.' Jay doesn't seem concerned, so I'm not either. 'It's why Ans lets me do most of the talking when they ask questions he doesn't want to answer. We've got it all worked out, so he can indirectly lie to them when he wants to. But leaving might be a good idea anyway. They said they left early and they're ten minutes away.'

Oh, no. I stand in a hurry, stuffing my gear into my bag as quickly as possible. My fingers brush over the 'Reinforce' rune he made for me, and in that moment I don't want to leave. He must see it, because he reaches towards me again.

It reminds me that this is not the time. There's no room in my life for a boy right now.

I toss the backpack onto my shoulder before he can say anything to change my mind. 'Talk about a narrow escape! Lucky they called. Tell your brother I wish we had more time to talk about video game art, but we'll do it another time.'

He pulls his hand back. 'Good luck with the Future Devs Showcase in Sydney next week,' he says. 'I know the publishers will love your game. I expect good news when we meet for our final battle, you hear? Go get that game in front of a crowd.'

'You know it.'

He gives me a small smile from the other side of the counter. 'Stay passionate, Udina. Trust yourself.'

The warmth from those words lingers as I leave the house

and get into my car, watching him watching me from the doorway. I'll back myself, and prepare myself for success at the showcase.

I'll prepare myself for the future I've dreamed of for so long.

CHAPTER 18

Future Devs Showcase: 6 days left

My phone buzzes with a message from Jay while I'm driving home. By the time I finally pull into the garage and read it, the damage has already been done.

Jerky McJerkface

> After your hasty exit from my place, my parents figured out you came by anyway

Might as well get what amusement I can out of it, aka needle Jay.

Sam

> What gave it away? Your smooth-talking skills fail you?

They were just fine, thanks. But there was a cup of kat chai suen mui left on the counter and connections were made

Sam

You failed to remove all evidence from the scene of the crime

Sam

YOU LOSE

Sam

Try again? >Yes >No

No

I didn't lose, I . . . had a setback. You don't lose a game because you failed a boss fight the first time

Sam

Oh wow, you really can't handle failure, can you?

IT WAS NOT A FAILURE DAMMIT

Sam

Mmmmhmmm

Jerky McJerkface

What's your bet our parents are already talking to each other about this?

Sam

That's not a bet, that's a guarantee.

I'm on tenterhooks all Monday wondering if my parents will say anything. But nothing happens, and life goes on as usual save for Eva sulking over our parents' continued refusal to let her go on holidays with Tamara's family.

It makes for an awkward Tuesday night when our family goes out to dinner to celebrate my upcoming showcase. Eva stares stonily out the window in complete silence the whole way there, so our parents simply talk more and pretend nothing is wrong. It's mainly my mum talking about what Aunty So-and-So did the other day, and my dad going on about the badminton matches over the weekend and how good each of the uncles are.

We arrive to find the restaurant pretty quiet, not surprising given it's a Tuesday night. I can never remember the name, because we call it Leng zai's restaurant (aka pretty boy's restaurant) – a nickname that stuck after my Yi Gu Jie came here and saw the chef who ran the place. It does some of the best Malaysian food in Brisbane, which is admittedly not a very high bar. They also do a mean Peking duck, which is the main reason I requested we come here.

My parents don't even need the menu. My dad tells them immediately we want the Peking duck, with sang choi bao as the second course. The sang choi bao is minced duck and chopped up veggies and mushrooms wrapped in crispy lettuce, and far superior to the other option of duck meat noodles. He also orders my favourites of assam fish – succulent fillets of fish in sweet and sour tamarind sauce – and a dry rendang curry, to go with the rice. They're really spoiling me tonight and I couldn't love them more. Even Eva thaws a bit when she hears the order.

Truly, food is the great peacemaker.

A waiter brings out the jasmine tea and I pour it into small cups for everyone, each of them knocking the table with their knuckles in thanks as I pass it to them. When we were children, my Dai Gu Jie told us this tradition originated from an emperor who went on tour in disguise, and at one point poured tea for a servant. The hapless servant, unable to kowtow in thanks as custom demanded because the emperor was meant to be incognito, tapped his fingers on the table instead. I suspect it's simply an old folktale that got passed around, but who knows? Honestly, who knows why we do half the things we do, anyway? Not my parents, that's for sure.

I'm pouring the last cup of tea for Eva when the door opens and I catch a glimpse of a familiar pointy head of hair. *Oh, no.* I take a sneaky glance as I pass the cup to Eva and, sure enough, it's Jay. Not only Jay; *his whole family* is with him. There's electricity in the air as our gazes collide.

The electricity of sheer terror.

Do his parents still think we're dating? Do they hate me because they think we're hiding it? Or worse, are they looking at me like 'Hello, future daughter-in-law'? This could be awkward.

I quickly turn back to my parents. 'Do you want to see the trailer of my game that I'm using for the showcase? It took me a while to make, but I'm really proud of it.'

If I can keep them looking down at my phone, maybe they won't notice Jay and his parents.

Then Eva says, very deliberately, 'Hey, isn't that your not-boyfriend Jaysen? And his family?'

Not satisfied with that, she stands up and waves at them like they're old friends. I swear, if I offed her at this very moment, not a single jury would convict me. And of course, Jay's parents come over, Jay and Ansen trailing behind. My parents seem quite pleased with this development, while Eva's obviously smug. I wonder if this is her revenge for our parents' – not even *my!* – comments about how I never went on trips with friends. Even if she truly believes Jay and I aren't a thing, she'll take advantage of everyone else's misunderstanding.

'Anna, Michael!' Jay's mum says, giving their names a familiar Cantonese lilt. 'What a coincidence to see you here.'

The way she says it so cheerfully is a dead giveaway. Coincidence my ass. I'd bet the workshop ticket this was planned.

I glance at Jay to see he has his best gwai zai smile pasted on. 'Aunty, uncle, lei hou.' And not satisfied with just that, he adds, 'Samantha has told me a lot about you, and I can tell she really respects you.'

All in flawless Cantonese, the show-off. Also, the liar. I haven't told him a thing about them. My parents look very happy, though, and my mum definitely likes him from the way she smiles at him like she wants to invite him over to feed him.

I'll be damned if I let him out-gwai me. 'Aunty, uncle,' I say to his parents, 'thank you for letting me visit on Sunday. Your house is so lovely, and Jay and Ansen were such good hosts.'

My Cantonese isn't as good as Jay's, though, so I end up saying 'hosts' in English. *Ugh.* Feels like I'm already losing this particular round.

'Esther, Edwin, why don't you pull over the table so you can sit with us?' my mum says. 'Our two families can have dinner together.'

No, no, no, no, no. What fresh hell is this? Now I'm a thousand per cent convinced this 'coincidental meeting' is a total set-up by both sides. The flash of horror that sweeps across Jay's face mirrors my feelings, though he quickly covers it up with his gwai zai smile.

'One moment,' Jay's mum says to mine, then she turns to Ansen. 'You'll be okay?'

It's good to know Ansen wasn't in on it, though he'd probably have warned Jay if he knew. All we can hope for is that he'll come through for us and say he'd rather our families dine separately. Jay's glance at him conveys the same emotion, but Ansen doesn't seem to notice our pleading stares.

He sighs. 'I'll be fine, Ma, and if there was a problem I'd tell you. You don't have to ask me about everything. I know how to handle things if I get overwhelmed.'

'Are you *really* sure, Ans?' Jay asks with a hint of *Say no, dammit* in his tone.

'Geez, gor, don't you start fussing over me too.'

Aunty Esther doesn't argue. 'If you're sure,' she says happily.

'Don't make a big deal out of this, it's embarrassing,' Ansen says in exasperation. 'Can we please sit with Sam and her family now?'

Behind them, Jay's smile is fixed and brittle, and it's obvious he's trying not to facepalm. A waiter pulls the two tables together for us, and Eva and I are unceremoniously shunted to the other table so the four adults can sit together.

I quickly grab the teapot and start pouring tea for all of them. *Take that, Jay!*

My dad and their dad immediately start talking about what we've ordered and additional dishes to order. Meanwhile, our mums are talking about – what else – us.

'Your two boys, everyone says they're very smart,' my mother comments casually, because the highest compliments are ones stated as though they're a matter-of-fact.

This is, without a doubt, a leading question.

'Ansen is very talented at art,' Jay's mum replies, accepting it with a small smile. 'He joined a sketching group for fun and his art's been on display at The Wesley Hospital before. He wants to make art for video games in the future, he says.'

The fact that she's not brushing off the compliment in a show of humility means she's ready to start the Jaysen sales pitch after the Ansen preface.

Sure enough, her next words are, 'Jaysen was also offered a spot at Monash University in Melbourne for his degree, but decided to stay in Brisbane to help us out. It's good having him around the house to keep an eye on his brother.'

'So gwai,' my mum gushes.

Across from me, Jay and Ansen fidget in embarrassment.

'Not that I need looking after,' Ansen mutters, and Eva gives him a look of shared commiseration.

'Eva is in Year Eleven and a very talented musician,' my mum says, not to be outdone. 'She plays in the church band, leads a group of youth at her other church, and is in the school's top choir and strings ensemble. Samantha just graduated and will be going to the Queensland University of Technology this year. She got into a scholarship course for the top students in the state, you know. She worked so hard for it. We're celebrating tonight because the game she made was chosen for a special showcase to video game publishers. Only one hundred game creators were chosen from all of Australia!'

'Wah, both of your daughters are so talented,' Jay's mum says as she smiles at me and Eva. 'Your parents are lucky to have the two of you as their daughters.'

'Thank you, aunty,' we chorus.

I wonder what she would say without the 'Sam has a scholarship' qualifier. So I add, 'I'm very proud of the game I made, and I hope I'll make my parents proud with it.'

'Aiya, so modest,' she says. 'I'm sure they're already proud of you, with your scholarship.'

When she turns back to converse with my mum, Eva elbows me. 'She *likes* you. You're in, now.'

Jay gives her an exasperated stare. 'You. This might be some diabolical plot by both our parents, but don't you make this worse.' He adds in a low voice, 'For the record, my mum likes just about every good girl who goes to church and is polite and treats her parents well.'

Eva giggles. 'They're low-key trying to sell you guys to one another. You need an anti-pitch, jie. How about: don't expect her to make dough in the kitchen . . . or in the boardroom either.'

Jay snorts and it takes all my willpower not to throw something at him. I'm not going to be the first to drop my mask of gwai.

Ansen turns to point at Jay. 'Then Jay's anti-pitch would be . . .'

He pulls out a pen from his pocket and does a quick sketch on his serviette. Before our eyes, Jay materialises in a hard hat, wielding a hammer. On one side is a box that says TO FIX, on the other one that says FIXED. Except everything in both boxes is new and unbroken, with sparkles for emphasis.

I laugh so hard that all our parents and the people at the other tables turn and stare. Before Jay can get his hands on the serviette I snatch it away and stuff it in my pocket.

'Ansen just showed us a very funny joke,' I tell our parents, even if it doesn't quite sound believable because the two of us are the only ones laughing. Eva is confused, Jay grumpy. I add in English, 'It takes a certain sense of humour to get it.'

That earns me two kicks under the table, but it's so worth it.

Aunty Esther tries to smooth things over, turning to our mum. 'Sam is so gwai, surely she must have a boyfriend already.'

I stifle a groan.

'Why not me?' Eva mutters under her breath. We both know it's because she's 'too young' till the day she graduates from high school – then it's a race for a boy.

I derive some amusement from the way Jay looks at his mum after that comment. If he wasn't in front of an aunty and uncle he would totally pull her aside right now and tell her to stop it.

Our mum shakes her head. 'Samantha doesn't have a boyfriend yet; she's only just graduated high school. I think it would be good for her to find a nice boy she can get to know during university, then settle down with after.' If that's not a pointed hint, I don't know what is. 'How about your sons?'

Aunty Esther's gaze cuts over to Jaysen and Ansen, and a pleased smile spreads over her face. 'Oh, no, neither of them have a girlfriend at the moment. Jaysen's never dated and Ansen's still so young, you know?'

'Ma, enough already,' Jay says, and Ansen nods in firm agreement.

'We're just talking about our children, that's what parents will do,' Aunty Esther says. 'It's no different from me talking about how Ansen goes to that sketching group or how you stitch those things with wool.'

'It's very different,' Jay says immediately. His gaze flicks over to my parents and he slips back into his gwai zai mode. 'Aunty, uncle, you should ask them about the place we stayed on the Gold Coast last holidays. It was a nice apartment for a family holiday with ocean views and everything.'

After all the years dealing with Eva, our mum has learned to go with the flow when it comes to redirects. 'We've been looking for a good holiday rental!' She turns to his mum. 'Esther, how did you find it?'

That, thankfully, is that. Then Eva's gaze drops to my bag with the crocheted rune keychain, and her eyes widen in understanding. 'Waitwaitwait. Did you make that keychain for my sister?'

One glance at Jay and we've already agreed on a tactic. Deny everything.

'No,' he says.

'Yes,' says Ansen at the same time, then cuts himself off from saying anything more when he realises what Jay's said. But when he sees the 'time to give them all the crap I got' grin spreading across Eva's face, he mirrors it. 'Jaysen made it especially for your sister.'

Eva cackles. 'Oh, *did* he? I think we should ask both of them more about their feelings, don't you?'

Ansen nods, his grin spreading wider. 'It's important to be aware of your feelings and understand them. That's what my counsellor says.'

'Hear that, jie?' Eva nudges me hard with her elbow. 'Would you care to tell us about your feelings?'

I squint as though in deep thought. 'I feel . . . like you'll both be lucky if you live through this dinner.'

To my utter relief, the Peking duck arrives not long after, so the two of them are distracted by food. I realise to my dismay that doubling the number of people means that instead of eating a good portion of the twelve or so pancakes that come with it, they now have to be shared out, with our parents given priority. My original four or five drops to one lousy pancake, since I insist that the adults have the second serving like the gwai lui I'm pretending to be. Jay does the same. Eva and Ansen take seconds without a care for what anyone else thinks of them.

Later, the rice arrives, and before I can react Jay gestures at the waiter to place the stand with the rice pot beside him. Damn it, now he gets to be the one filling all our parents' bowls. I settle for topping up everyone's cups of tea instead.

By the end of dinner I'm exhausted from keeping up the act, but if we're comparing approval ratings surely mine must be on par with Jay's, if not above. I've insisted the adults take from all the shared dishes first, offered the last morsels of fish and meat and mushrooms to them, and kept their tea cups topped up. He, meanwhile, has been the master of the rice, and charmer extraordinaire. His perfect Cantonese irks me to no end.

After they bring out the complimentary plate of sliced fruits, my mum tries to 'go to the bathroom' (i.e. secretly pay the bill). Jay's mum immediately stands to join her. So she has to actually go, passing the baton to my dad with a Look. My poor dad, who's hopeless at deception, stands up straightaway and makes a rush for the counter, except he's forgotten they have to total up the bill, so Jay's dad catches up to him. The four of us kids remain at the table, waiting to see the winner.

'Wow, you're really trying hard to impress,' Eva mutters to me as we watch the back and forth of brandished cards, the 'aiyaya how could I possibly let you's, and the poor waitress who has to take payment. 'Don't want to alienate your future parents-in-law?'

'How many times do I have to tell you they're not? This is all for the sake of the sole ticket to the Art of Game Design workshop, and nothing more.' I wave my hand in front of Jay's face. 'Jaybird. Tell my annoying sister we're not dating, please.'

'We're not dating,' he says immediately. 'Can everyone stop with the assumptions already? It's bad enough with both sides conspiring.'

I point at him accusingly. 'You shouldn't have put on that gwai zai act, then.'

'You did the same!' He crosses his arms. 'Did you think you were really going to beat me in that?'

The nerve of this guy. 'Excuse me? I totally did. Did you not see their tea cups? I gave your dad the last piece of fish! Literally spooned it onto his plate!'

He shakes his head. 'Amateur. I made conversation with your parents, asked them about what they did and even talked about the latest badminton tournament in Kuala Lumpur with your dad.'

'Well, *your* mum said how much she liked the kat chai suen mui I made for you guys,' I retort. 'And I gave full credit to my parents instead of taking any for my own.'

'Yeah, but I—'

'Don't worry, Jay's always this bad,' Ansen tells Eva.

'My sister isn't any better,' she replies, and they both laugh.

'Excuse me?' Jay and I say together, though we start and end at slightly different times.

Back at the counter, it seems my dad has triumphed, whipping his card over the reader before Jay's dad does.

'Game, set and match,' I tell Jay.

He doesn't look happy. 'Next time.'

'Oh, there's going to be a next time?' Eva asks with far too much innocence to actually mean it. 'So our two families will be joined eventually?'

Really. I'm going to kill her.

When our mums return, Jay's mum shakes her head when his dad gives her a helpless shrug to indicate he wasn't able to pay the bill.

'Thank you for the dinner, Anna and Michael,' she says. 'You must let us take you out next time. There's a new Malaysian place that opened in Logan that we really like.'

'Yes,' my mum agrees, 'we must do this again. It was lovely having dinner with you.'

In the car on the way home, all my parents talk about is how wonderful Jay and his family are.

'Aren't they great?' my dad asks me in a totally unsubtle hint. 'Esther and Edwin would accept you as their daughter-in-law.

They would support you making your games. Did you see how Esther didn't mind that Ansen wanted to make art for video games? He could draw for your games! And you can tell their son Jaysen likes you, the way he was watching you all dinner.'

'You like him too, don't you, Sun Sun?' my mum asks, teasing but also serious.

'No,' I say, and turn to face the window to end the conversation. I'm definitely not thinking about Sunday and his hand covering mine, and how easy it would be to fall into him, the rest of the world be damned.

Instead I close my hand around the 'Reinforce' rune he made me, and try to convince myself it's been cast on my heart to protect it.

CHAPTER 19

Future Devs Showcase: 3 days left

I sit in my room staring at the course deferral form I printed out after last night's two-family dinner. I've filled in all my basic information, but none of the details. If I defer, I'll still have a place in the university course, though the deal-breaker is that there's no scholarship. Maybe that's what I need, the kind of resolve I can't back out of? Especially not because of a boy.

If I can't fully commit to my future and focus entirely on making games that are even better than the previous ones, I don't deserve success. There is a future out there I need to work harder for. It's just that every time I have to put pen to paper, and write in actual words the reason for my deferral and that I understand I'm forfeiting the scholarship, I think of how disappointed my parents will be and end up writing nothing.

I've wasted so much time tonight staring at my piles of level design sketches, building up the confidence to fill this out, then chickening out again. It would be so much easier to fill this out if I was anywhere else. If I was far away from my mum washing-up after dinner in the kitchen, and the news blaring in the background as my dad half-dozes on the recliner after a long day at work. If I'm removed from all the reminders of what my parents have sacrificed for me and Eva.

Here, our mum's mostly a housewife who teaches music on the side. Back in Malaysia, pre-children, she ran a branch of a large music school. Meanwhile, our dad was a regional manager at a large engineering company, while over here he's a mid-level project manager in a local government office. In Malaysia, though, everything from university entry, professional qualification exams (like the bar exam for lawyers), and even a number of jobs, heavily preference Malays.

They wanted their own children to have the best chance at whatever they wanted to do, so they left it all behind to move here. I accepted the scholarship because of how happy they were, the expressions on their faces that said, *This made everything worth it*. That moment where all their hard work and sacrifices culminated in a joyful, tangible result.

It's the moment I'm chasing with *Vinculum*, the moment where everything pays off and I finally step onto the stage I've been staring at for years.

Both of these moments cannot coexist.

I lean over my desk to open the window wide, letting the gentle summer breeze come through. While Brisbane summers are usually disgustingly hot and humid, the wind tonight is cool and dry, a pleasant change in the air.

I'm making another attempt to fill out the deferral form when my door creaks open.

'Sun Sun, are you free?'

My mum pretends to ask permission, but she and my dad have already let themselves in. I hastily position my chair so my body blocks the form I was filling out, as they settle themselves on my bed with serious looks.

'We wanted to talk with you about the Chua's eldest son,' my mum says. 'That Jaysen boy.'

I narrow my eyes and glance between both of them. 'What about him?'

My dad glances over at my mum with his typical 'you do the talking' tilt of the head.

'I was talking to Aunty Esther today,' she says, 'and we don't understand why you and Jaysen were so secretive about your visit to their house on Sunday.'

Because we were trying to avoid a situation like this, I think.

Instead I ask, 'And . . .?'

My parents watch me carefully as my mum continues: 'If the two of you maybe made some . . . decisions . . . that you're scared to tell us about, we promise we won't get angry. As your mummy and daddy we want to help you if you don't know what to do next.'

I stare at them. And then laughter bubbles out, on the borderline of hysterical because yes there's something I'm terrified to tell them about, yes there's something I've been trying to find the words for all night, but this . . . *this is not it.*

'No!' I wait till the laughter runs its course. 'We haven't done anything of the sort. You can ask his brother, he was with us all Sunday. We're in the middle of a very serious competition, okay?'

My dad's brows furrow. 'Why are you fighting with the Chuas' son?'

I sigh. *Because if I can attend a workshop hosted by the Farrows and have my heroes talk about my game, it will elevate my career. I won't be a disappointment to the two of you. I'll be able to remain the good Asian kid.*

'Because there's one ticket to a very exclusive game design workshop in June that we both want,' I tell my parents, 'and we're competing to see who gets it. Like I said, we're not dating, we're fighting.'

Neither of them is convinced. My mum's brows furrow in the same way as my dad's. 'Why can't you buy another ticket?'

'You have the chance to interact with the game developers at the workshop, so the total number of places is limited.' I spread out my hands. 'Now do you believe we didn't get up to anything?'

My mum lets out a huff that's half laugh, and this time the look she exchanges with my dad is one of 'What did you expect?'

'We believe you, Sun Sun,' she says. 'But I also wish you would give this boy a chance. I talked to Aunty Deonna to find out more about him. She goes to the same church as their family and says he's always very polite, a very gwai zai.'

I give Jay this much, he's hidden his true personality from the adults very well. They don't know how he was so determined to win he made me throw up, or how he doesn't stop rambling when excited or nervous, or even how frustrated he gets at the expectations and responsibilities they place on him. Forget about the gospel of grace at church, all our Asian parents subscribe to the gospel of gwai.

'Why can't I simply be friends – or frenemies – with him? Is that so strange to both of you?'

Both my parents shake their heads with the frustration of someone who wants the other party to just *see*.

'All you focus on is making your games,' my dad says. 'Soon you'll go to university where you'll meet a lot of people and discover many new experiences, and we don't want you to miss out simply because all you can think about is making games.'

I'm starting to wish that my 'big secret' is that I slept with Jay, instead of it being that I don't want to go to uni so I can spend all my time making games.

'You know how serious I am about becoming a game developer,' I say, trying to keep the desperation out of my voice. 'And you know what it takes to become a professional in your field.' I turn to my mum. 'Musicians like Yo-Yo Ma, how much do you think they sacrifice and practise to be the best?'

My mum sighs. 'Sun Sun, that's a rough road with no guarantees. Unless you're a genius, then it also depends on luck.'

I gesture at my shelf of awards I've won in coding contests, game jams, school competitions. 'Isn't this enough to prove my talent? From primary school and all through high school, everyone's said I'm a great coder, and I put in the effort too. Instead of spending my holidays lazing around, I use them to work on my games and get even better. I'm going to a showcase where only a hundred people my age were chosen. Maybe I'm not a genius, but I'm really good at making games and you know it.'

'We understand.' My dad has a complicated expression on his face. 'You're still young, though, and life isn't always that simple.'

'I swear to you, I will achieve my dream of becoming a successful indie game developer before I consider any boys. Jay included. *This* is what I'm sacrificing for.'

I sweep my arm behind me to point at the game code on my screen, except I'm so agitated I accidentally knock some of my figurines and design papers off my desk.

'What's new?' my dad says, grinning at me, and the mood instantly lightens up.

My mum comes over to help me gather everything, and that's when I remember the deferral form was on top of my piles of scribbled designs.

Before I can grab the papers from my mum's hands, she holds up the form. Horror mingles with dismay as she looks at me.

'Sun Sun . . . what is this?'

CHAPTER 20⊙

Future Devs Showcase: 3 days left

Shit. Shit, shit, shit. My parents weren't supposed to know, not yet. I'm not ready for this conversation. I'm not ready to present a series of compelling, logical arguments, because their foundation rests on the publisher interest I'm sure to get at the Future Devs Showcase.

'I . . .' I glance back and forth between her and my dad. 'It's something I'm thinking about.'

'Sun Sun, you don't want to go to university? You want to reject the scholarship?' That's definitely panic in my mum's voice as she hands the deferral form to my dad. 'This is your future!'

How do I begin? 'I'm . . . I'm not sure if it is.'

'Sun Sun, we know you love making games, but the scholarship course will give you so many more options in the future. You're so smart, why are you wasting your potential?'

I give up on trying to explain myself in Cantonese, and switch to English to make my arguments. 'I'm not wasting it; I'm making full use of it! Isn't it better to do something I'm passionate about?'

'Passion is good, except it doesn't pay the bills.' Yep, my mum's panic is still there, and I wish so much I was truly the kind of daughter who could be happy with that kind of life. 'You need a backup plan, and this scholarship is the best plan there is.'

The part of me who is Australian, who has grown up with gwei lo values all around me, isn't willing to give in so easily. 'One that makes me miserable?'

My dad's not angry, just confused. 'How do you know it will? You haven't even started university yet.'

All I'm able to do is explain myself as best I can, and hope they come around. I don't want to fight with them. 'Because I've seen the courses, and after all these years coding I know what they'll cover and why I'm not interested.'

'Okay,' my dad says in a tone that's obviously meant to be placating. 'You're not interested in that course. How about another one?'

There's only one course in Brisbane that comes close. 'Bachelor of Games and Interactive Environments, with a major in Game Design. Does not come with scholarship.'

My dad sighs. 'And what kind of job can you find with that?'

'Probably one as another cog in a game company where I'll make games I don't have any interest in and am always crunching overtime to push the next game out.' I shrug helplessly. 'That's why I could do it and *then* branch out to make my own games, but it's a waste of three years of my time, and your money – or mine, if I take a government loan. For what? To study things I could instead learn from my own experience, being within the industry?'

My dad's not giving up, and he's got that 'let's-reason-it-out' attitude going. 'So why can't you take the scholarship anyway, and at least have a free degree that will make you employable?'

Employable, employable. As though it's all that matters because what Asian family wants a kid that leeches off them? Mixed in with my frustration is also shame. It poisons every thought, seeps into my determination, and it's unbearable.

'Just say that I'm a disappointment and a failure otherwise and be done with it! I already know that, so why don't you say what you think?'

'Sun Sun.' My mum's calmer now. She stands up and comes over to the gaming chair where my hands are clenched into fists, and covers them with her own. 'Do you think we see you that way? Do you see *yourself* that way?'

My dad nods. 'We only want you to have a plan other than making your own video games, one that can be a career if you ever need it. And me and your ma, we think the scholarship course is the best path for your future. That's all.'

'We're proud of you because you're hardworking, determined and so creative.' My mum pats my slowly uncurling fists. 'I thought you knew *that*.'

There's a lump in my throat that I can't seem to swallow. 'But it's not enough, is it?'

My dad puts down the form and comes over to ruffle my hair. 'Why do you think like that? Look at your mui, she—'

The words come out without thinking, words I've never dared to think about before. 'I don't want you to see me the way you see Eva!'

My parents are frozen. After a long silence, my mum is the first to speak. 'What do you mean by that? We love you and Eva equally.'

What *do* I mean by that? I've never really thought about it until now. 'I . . . I mean . . . that she's very gwei lo, right?' I pause, searching for why being seen that way causes me so much discomfort. 'She does what she wants with her friends, and doesn't really consider how much it worries you, or whether it makes you happy or proud, or . . . just, does she ever think about the sacrifices you both made to raise us in Australia?'

It's always something that's been in the back of my mind, which drives my choices. While I've pursued my dream, I've also been very careful about how I go about it. I've been careful about trying to balance my desires with respecting my parents' wishes.

Eva, meanwhile, doesn't even seem to consider this. Grades? What of them, they're simply a means to an end. Spending time with parents? Sure, if it's a scheduled activity or they explicitly ask (they won't, they're *Asian parents*).

She doesn't understand, but I, the eldest daughter, the more 'Asian' daughter, the 'good' daughter . . . I do.

My mum wraps me in a hug. 'Sun Sun. Me and your ba, we love that you're always thinking about us. It doesn't mean we love your mui any less for being who she is. We find it harder to talk to her sometimes, and we might disagree more, but neither of you is a "better" or "worse" daughter than the other.'

It's not that I ever thought of myself as a better daughter than Eva, exactly. Just . . . more aligned with my parents. More properly Asian instead of Australian and so better positioned to understand them. It made me feel good about myself, if I'm going to be brutally honest.

'If we ever made either of you feel this way . . .' My dad's voice trails off, as though he's searching for the words. 'We're sorry.'

'Even if we think your decision to give up your scholarship to spend your time making games is an unwise and impulsive idea—' Wow, way for my mum to make her point yet again while trying to comfort me, '—we would never see you as a disappointment.'

I look up from my mum's shoulder to see a ghost of my dad's teasing smile. 'We see you as one of our irreplaceable daughters who's about to make a big mistake.'

'You don't know it's a mistake.' Unlike Eva and her music-as-hobby, I've thrown everything I have into pursuit of this dream. I've been recognised time and time again. My persistence and sacrifice will pay off. It must. 'It could be uni that holds me back from everything I could achieve.'

'Or giving up university could lead you down a painful path in life where you're struggling to keep a roof over your head, especially if something unexpected happens and we leave you and your mui behind too soon.' There's a sadness to my dad's posture. 'All we want, as your parents, is to ensure you have a good future.'

I stare down at the floor. 'You sound like you're already sure my game will fail.'

My mum pulls away, holding me at arm's length so she can look me in the eye. 'So you do well with this game. But will it be the same for the next game, and the game after that?'

'I'll have fans,' I say firmly, looking up again. All the more reason I need to get to the Farrows' workshop and get that publicity. 'It's about growing your fan base with every game, so they'll continue to buy every game you make. The people who discover my later games will go back and buy my earlier games.'

'Sun Sun.' The trace of sadness still lingers in my dad's expression. 'Life doesn't always go the way you plan.'

'Let me prove it to you at the Future Devs Showcase. Please. Let me show you how capable I am.'

My parents exchange a glance before my mum leans down to kiss my forehead. 'Then we'll pray for your success.'

CHAPTER 21

Future Devs Showcase: 2 days left

With time ticking down till the Future Devs Showcase, I'm desperately polishing up *Vinculum* for the final time (though really, is it ever final?) when I get a text from Jay.

Jerky McJerkface

I know you're busy but . . .
are you free to meet?

Sam

Sure, what's up?

Jerky McJerkface

Stuff happened and I need someone to talk to for a bit. I know it's sudden, it's just, I felt like maybe you'd understand and

Jerky McJerkface

Sorry this probably sounds weird

Sam

I'm free, I'd love to meet, and I'm touched you want to talk about whatever this is with me

Jerky McJerkface

You're the best! I can come pick you up so you don't have to run around

Sam

Absolutely not, unless you want our parents to start new rumours about us

Jerky McJerkface

Good point. How about somewhere at the shopping centre with the GamesMasters store where we first met?

Sam

> Sure, I'm up for a D&M at
> The Greatest Outdoors

When this started, a deep-and-meaningful was the last kind of conversation I ever thought I'd be having with Jay. How things change.

Jerky McJerkface

> You kid, but . . .

Sam

> Meet you outside GamesMasters
> in fifteen mins

I shut everything down, tell my parents I'm going out to get some last-minute items for my trip to Sydney tomorrow, and head straight there. It's not like I'm excited to see Jay or anything. He needs someone to talk to and he reached out to me, so of course I want to hurry and be there for him.

Despite my hurry, Jay's already outside the GamesMasters when I arrive. He seems exhausted and his hair is rumpled, though not in a suave Hollywood movie style. It's more a 'my hair would be a tangled, matted mess if it was any longer' style. When he spots me his eyes light up, and maybe, just maybe, mine do too.

'You look like total crap,' I say by way of greeting.

He lets out a small huff of amusement. 'Thanks.'

'The Greatest Outdoors, then? Or do you want to go to one of the small cafes here and hide out in a corner?' For all my teasing, I don't actually want to have a D&M at The Greatest Outdoors under the porta-potties. 'There's a "$50-is-pocket-change" level cafe here that no self-respecting Asian aunty or uncle would open their wallet for.'

'Done,' he says. 'My treat.'

We head over to the cafe, which is decorated in what seems to be an attempt at what I can only call post-modern chic. The interior is mostly black, the chairs plastic and 'artistically' shaped, with lampshade chandeliers hanging from the ceiling and splashes of abstract white decor all around. You don't even need the menu to know this place is pricey. My parents would definitely mock it as a waste of money.

We manage to snag a small booth to one side. After we order a tiny overpriced cake each to justify our presence to the wait staff, Jay lets out a breath and basically collapses in on himself.

'What's with the death-warmed-over look?' He did say he wanted to talk, after all.

He glances up from where he's buried his face in his arms. 'I . . . had a fight with Ansen. He went to his room and put his taiko drumming music on full blast, which he only does when he's really pissed or agitated. And now he's not talking to me.'

It's so unlike the Jay I've known this whole time that I'm genuinely worried, even if it seems like a bit of an overreaction to a fight. Eva and I used to get so huffy we'd ignore each other for an entire day or two.

'Surely you guys fought a lot growing up? Or still?'

'Yeah, I knew how to deal with that, sort it all out, you know? It's different this time.' He groans. 'It's your fault, by the way. He's been snippy with me since that day you came over. I say anything and now he's all "I didn't ask you to solve my problems". Have I been doing this big brother thing wrong the whole time? I figured you, at least, would give it to me straight. And . . .' He glances away and mumbles, 'I had the feeling after playing your game that you'd understand what it's like to suddenly find there's a distance between you and your sibling, and you don't know how to cross it.'

I didn't know a heart could squeeze in this way. 'Yeah, like you're in different worlds and you don't know how it happened, right? What was the fight about?'

Jay sighs, resting his chin on his forearm. 'My dad went to pick him up from his sketching group earlier than usual last night and saw two of the guys there making fun of Ans.'

Is it bad that I hope Jay's dad is as adept in Krav Maga as Jay, and as willing to use it? 'What'd your dad do?'

Jay's shrug is resigned. 'Brought him home, what else? Then talked with our mum, and said at dinner that they'd find him a new sketching group.'

'That sounds reasonable.'

The look he gives me is that of someone who's finally found an ally among enemies. 'Right?! He *should* get away from those pieces of garbage.'

'So what happened?'

'He refused. Flat-out said he wouldn't leave and that he

could deal with it.' Jay's expression is pleading. 'Wanting to get someone out of a bad situation isn't wrong, right?'

Does he expect me to give him absolution? 'I don't think I'm the one you should be asking about this. If it was your parents insisting, why's he angry at you?'

He reaches up and runs his hand through his hair. 'He turned to me and said I didn't think he should leave, wasn't that right?'

Oh. I see where this is going. 'And?'

'I said that he *should* leave, because he shouldn't be part of a group where he was bullied. Made a joke that I was too old to beat them up and run them out without doing jail time now. Before I could say anything else he went *off*. Said I'd always treated him like a kid who didn't know any better and I needed to butt out because he hated it. Oh, and that he hated me. Then he stormed off to his room and refused to let me in.' Jay lets out a low growl. 'He was super agitated, I could hear him through my bedroom wall, and I couldn't do anything. Why can't he understand that I don't want him to be hurt, that's all?'

The tone of that last line is so similar to when my parents were going on about how I shouldn't give up the scholarship. They genuinely want the best for me and wish for my happiness, except they believe my happiness is in getting a stable job, and ideally marrying a good boy to boot.

'You know, I want to take a gap year instead of doing the whole scholarship thing at uni.'

He seems confused. 'Ooo . . . kay? That's great?'

'My parents found out the other night. They think it's a terrible idea and that I'm making a big mistake.' I stare at the artsy chandelier above our table, trying to distance my emotions so I won't accidentally cry and make this about me. 'Logically, I get it. I'm giving up a free ride through uni to make games with no sure guarantees it'll pan out. On the other hand, I wish they'd step back and let me make mistakes and deal with the fallout. Assuming it even *is* a mistake. I don't want to have any regrets, and I want to do things my way even if they think they know better.'

Jay lets out a huff. 'That's different, though. It's not like you're being tormented by people. I mean, if you saw your sister in an abusive relationship, wouldn't you tell her to leave? Wouldn't you make her if she wouldn't?'

'Well, yeah. If Eva was willing to listen.' I give him a wry smile. 'First off, I've tried and failed at being the older sibling the younger one looks up to. Not the way Ansen looks up to you. So I could tell her, but I can't always make her do what *I* think she should do. The older she gets, the harder it gets.'

I continue: 'Even my parents struggle with how to handle those situations. Eva's in a cold war with them right now over going on a holiday with friends. Sometimes you can't fix everything. You have to let them go, and be there if they need you later.'

He stares down at the table for a long while. When he speaks, his voice is softer and more unsure than I thought possible for him. 'I know he has his own life, but it's hard having to watch others treat him like shit over and over just because he doesn't act how *they* think people should act. Especially when I have the power to stop them. To stop the hurt and the nonsense life's decided to rain down on him.'

'Paraphrasing what Eva told me when she was annoyed, if he understands what he's facing, then it's his choice, his consequences.'

'Are all siblings like this?'

'Heh. Probably. Maybe he has a reason for wanting to stay in that group. Did you ask him?'

There's a reluctant twist to his lips when he replies grudgingly, 'No. And I'm belatedly remembering what you said about not asking what you were trying to do with the game or what your goals were before saying anything, and . . .' He ends in a strangled, inarticulate noise.

'Go forth, Jaybird. You already know what you need to do.'

'Thanks, Udina. When I was pacing my room, not knowing what to do, feeling like a terrible big brother, you were the first person I wanted to talk to. I figured you'd already seen me at my most pushy and just told me to shush in a way that made me feel like it was okay to mess up, because I could trust you to tell me straight without feeling like you were disappointed in me. Does that make sense?'

When I nod because I don't have words for it – how does one find words when told something so small yet so immense? – he pauses and takes a deep breath. 'Sorry, rambling again. Um. I just felt like I could stop being the perfect Jay Chua everyone sees for a while and it wasn't a big deal to you. Like to my parents and aunties and uncles I'm the gwai zai, to Ans I'm his gor. But you already saw me at my most . . . Jay, good and bad, and didn't run.'

'I'm hardly going to run when you're holding my workshop ticket hostage. You're not getting off that easy.' I keep my tone light, teasing. Hiding everything that wants to burst out.

'I know, and I loved—uh, appreciated that.'

Jay continues to stare at me for a long moment. There's something about the way he's looking at me, a heady cocktail of soft and intense, that stirs butterflies in my stomach. There's a tugging, a longing that makes me scared of what he might say, because if he so much as suggests something more than friendship I won't be able to refuse.

I want to stay here in this bubble that separates me from the rest of my life when I'm with him. It's a time where I'm not thinking constantly about my game, or my future, or who I should be or want to be, or how I should act.

Even the appreciation goes both ways. Not only can I play games freely in a way I haven't in so long, but I can speak my mind without that little voice always second-guessing me. Maybe it's because I didn't give a damn what he thought of me when I first met him. Whatever it is, there's something about hanging out with him that feels right, like that 'ah-hah!' moment when you solve a puzzle. I don't want to leave, even though I really should get back to work on *Vinculum*—

I yank my gaze away.

From the corner of my eye, I see the shake of his head, as if he's clearing it. 'Anyway. I'll take your advice and have a proper talk with Ans.' He gives me a shadow of his cocky grin. 'I'm only admitting you're right this once, understand? This is in no way an admission that you're right about anything else. Especially when it comes to who will win this competition.'

It's his way of reassuring me he's fine; I never thought I'd be happy to see this version of Jay again. And the insults, they're safe. They're *friendly*.

'You go on being wrong about everything, Jaybird. I'll be there to say "I told you so" every time.'

After we finish our mini cakes that cost as much as a whole cake should, Jay convinces me to go to the arcade with him. Well, less 'convinces' and more 'obviously wants company, except he's too proud to say it and therefore acts (badly) like it's a casual request'.

We head over to a surprisingly busy arcade near the movie theatres. I gravitate towards the *DDR* machines, tugged by memories from the start of primary school when I'd play every day on the soft mats at home. It was the first video game I spent hundreds of hours on. These look to be the newest versions, so it's doubtful there are many songs I'm familiar with.

Jay taps me on the shoulder and it's only then I realise he slipped away while I was checking out the machines.

He hands me a card. 'I got us seventy minutes of unlimited games.'

'But—'

'No buts, we've only got seventy minutes, so play now, argue later.' He swipes his card and hops up onto one of the joined platforms. 'I saw you staring at the dance pads, so your choice of game is *DDR*, right?'

I swipe mine as well, and get on the platform beside him. 'Excuse me, my choice? You went and swiped your card without waiting for my confirmation. That means *DDR* is *your* choice, and it's my turn to pick a game next.'

'Okay.' That's surprising, an agreeable Jay. There's probably a catch. Sure enough, he continues, 'I should warn you, this is one of the games I used to regularly beat Ans in when we went to the arcade as kids.'

I select the two-player 'Versus' mode. 'You said he didn't really get into games till *Negatory*, so he was probably playing casually because his gor asked him to. Doesn't count.'

He raises his eyebrows. 'Them's fighting words. Let's do this, Udina.'

There's a ton of songs to choose from, none of which I recognise. We eventually settle on a pop song with a strong beat, and choose the middle level. It may have been over six years since I last played *DDR*. Still, it's like riding a bike . . . right?

Then the song starts, and wow, those arrows scroll up the screen a lot faster than I remember. I can still read them fine. My legs, however, can't keep up. I'm tripping over my own two feet, the solid platform feeling very different to the soft mats. My health bar dips into the red, then disappears completely. The song doesn't stop, so I keep going. Maybe I can bring the bar back up somehow.

When the song ends after far too long, I lean my poor

unfit body against the bar behind me. Jay looks to be in better shape – it's only now I remember he does Krav Maga and therefore exercises on a regular basis. Our scores come up, and of course, I failed miserably. To my surprise, Jay's barely scraped through. He glances over at me with a self-deprecating grin and we both start laughing.

'Wow, we suck now,' he says, and in that sharing of our embarrassment, I go from wanting to run and hide to wanting to try to do better the next time.

'At least you kept us in the game,' I say with a nod towards his score.

He shakes his head. 'Barely. If I'd missed one more arrow our run would've ended with both of us heaped in Asian shame.'

I hit the button to return to the main menu. 'There's more than enough time for that to happen this round.'

I scroll down, looking for a slower song with a similar level. Neither of us need to say to the other that there's no way in hell we're going to an easier level. Then I notice there are songs from earlier versions of the game, and I can see the light. I go straight to the *DDR Extreme 2* section and there are all the songs I remember.

My cursor hovers over the Captain Jack Grandale remix, one of the most popular *DDR* songs ever and my eternal nemesis. I lost count of the number of hours I spent trying to pass, then perfect, this song.

One pleading glance at Jay later, we're loaded and ready.

'If I'm being realistic,' he says ruefully as he grabs the bar behind him, 'our run's ending here unless you carry us.'

I chose this, so time for me to take responsibility. 'I gotchu.'

The song starts and we're off and running. This is the most intense cardio workout I've had in a long time. Thankfully we played the previous song, as my mind and body are finally remembering how to move to the arrows again. Although I'm still missing a lot of arrows, it's amazing what muscle memory can do.

At the end of the song I'm in the red but I'm still standing, dammit. Jay's bar is totally depleted.

Jay groans as he flops back on the bar. 'That was hell, Udina. Two minutes of pure hell. I lost about twenty seconds in. Are you trying to kill me so you win our competition by default?'

I collapse on my own bar and flap a hand in his general direction. 'It was never going to end well,' I say, and Jay snorts his agreement.

We try one more song which, to no one's surprise, we end up failing spectacularly. Definitely time to wave the white flag. Fetching our bags, we find a wall to lean against and recuperate. We finally settle near a row of basketball-throwing games, where a young boy is attempting to get the basketballs into the net with little success.

My phone buzzes with a message, and I check to see it's from Aneeshka.

Aneeshka

My new game is not gonna be done by Saturday there's so many bugs kill me now dfjaskljasklfjaskldfjaskldfjkl

I don't want to be that rude person on my phone when I'm meant to be spending time with someone. I send a quick, *You can do this, and you have your original game as backup!*, then put the phone back into my pocket.

Except the message reminds me that the showcase is in two days' time, and instead of working on my game I'm goofing off at the arcade with Jay. Not for my game, but because I really like hanging out with him and I don't want to leave. It terrifies me, this losing myself to a possible significant other.

'Hellooooo? Udina?' Jay flicks my forehead and it stings. 'Good, you're back. What's with the sighing and distant stare at the door? Is it this place or me? If it's me, I'd appreciate it if you said it was this place for my ego's sake.'

'No,' I hasten to assure him. 'It's just . . . the big industry showcase is this weekend. My future depends on whether I get publisher interest, but I'm here messing around at the arcade instead of focusing on *Vinculum*.'

It's the first time I've talked openly about the invisible, unspoken pressure to justify my choices and prove myself. Will he understand, or shrug it off like everyone else does?

To my relief, he nods. 'If you want to do something that's not Asian Standard Life Plans, you have to work the hardest and be the best or it'll never be enough.'

'Yes!' It's half relief, half affirmation. 'I've spent my life being proud because my parents are proud, you know? Because I have to be the kid who fulfils their expectations, since who else will?'

'I get that.' Jay crosses his arms and closes his eyes with a sigh. 'Expectations are . . . something, all right. My whole life

I've been told that because I'm the big brother, I have to set the example. Be the best, so Ans has someone to look up to. Be the one who fixes the problems, like when my mum had to deal with banking stuff and didn't understand what they wanted, or when my dad nearly lost his licence for speeding and I had to write a letter for him pleading his case. Make sure Ans had the support he needed from his teachers at school, since I was also there.' He glances over at me, a spark of mischief in his eyes. 'Or the period when he seemed down, so I decided to find him a ticket to the Farrows' workshop.'

'Oh, *now* we're throwing out the excuses,' I say, then poke Jay in the side as he squirms away.

He catches my finger, then lets go and tentatively touches his hand to mine, asking for permission. I intertwine our fingers in response. They fit against each other as though they belong, as though this has always been their default state. As though they're the bits of us freshly revealed, falling into place.

'No excuses, just fixes. That's me, I'm the fixer. I handle the painful things and the hard things so the people around me can be happy. At least, that's what I've always believed. And I wanted to sort out Ans's current situation, till an annoyingly convincing girl told me I should step back. More than once, come to think of it.' He squeezes my hand. 'All that to say, I get that about falling into a role then feeling helpless when you realise you can't fill it anymore. Or that maybe you never could.'

It's strange to think that the cocky, confident Jay I've seen till now would harbour the same kinds of insecurities as me. Maybe he's simply better at hiding it. But like our *DDR* embarrassment, sharing them makes me feel lighter. Less lonely.

Seen.

'What do you mean, you never could?' I ask eventually. 'You fixed all those other things, didn't you?'

He shakes his head. 'Thinking back, I'm sure my parents could have worked things out themselves eventually. And Ans, he's never really needed saving, he only needed to find the right crew – even if it took him awhile. Now he's made some great friends at school and maybe even through his sketching group, if he doesn't want to leave. None of it was me, it was all him.' His callused thumb strokes the back of my hand and it's so unexpected, so light, that I shiver. 'I saw how much love you poured into *Vinculum* and thought, wow, I want to do something for me and me alone. Well, maybe I can. Could be that these roles and expectations are things we created for ourselves, hey?'

I suck in a breath to clear my mind. 'What's left if we let them go?'

He swings our joined hands back and forth. 'Whatever we want to make of it, I guess.'

'You mean there's a world out there where I can focus on making games and achieving my dream of becoming a prominent developer without guilt? Where you can sit back and not be the oldest kid who's responsible for everything, and let everyone else sort out their own lives?'

Jay laughs. 'We were raised in Asian households; there'll always be some guilt. It's almost cultural at this point.' He continues stroking the back of my hand. 'You'll need to keep reminding me that those ties with the ones I care about are still gonna be there even if I can't make everything right.'

The casual acceptance of this fact (and his reference to *Vinculum*!) lifts a heaviness in my heart I've lived with for so long that I'd forgotten it was there.

I stroke his hand with my thumb as well. 'Don't you worry, I'll make sure the game's so successful you'll remember that every time you see it mentioned.'

Jay gives my hand one last squeeze, and turns to face me. 'Tell you what, let's take a raincheck on the arcade. Go home, work on your game, steal the showcase and convince your parents about the gap year. I'll go talk to Ans. When we've successfully completed our quests, we'll come back here to celebrate.'

He *understands*. And he's encouraging me to give it my all because he will too. I could kiss him. If we were actually dating, that is. But everything can wait until after. Perhaps during our next date. Because that is what this is, isn't it? Even if I'm not ready to admit it yet.

'You're on.'

CHAPTER 22

Future Devs Showcase: 1 day left

Sam

> THREE HOURS THREE HOURS
> I FINALLY GET TO SEE YOU IN
> THREE HOURS

Aneeshka

> HOW IS THE SHOWCASE TOMORROW
> I AM DYINGGGGGG

Aneeshka

> You were right, making a new
> game was a terrible idea. Help!

Aneeshka

One of the guys on the indie dev
discord did a ranking of the games at
the showcase and I KNOW it's a guy
who's a jerk, but he put *MetaVision* right
down the bottom with 'needs polish'
which is actually fair because
I haven't done any work on it???

Aneeshka

Now I have one partly polished game
and one super basic game and a ton
of banners I spent way too much
money on for both and argharghargh

Sam

MetaVision was already a solid game,
and publishers will see that even if you
don't have music yet

Sam

You already spent so long working on it,
I'm not letting you panic and sabotage
yourself now

Sam

Besides, this mysterious new game of
yours might even be a sleeper hit

Aneeshka

I hate it. I hate it all.
What was I thinking???

Aneeshka

Throw me in the trash and set me on fire
I am done

Aneeshka

I will ABSOLUTELY DIE if I prove that
guy right with his ranking crap

Sam

When I get there we're having an
emergency strategy session ASAP

Sam

We're the dynamic duo, remember?
We can do anything, including making
this work.

Telling Aneeshka 'I told you so' would be a terrible idea, though it doesn't stop me from thinking it. Still, I'll make sure she's ready for the showcase one way or another, even if it means both of us pulling an all-nighter. Maybe she'll finally see that her new friends don't actually know that much about making games — not as much as I do, anyway.

Luckily, we're sharing a hotel room in a place that's right next to the convention centre where the showcase is being held. It's fancy and expensive as hell, but until Aneeshka finds a place to stay that's not a family friend's bedroom, it was the easiest way to convince my parents to let me travel to Sydney on my own and prove I'd be 'safe'. As a bonus, the location's incredibly convenient and will save us from having to wake up too early.

'Are you sure you have everything, Sun Sun?' my mum asks for the tenth time, patting my carry-on duffel atop the suitcases beside the garage door.

There are *so* many items required for a convention booth. One suitcase has my gaming PC, fully protected in foam. I've stuffed swag for my game in there too – illustrated postcard flyers, business cards and stickers of the two sisters reunited. The boxes for them take up the remaining space in the huge suitcase. Even if I don't give them all away at Future Devs, maybe I can save some extras to gift the Farrows when I meet them at the workshop.

The other oversized suitcase has three monitors, also protected. The protection takes up more space than the monitors themselves. There are two for the game demos, so I can run one from my desktop and the other from my laptop, if I get enough interest. The final one is for the basic gameplay trailer I cut together. Finally, there are two banners in long black pouches, which can be slung over your shoulders like weapons. All my actual travelling gear like clothes and toiletries are stuffed into my carry-on.

I'm ready to reveal my baby to the world, and be done with all expectations the same way I'm done with high school.

'I checked and checked again last night,' I tell my mum. 'I even wrote a list and crossed everything off.' I think. 'The important stuff for my booth is packed, and anything else I can buy when I get there.'

She turns to patting my backpack. 'Your purse? Your mobile? Your boarding pass? Your passport? Oh, and a face mask just in case?'

'They're all there, I checked. Except for my passport; I don't need that for travelling within Australia. Only my driver's licence for ID.'

'She knows what she's doing, Mummy,' Eva says as she leans over the banister at the top of the stairs, eyes lidded from the remnants of sleep. 'Good luck, jie.'

Our parents are only dropping me off, because airport parking is expensive and Asian-parent economics says why pay to say goodbye at the airport when you can do the same at home for free?

'Did you print your confirmation for your hotel booking?' our dad asks.

'Kind of.' I hold up my phone. 'No need to print it, it's all on my phone.'

He's not convinced. 'But what if your phone runs out of battery?'

'Then I tell them my name and show them my ID. I'll be fine, I promise.'

'Make sure you call us as soon as you land,' he says.

'And after you've checked into your room,' our mum adds.

They're nervous because this is the first time I've travelled on my own, even if it's only a short flight away. 'I will, I promise.'

Our mum grabs her handbag on one of the bar stools tucked under the kitchen counter, and roots around for a bit before pulling out a lipstick case. She hands it to me.

'Take this with you,' she says. 'You always say you're too lazy to bother with make-up but a little bit will really freshen you up and you want to look your best when presenting your game. Your appearance is important, because it's all about being professional. It will make people approach you.'

I'm about to tell her that no one will care, because the focus is my game and not me. No one cares how the developer looks as long as the game is on fire. But Eva gives me a meaningful glance that says, *Shut up and take it, okay?* and it reminds me that in some ways, she understands our parents better than I do. Even if it's hard to admit.

'Thanks, Mummy.' I put the lipstick tube in my pocket and give her a hug. 'I appreciate it.'

I glance at Eva again and think about everything Jay and I talked about yesterday, that if he understands Ansen's *why*, it'll help him let go. For all my pride about being more 'Asian' than Eva, and being the 'better' kid because I get our parents more than she does, maybe this goes both ways. Maybe in order to let us go, our parents need to learn to understand us too.

'If you trust me to fly to another city and stay in a hotel with Aneeshka,' I say to them, 'maybe you can trust Eva to go on a short holiday with her friends when there are parents present.

And you can get to know them for your own peace of mind. Eva respects both of you enough to abide by your decision on whether or not she can go, can't you put in some effort to go to a party she's invited you to, and get to know them before you decide?'

I don't know if I would've been able to say such a thing before giving Jay that advice, or before admitting that maybe I *like* being the 'good kid' even if I'll privately commiserate with Eva. Her eyes are wide open as they shift between me and our parents, all traces of sleepiness gone.

Our parents exchange a look of *She has a point but we don't want to admit it.*

Time to push them a bit more. 'It's a party, so there's lots of good food and drink. All free. They live in a big fancy house; I saw it when I went to pick up Eva once. You'd get to see *inside*. And then gossip about it with her.'

Their next glance is a borderline *I might be interested if you are . . .*

Eva's full of energy now. 'Let's get jie's luggage into the car, and decide what to do when you return from the airport,' she says, running downstairs and hefting one of the suitcases into the garage.

We have to fold down the back seats to fit everything in, but all my gear is safely loaded in the end.

'Ready?' our mum says, but from the way she lingers by the boot it's clear she's reluctant to send me off.

'Do you have something to catch the game publishers' attention?' our dad asks. Great, he's dragging this out too. 'Back in Malaysia when I was working for an engineering company, we had to sell connectors for high voltage power lines.' He switches in and out of English when referring to the technical components, and I'm pretty sure he's never referred to them in Cantonese either. 'I took them to the field, rolled up my sleeves and showed them how well it worked in person, even though I'd never worked with high voltage power before.'

Eva tilts her head and gives him a genuinely curious look. 'How are you still *alive*? Especially with all the nonsense you pulled when you were young.'

Our dad taps her on the nose. 'This is why I tell you: do what I say, not what I do.'

'You're terrible, Daddy,' Eva says with a sigh.

He turns back to me. 'Sun Sun, that demonstration? I followed it up with a full colour presentation with animation on a laptop, which was a very rare and expensive thing back in the early nineties. They remembered us, even if it was just for the laptop.'

'That's great, Daddy,' I say, even though his well-intentioned advice is way out of date. And borders on lethal. 'Wait till they see my game.'

It'll do all the speaking for me, and prove to them I have a viable career plan. I don't need any bells and whistles – the swag is just for fun. 'They won't forget me when it's done.'

Eva snickers. 'Make sure it's for the right reasons, and not because you electrocuted yourself.' She reaches behind our dad and grabs my wrist. 'I wrote amazing music for an amazing game, if I do say so myself. You go show them the game that's gonna be the next *Negativity*.'

'*Negatory.*'

'That's what I said.'

I grab her wrist as well in a monkey grip and pull her in, squeezing our dad between us. With my other arm, I drag my mum into the group hug. Even if it's not the unconditional support I would have wanted, my family's poured so much love and faith into this dream of mine. Now it's my turn to show them how far I can go.

'I promise that I'll make you all proud.'

Let's get this game in front of a crowd.

CHAPTER 23

Future Devs Showcase: 1 day left

When I arrive in Sydney, I take a taxi from the airport to the hotel, even though every fibre of Asian in me rails against the cost. But there was no way I'd be able to wrangle all my gear onto the train, then walk it to the hotel. So, taxi it is. I message the taxi's licence to my parents and turn on Facebook tracking so Eva can show my parents I'm not being driven to an abandoned warehouse and murdered.

In the taxi, I get a message from Jay.

Jerky McJerkface

I took your advice and talked to Ans

Jerky McJerkface

That was interesting

Sam

Don't keep me hanging! I'm invested in the Chua brothers' relationship now!

Jerky McJerkface

What'll you give me for the ending?

Sam

Advice and more advice, even if you don't want it

Jerky McJerkface

You're going to say it's because I need it, aren't you?

Sam

You said it, not me

Jerky McJerkface

It's a deal, then

My phone rings, and I immediately answer. Jay doesn't even bother with small talk before picking up where he left off.

'I started by telling Ans that if he really didn't want to quit the sketching group, I'd use my Eldest Sibling Privilege to back him up with our parents.'

I can hear the capitals in that, and make a mental note to tell him that I used mine this morning and it worked out rather well.

Jay continues, 'After I made that clear, I asked why he didn't want to leave. You won't believe what happens next!'

My groan must be especially loud, because the taxi driver eyes me with concern in the rear-view mirror before I give him the 'everything's fine' wave.

'I changed my mind, Jaybird, I don't need the clickbait ending.'

'Too bad, you're already in too deep.' He pauses for dramatic effect, and I'm about to tell him to hurry it up when he finally says, 'It turns out Ans has a girlfriend there! That little brat, now I learn he's excellent at withholding information if he's never asked about it.'

I lay my phone on my lap to give him a golf clap, then pick it up again. 'Jaysen Chua, newest reporter for the Asian Gossip Network. Good on Ansen, though.'

'No, no, no, you don't get it. This is *big news*!' He sounds scandalised. 'My baby brother beat me to having a girlfriend! Whatever happened to "older brother sets the example"?'

A response comes to mind immediately. *You could catch up if you wanted.*

Those words would be so easy to say because they feel so right. I stop them before they come out, though. Do I really want to start something with Jay over the phone? The timing is off as well. I swore to my parents I would put my career before boys, and it would be embarrassing to go back on that. I'll only have to wait till after this weekend, anyway. That's how confident I am.

'Udina?' There's concern in Jay's voice. 'You still there? I'm not . . . I'm not hinting at anything, if that's what you were worried about.'

Crap. I forgot he was waiting for a reply. 'Sorry, what'd you say? Reception dropped out for a moment there. Sounds like it's back now!'

'Oh, it was just your reception. I didn't say anything much.'

Liar. I'll let him get away with it this time, though.

'So, Ansen's staying on at the sketching group despite the bullies because tru luuuuuuurve?'

He laughs. 'Exactly that, in that tone and with that emphasis. I wanted to talk to the person in charge at least, except he wouldn't even let me do that. Said he and his girlfriend Petra could handle it, and he didn't want me to make a big incident out of it, because apparently I would.'

'You totally would.'

'Ye of little faith!' He doesn't sound annoyed at all, though. 'I think it's a bad idea, but yes I will listen to him and trust he can handle it if he says he can. Though you better believe I'm gonna charge in swinging if he so much as asks, or if he's in danger. Hope you're ready to bail me out.'

'All royalties from sales of *Vinculum* will go to the Jaysen Chua Bail Fund.'

'I wish I was there for moral support, or even handing-out-flyer support. You got this. Go stomp the competition, Udina.'

I wish he was here too, and that thought surprises me. Also, how typical that he'd call the showcase a competition.

'Does everything have to be a competition with you? This is a showcase.' I pause, and gather up all my confidence. 'I mean, I plan to be the centre of attention, but there are no winners or losers.'

'You optimist, you.' That's definitely fondness in his tone, right? 'There are *always* winners and losers.'

We talk until I arrive at the hotel, upon which I have to hurriedly hang up so I can pay the driver and unload all my things. Aneeshka only left the place she's currently staying after I got into the taxi, so I'm the first here. I check in, text my parents again to let them know I am still in fact alive, then text Aneeshka with our room number.

The place is super plush with two twin beds and a great view of Darling Harbour. I take a picture for my parents as well, because apparently if a place looks luxurious, it's safe. I have so much gear it barely fits into my side of the room, and when Aneeshka arrives she'll have even more since she has two games. I make the executive decision to take over the one small desk before she arrives, and set up my laptop.

The showcase is really happening. Tomorrow, my game will be seen by the people who matter. I came up with an idea for a nifty tweak to one of the levels to make it more 'ah-hah!' and less trial-and-error while chatting with Jay in the taxi, so I'll implement that for tomorrow's demo.

I'm jolted out of focus when my phone buzzes against the side of my wrist. I glance down to see a new text.

Aneeshka

I can hear you typing away in the room. Let me in! I've been knocking for the past minute!

Oops. I run to the door and fling it open, upon which I am greeted by the most enthusiastic hug in history.

'Saaaaaaaaaaaaaaaaaaaaaaaaaaaaaam!'

I wrap my arms around her and we do an excited two-person-jumpy-huggy thing while squealing. She's not much taller than me (thank you Bengali genes for keeping us at height parity), and the perfect hugging height. Even when we went through our growth spurts at school we remained about equal despite her constant insistence she was a centimetre or two taller. When we finally release each other, I step back to take in her new look.

The large red streak is a bright pop of colour against her black hair and brown skin, and she's styled it in a way that perfectly accentuates it. She's got more make-up on than I've seen her with before, but it all looks natural. Everything about her is so stylish, worlds away from school uniforms and braided hair. It's Aneeshka, even if it's not quite the same Aneeshka I remember. As though in the mere month she's been away she's already grown up without me.

I swallow those feelings down, reminding myself that she's here for the Future Devs Showcase with me so nothing's changed *that* much. If anything, I should be happy she's growing and evolving into the person she always wanted to be; the person she was meant to be.

'Your hair looks amazing! *You* look amazing!' I glance around at the conspicuously empty hallway. 'Where's everything for your booth? Surely you didn't fit it all into a backpack.'

'It's with the bellboys.' She enters the room and glances around admiringly. 'This place is *fancy*. I better let my parents know how fancy so they'll get off my back. Which bed's mine?'

I point at the one closest to her, which isn't surrounded by bags. 'I got here first so I shotgunned the window bed.'

She tosses her backpack on the ground, kicks off her shoes and flops down on the bed. 'It's hard to care when the beds are this soft.' She sees my expression and knows me too well, because she adds, 'Hey, don't give me that face, this is a temporary hotel bed so outdoor clothes are fair game. You won't die and neither will I. Well. I mean, I will die tomorrow because of my crappy game, but not because of the bed situation.'

Finally, *finally*, it feels like we've returned to the same orbit once more. No weirdness where she's building a whole other life I'm not a part of. No other friends who could totally take my place as her gaming buddy and fellow dev. Just me and her and all our in-jokes no one else gets, and the dream we've shared for years.

I grab her arm and pull her upright so she's seated. 'Let's see this mysterious game of yours.'

She buries her face in her hands. 'It's a mess. I mean, I told you it's a mess, right? No one should be seeing this. Will you pretend it never existed if I say you were right and hacking together a game in three weeks was a terrible idea?'

'Nope.' I gingerly seat myself beside her. 'Because I'm sure it's not as bad as you think and also, you've kept me in suspense for three whole weeks. There's no way I'm simply forgetting about it.'

'Okayyyy.' She grabs her backpack and pulls out her laptop case. It's covered with little felt characters from books and video games, all of which she made herself. 'Don't say I didn't warn you. Prepare to be severely disappointed.'

I move my laptop aside so she can set hers up on the desk, and move one of the chairs to one side. She pulls out two controllers from her backpack and turns them on. That's a bit of a surprise.

'It's multiplayer?'

'Yup. I wanted something that would be fun for two people. Like *Keep Talking and Nobody Explodes* or *39 Days To Mars*.' She sees my expectant gaze. 'Or, yes, *Portal 2*. Ancient as it is.'

It's certainly a change from her previous focus on single-player games. I wonder if it's the influence of her new friends, then push the thought aside. 'So is it shoot-y? Puzzle-y? Social dynamic-y? Competitive, or co-op?'

She hands me a controller. 'You get to shoot *and* strategise on a map-wide scale. In lieu of a better name, this is called *Turn and Run*.'

The screen loads, a split-screen with first-person view, and we're plopped into a level that seems like something Escher would've dreamed up. It's basic and blocky, but even with her limited timeframe she's managed to give the objects a pencil-sketched appearance. All I can see are my character's greyscale hands holding a metallic sphere, which fits in perfectly with the rest of the world.

'Hold on,' Aneeshka says. She presses a button that zooms out to a map screen – again with the hand-drawn aesthetic, and a dot that shows my character – then selects a section and taps the left trigger. 'This rotates the selected part of the level. Clockwise only, so you need to wait through three more rotates to get back to the original orientation.'

The world shifts around my character, and my available paths on the screen change. She grabs my controller and navigates me to a sphere, which my character picks up. In the top left corner of my half of the screen, a timer starts counting.

'You can open new paths, or block a path from the other person to you,' Aneeshka says. 'The catch is, you're completely defenceless while you're on the rotate screen. If the other person sees a path to you, you're vulnerable.'

She returns my controller and I run along the path, using the landmarks on both my screen and Aneeshka's to orientate myself and get in proximity of her. Just as I catch sight of her character – which is a bunch of blocks in a vaguely humanoid shape, another thing I'm guessing she didn't have time to refine – she taps into the rotate screen, and now the path changes so I can run past her, but I can't touch her. I go to the rotate screen to change it back, then find she's running somewhere else as I do so. Before I can work out where her character's gone, she appears behind me and grabs my metal sphere upon contact. My timer pauses, while hers starts. She sprints away and hits rotate on her square before I can react, and disappears as I'm strategising my next move.

'The only mode I have at the moment is capture-the-flag, and I want to add others like deathmatch,' she says as I take chase, trying to track her through labyrinthine passageways by watching her screen. It helps when she rotates, as her map screen shows her current location, though she's already changing the paths before I can work out a new route to her. I could bring up my own map, except then she'll see where I am.

I spot a shortcut in the new orientation, though, so I chance it and take a hard right. Lucky me, I spot her dead ahead. I've almost got her when she dodges away and does a quick rotate, laughing at my outraged expression. We keep chasing each other, trading possession of the orb, until she finally hits two minutes.

'I win!' She turns and grins. 'Get the gist now?'

Jay is rubbing off on me because I'm damned if I'm going to let it end this way. I think I'm starting to understand the odd way the paths twist, too.

'Again!'

And then after a close match that I would've won if it wasn't for a last-second rotation: 'Again!'

I can't count how many times we play, but it's a joy every time. She's only got one map so far, yet it's enough for a solid gaming session. The pure genius of this isn't just in the concept, it's the perfection of the level design where rotating paths doesn't interrupt the flow, only changes it. Who cares if it's still a bit janky, there's no background music and the art is basic blocks? It's the joy of a chaotic game of tag where we're seated side by side and trying to physically disrupt the other person or force a rotation.

There's a simple, beautiful elegance to the level designs, which have enough complexity to present you with something new every rotation, and also force you towards each other eventually, like being on the same side of a möbius strip. We play over and over till we're interrupted by a knocking on the door and the call of, *Your luggage is here!*

As I help Aneeshka move her bags in, because we feel bad standing around while the bellboy – well, bellperson – does all the work, the game is still on my mind. If I'd rotated one particular tile an extra time, could I have found a way to ambush her? What if I tried using a sniper rifle after I rotated *that* tile?

'What did you think?' Aneeshka finally asks, glancing over at the screen where, conveniently, she currently has possession of the orb.

The answer is easy. Already I want to play the game with Jay and Ansen. Assuming, of course, we don't kill each other in the process, but that's all part of the fun. I'm planning to beg Aneeshka for a copy 'for playtesting' at the end of this weekend. Turns out her new friends were right, much as I hate to admit it.

'This is it,' I tell her. 'Girls can't make good games, my ass. This is the game you go with for the showcase.'

CHAPTER 24

Future Devs Showcase: Judgement day

I stand in the middle of my booth – yes, *my* booth! – surrounded by banners, with a swag table out front and a monitor showing off a supercut gameplay trailer. Just inside, my desktop and other monitor are set up with a controller decal-ed with my game's logo, and fancy-looking gaming headphones. It sits on the menu screen, waiting for the first player.

There are advertisements for PopSplosion everywhere, even though it's still a few months away. Most of them feature the Farrows front and centre as one of their special guests. Whoever put these up knows their audience, all right. They're on a few panels that are open to the general public, but I'll bet every single person at this showcase would sacrifice their firstborn game to attend their workshop, if they don't already have tickets.

The low murmur of activity echoes through the convention hall, carrying through the metal beams in the high ceiling. Around me, everyone else is setting up their own booths. Some have motion controllers, others VR. There are one or two just down the row that look particularly interesting, with almost the entire booth dedicated as a space for the person in the VR headset to move. Across from me is someone with an augmented reality headset that I'm itching to get my hands on to try, and I've heard whispers about an amazing game using a controller that detects your hands' movements in a space above the sensor.

There's also a large booth out the front about accessible games, which shows off all kinds of alternative control methods for mainstream games, as well as ones made specifically with disabled gamers in mind. It's so exciting to see the range of games on display all throughout the hall, and even more so to be one of them.

I peek out to see Aneeshka finishing off her own set-up a few booths down. Her original *MetaVision* game is tucked away in a corner, and *Turn and Run* is pride of place out front. She's got a low-key dressy style going, with a slim-cut button-up shirt tucked into long black pants. I tried to imitate her, except T-shirts will never reach the same level as button-ups. Neither of us bothered with make-up this morning, yet she still manages to appear impossibly fresh. She catches my eye and we exchange grins full of nervous energy.

'Hey, let's go take a peek at the booths near the front,' she says, coming over. 'See if that guy boasting about getting a booth up front on the Discord was nothing but hot air.'

My booth is all set up, and my gear should be safe because it's exhibitors-only at the moment.

I grab her hand. 'Let's go. What's your bet it's nothing more than a fold-out table with a laptop because "his game is too good to need any extra promotion"?'

It isn't.

Boy, does he have money to burn. We're talking multiple monitors on stands, a panel that covers the entire back wall, a woman cosplaying one of his characters handing out swag, two helpers in shirts printed with the game's logo, even some kind of custom flooring. For someone who's supposedly an 'up-and-coming dev', it seems more like a fancy PAX booth.

We stop and stare a little too long, because he swaggers over. 'Like what you see, ladies? It's smart of you to approach me before the doors open and the publishers are lining up at my booth. Don't worry; I'll remember your cute little faces.'

'I don't think we'll remember you, though,' Aneeshka says. 'We've met too many mediocre white men in the industry and the faces all start to blur together, you know?'

I can't help it. I burst out laughing. This is why she's my best friend.

He glares at us. 'You just wait. I'm going to have all the publishers blackball the two of you. They'll do anything I ask after they see my game.'

'Sure,' I say. 'Still better than no balls like you, though.'

It's Aneeshka's turn to crack up. Payback accomplished! I grab her hand and we walk away, ignoring his dire utterings about 'lesbian bitches' and 'never work in this industry again'. We've heard those curses one too many times, and know better than to respond to them by now. Her hand is clammy in mine, and I realise she was just as nervous as I was.

'He doesn't actually have the clout, right?' she whispers to me once we're out of earshot.

I let out a nervous giggle. 'Probably should have checked that before we dissed him. But he deserved it.'

'I know! He must know we're also devs chosen for the showcase, and he treated us like his stans. Whatever happens, it was worth it.'

'Exactly.' I can at least pretend that I'm not concerned he might be able to make good on his threat given the sheer amount of money he's spent on his booth. 'We'll have our revenge simply because we're better devs.'

I peel off at my booth, and she gives me a nervous grin and a thumbs up. 'We got this.'

That's when the nerves hit. In five minutes, the doors will open and the showcase will begin. It runs over Saturday and Sunday, and scouts from indie publishers curated by the organisers will be coming through to find promising games, along with invited members of the press.

This is it. These two days are where my career begins, and meeting the Farrows at their PopSplosion workshop will be where it takes off.

Pulling out my phone, I re-read the messages in our family chat, scrolling past the photos Eva sent last night of our parents at Tamara's party. Our parents aren't in costume like the people around them, but they seem to be having a good time posing for the camera. There's even one taken with a couple Eva says are Tamara's parents, and they seemed to be getting along well enough.

Eva's sent me a private message saying that Tamara's parents went out of their way to talk to our parents and convince them to let her go with them on holiday. They haven't agreed yet, she says, but they're wavering.

There are other random messages in the family chat from this morning, too. Eva sends me a ton of 'You got this' gifs. My dad says he'll make me an entire carton's worth of his special egg to either celebrate or cheer me up. My mum says to do my best and it's fine no matter what happens. Is that a hint of 'I hope it doesn't go well and you end up at uni' I detect in both of my parents?

My mum also reminds me to drink a lot of water and eat properly because I need to stay healthy to sell the game. And then reminds me to put on the lipstick and says to send her a picture when I do.

Closing my eyes, I take a few deep breaths. Ever since I was selected for the showcase last year, I've poured all my energy and passion into *Vinculum*. I've analysed all the things I love in my favourite games and worked on bringing those elements in. The publishers will see and appreciate this labour of love.

My phone buzzes with a new text.

Jerky McJerkface

Don't let this boss battle smash you, Udina. Oh, and Ans says you need to hurry up and get a publisher so you can make more games.

I knew I liked Ansen more than him.

Sam

And what do you say?

Jerky McJerkface

That they have no foresight if they don't show any interest in the partner of the guy who set an escape room record

Hah! He's dreaming; he knows exactly who did the bulk of the thinking to get us that record. But before I can respond, a second text comes in.

Jerky McJerkface

By partner I mean partners in crime. Not the kind our parents are shipping. For the record.

I'm both relieved and disappointed, and even more disappointed that there's disappointment in the mix. Get yourself together, Sam!

Sam

Let's get the titles correct, here. I think you mean they'd be short-sighted not to show interest in the mastermind who set an escape room record with the help of her minion.

Whatever gets you through
the showcase, Udina

Laughing to myself, I pocket my phone. Odd how the normality of Jay's insults calms me more than any of the supportive stuff. I wonder if he knows that, too.

The PA blares to life. 'Good morning, Future Devs! The doors are now open!'

I pace nervously around my booth, unsure if the tickling in my stomach is nervousness or too much milk from the latte I downed this morning. I don't even like coffee, but I was hoping the caffeine would turn my nerves into nervous energy. Time for the hard work and sacrifice and no time for anything except homework and coding after school to pay off.

Here. We. GO!

Our row is somewhere in the middle, so it takes a while for anyone to reach us. I wipe clammy hands on my cargo pants and put on my best customer service smile. The first two attendees appear, ambling along and taking in each booth. They don't stop at any, though one of them takes the postcard I hold out, glancing at it and stuffing it in her tote bag. It's a start, I suppose.

Over the next fifteen minutes our row starts to fill up. People stop to play, and it's with no small pride that I see a small crowd growing around Aneeshka's booth. I get some interest too, with a few more people taking stickers and postcards, and one or two asking me more about the game and playing the demo for a few minutes.

It's not the overwhelming reception I was hoping for, people battering down the booth walls to play my game. I wonder how that creeper from earlier is doing, then banish that thought from my mind. Like I told Jay, this isn't a competition. He couldn't have blackballed us so early on, surely. Anyway, Aneeshka's getting interest, so it must have been an empty threat. Which means the problem is me. I mean, my game.

I remind myself it's still early, and every person who passes by is another glimmer of hope that makes me stand a little straighter.

'The music is gorgeous,' someone says, and I immediately message Eva because it'll make her day.

There's a trickle of people through, all of whom play a few minutes of the demo and move on. Which I tell myself is still fine – not every game is for everyone. And as Jay said last weekend, if just one publisher shows serious interest, or one media outlet mentions *Vinculum*, that's a win. Publishers, media, they show some interest, but none stay. None ask me more questions, or give me their card after playing a few levels.

There are other booths around me with fewer people stopping by, so I'm not doing terribly. It's just that the crowd around Aneeshka's game keeps growing. Which is great for her and I'm happy, I really am.

I'm not disappointed at all.

It's nearing the end of the first day when a woman stops at my booth, scanning the banners and flyers. The lanyard around her neck is green, meaning she's with a publisher, but her card is flipped around so I can't see her name or which company she's from.

'What's your game about?' she asks.

I launch into my pitch: It's a narrative puzzler about two sisters in separate worlds finding their way home, with a core mechanic of one controller for two characters. She nods with interest, and I show her over to the demo where I restart the game and hand her the controller.

As she leans forwards to pick it up, her lanyard swings, and I spot the publisher name.

Blackbird Interactive.

Yes. YES! Someone from *the* indie publisher I've always dreamed of has shown interest in my game and is about to play it. Please, oh please, don't let any random new bugs appear now. Please let all my hardware work perfectly.

I'm shaking as I watch her play. She blitzes through the early levels, but because I'm standing behind her I can't see her expression. Are they too easy? Too hand-holdy? She takes a bit longer in the later levels, and this has to be a good sign because no one else has played for this long yet.

After another few levels she puts down the controller, and I try not to look too eager as she turns to me.

'Not bad,' she says. 'You're a promising developer.'

Before I can say anything more or ask her if Blackbird invests in promising developers, she gives me a friendly nod and exits the booth. No card, no serious sign of interest, nothing.

I breathe, then breathe again, wondering why the air isn't reaching my lungs the way it normally does. This snub hurts more than all the rest, because I actually hoped this time. I thought that maybe this was it, maybe I'd actually get interest from the publisher I wanted to work with more than anything else, and for a sliver of a moment I genuinely thought it would come true. I let down my guard, and disappointment was the result.

But I'm not willing to give up. There are many other companies out there, or I can self-release on Steam if I get enough interest from the press this weekend.

It's not over yet.

Aneeshka and I order room service that night to celebrate. For *her* to celebrate, at any rate. She has a number of cards from interested publishers, some of whom are even willing to pay her to develop the game further.

'It would be crass to go up to that creeper's booth and fling them at him like a wad of cash, wouldn't it?' she asks between mouthfuls of super-spicy arrabbiata pasta.

I stab my fork in her direction. 'Crass, maybe. Satisfying and oh-so-worth-it? That's a yes from me.'

Aneeshka twirls her own fork. 'I might have subtly got information on his game out of a few of the publishers who came around, and even though they didn't say it directly, I got a very strong vibe of "all looks no substance". Though I think some were still interested because they think the looks will sell.'

Great. I'm not even at a creeper's level. While I'm glad that we — okay, that *Aneeshka* — smashed him and totally disproved his sneering insinuations that women are terrible developers, why couldn't it have been me too? A slightly bitter part of me thinks that Aneeshka doesn't even want to drop out of uni, so it's not like she needs the success as much as I do. But I push that thought aside and focus on the happy ones. Like, my best friend in the world is going PLACES!

Aneeshka's already moved on from the creeper. 'Can I still call myself an indie developer?' she asks. 'Let's say I'm being funded by a publisher during development, and they want creative control. Example, someone from Sony said they'd be interested. So if I take the cash and let them have the final say, does that make me a sell-out?'

I swat her gently. 'You would *not* be a sell-out if you took money to develop your game. You would be someone with sound financial management practices.'

She passes me another card from a company called Fellow Traveller. Another one I was eyeing because they're based in Australia. As the team who published popular games like *Screencheat* and *Hacknet*, it's no surprise that they're interested in Aneeshka's game.

'Can you believe they wanted to work with me? When I've loved their games for, like, forever?'

I push my plate aside, appetite disappearing.

'Of course I can believe it, *Turn and Run* deserves it!'

I mean it, but it also hurts. One of their scouts played my game for a few minutes and walked away with no further interest.

Aneeshka leans forward. 'You said they were one of the companies interested in you, right?'

I might have lied a bit about how my day went. I didn't want to bring down Aneeshka's mood by crying, because if I let even one tear out, the rest will be close behind. I'm a big girl. I can handle my feelings on my own.

'They were really interested! Blackbird Interactive too!' I try to sound excited, hoping she can't see through my lie. 'I'll be sending a detailed info pack with data and screenshots after the showcase.'

'Yes!' She pumps her fist in the air. 'You'll get more interest, for sure. I told everyone who talked to me that they had to check out your game too.'

That explains why I had a steady flow of people through my booth, even if they didn't stay long.

Aneeshka continues, 'I just know we'll both be signed with reputable publishers soon. Imagine if we released at a similar time! We'll rub it in the face of every guy who creeps on us so hard they'll never be able to look either of us in the eye again. I wouldn't want to take this journey with anyone but my best friend. We'll promo the hell out of each other and give dude bros the most dismissive side-eye.'

I put on my best grin, ignoring the sick churning in my stomach. 'That would be the best.'

It's not jealousy, I tell myself. *I couldn't possibly be jealous of my best friend, especially since I know how much hard work she put in.*

'I had some great ideas from talking with some of the scouts today,' I tell her with all the energy I can muster. 'Gonna try to get them in before tomorrow.'

Truthfully, I had exactly three conversations, but I need to escape the current one. If it goes on for too much longer she might see through me, and I want her to be happy and excited tomorrow, not pitying me or feeling guilty for her success.

'That's a good idea,' she says. 'Someone from Blackbird showed me a picture of one of Escher's works that I want to try to turn into a level, somehow. I can't believe this is all happening, it seems so surreal.'

I point at my laptop. 'Better get cracking so I don't look like a zombie tomorrow.'

'Good point,' she says. 'Work first, celebrate properly tomorrow night.'

Honestly, I don't know what else I can do with my game. So I settle for small tweaks, areas of friction I noticed while watching people play through the first few levels. I tweak and I tweak as Day One tips over into Day Two, as Aneeshka shuts off her laptop and gives me an excited *Can't wait for tomorrow!*, as she snuggles under the covers and admonishes me to get a few hours of sleep at the very least because there are more publishers and press waiting for us. It's not until her breaths settle into the slow rhythm of sleep that I finally close my own laptop and put my glasses on the bedside table.

It's the long silence of the night, when darkest thoughts are given free rein. I can't stop the 'why's from creeping in, even though they're completely irrational. Why her game, and not mine? Why isn't my game good enough when I have just as much passion?

Why am I not able to make it on my own?

I won't cry, I tell myself as I lie in my bed and stare up at the ceiling. *I'm stronger than this. I'm not envious or upset by a single setback.*

Not one bit.

CHAPTER 25

Future Devs Showcase: Judgement Day, Round 2

The second day of the showcase has fewer attendees. They're mainly scouts and press who couldn't make it yesterday, or some who came back for a second look at games that interested them.

A guy with a green scout lanyard leads another person towards my booth.

'There was a game Freya couldn't stop talking about yesterday,' he says, and his companion glances around with fresh interest.

I expect them to walk past, till they stop at my booth. *Wait. What?* Someone was *that* interested in my game? Even if they're a smaller publisher, I don't mind as long as they're just as passionate about *Vinculum* as I am. Maybe I can still turn this around.

I give them my brightest smile as they watch the trailer. I'm itching to pull them to the game itself so they can play it. Patience. Get them drooling, then hook them.

Halfway through the trailer, the woman scout furrows her brows. 'What was the name of the game again?'

He checks his phone. '*Turn and Run.*'

My heart throbs like it's being sucked into itself, a black hole absorbing all excitement and hope that existed before this showcase. It's hard to breathe, but I have to act normal. Don't let my smile falter.

'Oh, it's that one over there,' she says, pointing at the line at Aneeshka's booth. Turning to me, she adds, 'Sorry about the mix-up – your game also seems great, of course.'

'Do you want to give it a go?' I ask them, trying not to seem desperate or pushy.

She glances over one more time before saying, 'Sure, why not.'

The two of them give the demo a cursory play, and it's obvious they're simply being polite the whole time.

'You should be proud of the game you made,' the lady tells me after she puts down the controller. 'Good job.'

The guy with her nods in agreement, though neither offer cards nor anything more. I watch discreetly as they leave my booth and join the growing line at Aneeshka's. It's clear that she's one of the biggest standouts in this showcase.

One person. One publisher. That's all I ask, all I need.

I don't look at my phone, either, which has a lot of new messages from my family (aunties and uncles and cousins too) wishing me good luck for the second day. I sent my parents enough of a reply that they know I'm alive, though I didn't say more. Couldn't. I don't want them to know they were right.

There's also a text from Jay I haven't responded to. After all my big words to him about not needing or wanting his help, it turns out that he – like everyone else in my life – was right. I should have let him help with my game because clearly I don't have the ability. I'm sure he wouldn't rub it in, but it's still humiliating after giving him an entire lecture.

The day drags on. I want it to be over already. I don't want to spend one more night here, because I'll have to celebrate with Aneeshka and pretend I made it too, when all I want is to curl up under the blankets and block out the world. It's not her fault, and I'm glad she's receiving all the accolades she deserves. Right now, though, the sense of utter futility is drowning out all other emotions.

At noon, I duck into a corner and use my phone camera as a mirror to apply the lipstick my mum gave me. Maybe she's right, and potential publishers have turned away because I don't look fresh enough. It does brighten my pale, chapped lips.

I return to the front of the booth with my best smile. To my surprise, it works. A member of the press who's walking past stops as I smile at her.

Then she pulls me over, like we're sharing a secret, and says, 'Just thought you'd want to know, there's some lipstick on your teeth.'

'Thank you!'

I pull out my phone, and sure enough, there's a smear on the edge of one of my front teeth. Turning aside, I rub it off with my tongue, and when I turn back, the lady's gone. Great. There's a lump in my throat, a scream struggling to escape. I force it down along with the hot tears pricking at my eyes.

Then I see her. The woman from Blackbird Interactive who played my game longer than anyone else yesterday. I run out, my fears about people stealing my computer or monitors or swag be damned. As far as I'm concerned they can have it all and good riddance.

I'm about to tap the lady on the shoulder when I realise she might not like being touched and it could be seen as creepy.

So instead I say, as politely as I can, 'Excuse me!' She doesn't turn, but someone else does. 'No, not you, sorry, um, excuse me, not you either, I'm just . . . *excuse me!*'

Oh, no, that was far louder than I intended. And of course it's the one that makes her turn. She must think I'm so rude.

'Were you trying to get my attention?' she asks. Thankfully she doesn't seem hostile. 'You could have just tapped me on the shoulder.'

My words are slipping away fast and I snatch at them desperately. 'Yes, sorry, I was going to and then I thought you might not like it and—' I'm turning into Jay the rambler. I stop. Swallow. 'You played my game for a while yesterday, and I was wondering if I could ask your opinion on something. I completely understand if you don't want to or if you're too busy scouting games and all—'

'It's fine,' she says, and seems like she genuinely means it. 'My whole reason for being here is to support up-and-coming devs, so I'd be more than happy to answer any questions.'

'Thank you so much!'

She follows me back to my booth, where nothing is missing. Of course not, who would want to steal anything from my game, anyway? She stops and gazes at my banner and gameplay trailer for a while.

'Oh, yes, I remember your game,' she finally says. 'I thought you had a great deal of potential.'

I take a deep breath and squeeze out the words too shy to emerge. 'Then . . . then why did you pass on my game for Blackbird?' Oh dammit, that didn't come out how I intended. 'I don't mean it as an accusation, quite a few scouts played my game yesterday, except no one played for long. So I'm trying to understand what's wrong.'

She looks uncertain and maybe a little nervous too. 'There was nothing wrong with your game,' she finally says. 'And choosing games we want to publish is a very subjective thing.'

'Please.' I'm begging now, because I have no more pride to lose. 'Please be honest with me, because I need that more than empty platitudes at the moment.'

She lets out a huge sigh, probably regretting that she agreed to my request. 'Okay. Just keep in mind that this is only my opinion and not Blackbird Interactive's.'

'I know, and I'm grateful, truly.'

'Your game is well-crafted and polished,' she says. 'That much is a fact. You show excellent grasp of puzzle design, even if some of the levels are slightly superfluous. You've made a solid game you should be proud of.'

I hold my breath waiting for the 'but'.

'But there's nothing particularly unique about it. There are thousands of puzzle games on Steam at the moment, and your game doesn't have that one element that would make it stand out from the rest. There are a lot of solid games, a number of which even had successful Kickstarters, yet never really got the sales numbers. Now that it's easier than ever to simply publish your own games through Steam, getting traction in the flood of games that are competing with you for attention is a much harder prospect.'

She points to the queue at Aneeshka's booth. 'You should play that game, and you'll see what I mean. It brings a unique twist to competitive first-person shooters, the way *Screencheat* did by making players invisible so they're reliant on watching the other screens to find their opponents. It's also a unique mash-up of genres. A great example is how *Negatory* brought together elements of exploration, visual novels and JRPG fighting.'

'She's . . .' Why is it so hard to say that the developer is my best friend? Instead I settle for, 'I've played *Turn and Run*, and I see what you mean. Thank you for your honesty, I know it must have been hard.'

She pats me on the shoulder. 'I'm sorry I had to break it to you, and I hope you're not too discouraged. *Vinculum* is a good game. I honestly hope to see great things from you in the future.'

The tears I've been holding back all day are ready to burst. I manage to keep them in check as I thank her profusely a few more times till she leaves. I'm still fine. I should woman-up already and take the setbacks and failures in my stride like a promising developer would.

Why did you even bother trying? The whisper is insidious, and I can't shut it out. *You're not special like the Farrows. Nowhere near the same level as Aneeshka, who's created a game everyone wants in three weeks flat. You can work as hard as you want, but in the end you're plain white rice.*

Boring. Unimaginative. How do you combat that? Even though I can work on improving my skills, if my ideas can't even reach chicken rice level – forget about the chicken that goes with it – my skills hardly matter. I gave up on a normal high school life, turned down days out, spent all my holidays cooped up in my room working, researching, building and rebuilding. I went to game jams and entered competitions and won awards. I was so sure it'd pay off, that I could pursue my passion instead of spending four years attending lectures and working on projects to develop software I had no interest in.

And what did I end up with? Something that's not hot like *Turn and Run*, not so glitchy it's hilarious like *Goat Simulator*, just . . . good. I made a 'good' game that's utterly forgettable.

I stare at the 'Reinforce' rune Jay gave me, hanging tauntingly from my backpack as though telling me I'm worthless even with all the support everyone's given me. I unhook it from my bag and shove it to the bottom. That rune can't help me if my base stats aren't good enough to begin with.

I'm trying to find the passion I had for this game when I first started making it . . . the passion for making any game at all, really. Except it's gone, doused by the icy bucket of reality. The best I can do is work for someone else and make software with clear requirements and purpose. How could I even dream of going to the workshop at PopSplosion and pitching this run-of-the-mill nothing to the Farrows? I should be grateful I saved myself the embarrassment.

I pull out my phone and send a message to Jay.

Sam

> I forfeit. The Art of Game Design workshop ticket is all yours. Uh, Ansen's. Congratulations, you win.

His answer comes back almost immediately.

Jerky McJerkface

> Udina? What happened? Are you okay? Give me a call. Whatever it is, we can work something out. Or I can come to Sydney and we can sort things out in person.

The last thing I need, the last thing I *want*, is some guy swooping in to save the day. Sure, he's not one of the dude bros that are so sure they know better than me. But he's still trying to fix my situation, to make it better and if I let him I would only despise myself more.

Sam

No need. It's over.

Then I turn off my phone, and leave it off.

CHAPTER 26

The rest of the day passes in a blur. Thankfully, Aneeshka is too busy at her booth to come by mine, which gives me time to practise hiding my emotions. Wash away the tears. Let my eyes unpuff. Practise acting excited in the bathroom mirror. Get ready to go play the escape room she booked for us weeks ago as a post-showcase celebration.

I want to be The Most Supportive Friend, because she's stuck by me through everything, and talked me out of the depths every time I was convinced my games were terrible. She's seen her own share of failure, and finally grasped the success due her. She deserves to celebrate instead of commiserate, so what's a little lie in the face of it all?

It takes over an hour to pack up my booth, made longer because I have to sneak all my postcards and stickers into the bin while Aneeshka isn't looking. I'm done with this game, done with trying, so there's no point in keeping any of it. And this way, if she does look, it'll seem like I ran out of swag due to my popularity.

It's past 5 pm by the time we make it back to our hotel room, even though you'd think it was 3 pm thanks to daylight savings. Aneeshka's exhausted but buoyed by exhilaration; I'm exhausted but determined to match her mood so she doesn't suspect a thing. The escape room she booked is in the city, the opposite end from where we are.

On the light rail there, she's still riding high on our success. 'We're finally at a point where we'll soon be able to call ourselves professional devs!'

Every word is a fresh punch to the gut, yet I don't let it show. 'Exactly. All the times we got dissed at school for sitting in front of our computers all lunchtime, all those failures, this is where they led us.' I grab her arm and raise it in triumph. 'Tonight we celebrate!'

'Tonight we mark the start of the Sam and Aneeshka era with a new escape room record!' she adds. 'You know, if you're doing the full-time dev thing now you've got publisher interest, you could move to Sydney too. We could live together and properly bootstrap by starting our studio in a crappy old apartment with not enough space.'

I force myself to laugh at that, because the old Sam would find it hilarious. Thankfully, Aneeshka doesn't notice anything amiss because she's responding to a message on her phone. I can't wait till we get to the escape room – there'll be so much going on I won't have time to think about all this, and she won't have time to realise something might be up because she can read me too well.

'Hey,' she says, still typing, 'some of my new friends said they're free to join us for dinner after the game! Do you want to meet them? I think you'd really like them, and it also means we can order more food to share.'

Honestly, I don't want to. I don't even want to go out. But this is Aneeshka's night. I should be the kind of supportive friend I'd want if I was in her place, not a weeping mess who completely ruins any sense of achievement and overshadows it with guilt.

'Sure,' I say, trying not to sound too peppy either, another giveaway. 'I'd love to meet all these awesome friends you've been telling me about.'

'Done!' she says, and puts her phone away. Which unfortunately means all her attention is back on me. 'I *had* to book this escape room; a review mentioned it was a cross between *Portal* and *Keep Talking and Nobody Explodes*. If it wasn't made for us then no escape room will ever be. Maybe one day there'll be escape rooms inspired by our games too!'

'Wouldn't that be a dream come true?' All I can think of is the Blackbird scout's feedback. A *good* game. But nothing special enough to inspire players, let alone a whole escape room. So I turn the conversation to her game instead. 'Imagine something like *Turn and Run* where each room could be rotated to connect to a different one, and you have to line up, say, three rooms in a row to get something from one end to another.'

'Genius,' Aneeshka says. 'You're so good at creating puzzles, no wonder everyone loved *Vinculum* too!'

It's all I can do to squeeze out an excited grin for her. Upon arriving at the place I can already sense a nerdy vibe about it – there's a lightsaber hilt on one of the tables, and an Aquaman trident in another corner.

I should be excited the way Aneeshka is, except all I can feel is the cold, twisted lump at the bottom of my stomach. I can hardly focus on our game master's briefing – I sure hope there are no important specifics I missed – and laugh maybe a bit too loudly when they come out again in sunglasses as a totally unrelated secret agent to give us the game's introduction.

I hate that I should be loving this, but I can't even find the emotions. It's all I can do to focus on keeping up my energy for Aneeshka so she doesn't suspect anything.

'Everything okay, Sam?' she asks once we're alone in the first room, listening to an automated voice inform us that *Decontamination is underway, please do not move or the automated scourer may scour an eyeball.*

'Just nervous,' I tell her. 'I mean, we're gonna be professionals now instead of two excitable teens. We have a lot more to prove this time around, right?'

Thankfully at that point sirens go off, something drops with a loud clang that makes us both scream, and the game truly begins. Even if I'm stumbling through the whole thing in a haze, playing up the fun and excitement I don't feel.

It turns out that Aneeshka wasn't kidding when she said it took inspiration from *Keep Talking* – there are quite a few sections that require one person to convey deliberately misleading instructions to another person at a control panel. It doesn't take long to slip back into our old rhythm, as though nothing's changed and we're still kids dreaming of the future.

'Got it first go!' she yells from the other room after I've instructed her on how to position a set of switches.

We're making good time, flying through the puzzles, falling into our shorthand, and while we're in the game it's like everything's better. Even if I jump and cheer and am louder than usual, I can pass it off as the excitement of the whole weekend.

In the end, we're three minutes off the record, which seems to impress the games master. I mean, *I'm* impressed with us too. He spends some time taking us through the room, showing us all the Easter eggs and references, and both of us fall into our usual habit of taking notes to compare later.

We have our picture taken, but don't have time to debrief privately with each other like we usually would – Aneeshka's new friends message her to say they've arrived early at the cosy Spanish tapas bar where we're meeting. They all seem very friendly, even though I'm terrible at remembering names. I do, at least, get out all the nice-to-meet-yous and let them squeal over Aneeshka's recount of the weekend. I even manage an account of my encounters with various publishers that sounds promising, before pretending I'm too caught up by all the delicious food.

'When I was a kid,' Aneeshka tells her new friends, 'I didn't know many people who were into gaming. Not like you all. Then in Year Seven I met Sam, and the rest is history.'

She drapes one arm around my shoulders. 'It's so incredible to think we made it all the way here, together. You should've seen us blitz that escape room. There's a reason they called us the Dynamic Duo in high school, you know. First escape rooms, next the gaming world!'

I take a large sip from my glass of sangria to swallow down the sob rising in my throat. It promptly distracts everyone because wine was not meant to be swallowed in such quantities, at least not when you're unused to it like I am. It even gives an excuse for the tears in my eyes after.

'Yeah,' I say to Aneeshka when my coughing fit is over. 'What a journey, huh?'

'To all the success to come,' Aneeshka says as we clink our glasses of sangria, and I take a small sip this time.

She looks at me expectantly, and I realise I need to give a toast too.

'To . . .' Words fail me. To what? To being a worthless wannabe? To the end of a career that never even began?

'Sam?' Aneeshka pulls back her glass with a concerned frown. 'What's going on?'

Raising my glass again, I wait for her to pick hers up. 'To you.' *Wait, I'm meant to be celebrating as well.* 'To us! To the best damn team the world will ever see.'

'You sure as hell know it,' she says, but watches me carefully as we drink again.

Time to up my game. I start talking about my hopes and dreams for our future, the two of us going from dodgy apartment bootstrapping to becoming a leading Australian studio that'll grow the industry and make it viable to have a rewarding career as a game dev in Australia. All things Aneeshka and I talked about in the past. All things that are out of reach for me now.

I spin the story one last time, both for them and for myself, weaving in everything I ever wanted for us. For other girls who love games, who are fighting to be seen as a legitimate part of the industry without having to beat the boys first, who just want to do their own thing and still live up to their family and their community's expectations.

When it ends, reality returns with a vengeance. My parents were right after all. I should take that scholarship and settle for the backup plan that's turned into the *only* plan. Moving to Sydney to work on games is definitely out of the question.

'I had an amazing cocktail at an underground bar in Surry Hills the other night,' one of Aneeshka's friends say to her. 'It's exactly your taste profile.'

Firstly, taste profile? What does that even mean when it comes to cocktails? How often does she go out with them that they already know what she likes? And secondly, we've never talked cocktails before, ever. But from the way her eyes light up, it's clear she's itching to try it out.

'This isn't the one we went to last week with the cute bartender, is it? The one who had stunning legs?' Aneeshka laughs and wriggles her eyebrows while raising her glass. 'I'd let them serve me my perfect drink any day.'

'Nah, different place, though they did give me Chaos vibes. I mean the character from *Hades*, if that's your thing.'

'It's totally my thing.'

Aneeshka fits in so well with her new friends, from gaming to wider interests. At one point the talk turns to whether there were any hot gamers at the showcase, and I'm checking out because I don't understand how abs or legs or butts or boobs or faces can stir feelings in anyone.

She belongs here, and I don't. All I can do is sit here and watch her accelerate out of my orbit.

It seems like forever before we finally leave, everyone having had a bit too much to drink. I focus on wrangling Aneeshka back to our hotel room, and into her bed. It's a relief when I can tumble into my own bed and remove the happy facade. I'm so ready to go home.

Thankfully I have a 7 am flight (it was cheap!), and my low mood can easily be attributed to waking up far too early after our late night. She sees me out the hotel door making me promise to keep her updated on everything and to come see her in Sydney again *soon*. It's not until the door closes that I finally let my shoulders slump.

When I land back in Brisbane, my parents and Eva are waiting at the airport gate. Eva's in her school uniform so we can drop her off on the way home. They greet me with excited smiles as I walk out.

The first thing my mum says when I emerge is, 'You're not wearing lipstick!' Then she stops, takes a closer look at me, and asks, 'Sun Sun? Are you okay?'

She wraps me in a hug, and my dad and Eva join in so I'm wrapped in the biggest, warmest group hug I can imagine. And only now, finally, do I break. It starts with a quiet sob, almost a hiccup. Then another, and another, until they meld into bigger sobs. All the tears I managed to hold back for the entire duration of my Sydney trip come flooding out in the middle of this damn airport.

I rip off my glasses and cry into the closest shirt, and they all surround me like a protective wall, holding back the world. It's embarrassing that Eva's seeing her older sister in such a state. I'm meant to set an example for her, to be the person she can rely on instead of the one she has to care for.

My mum strokes my hair. 'It's okay, Sun Sun. Maybe things didn't go well, but it's not the end. You're smart; you have a lot of options.'

It's obvious what options she's referring to.

I let out a bitter laugh. 'You were right. Not wanting to go to uni was a ridiculous idea. I should get that degree and get a normal job like everyone else.'

There's nothing particularly unique about it. Every time I think about my game, think about making any game, all I can hear is that phrase.

My mum's hand pauses mid-stroke. 'Sun Sun, you know we don't want you to—'

'I'm okay now,' I tell them, pulling away so I can swipe my face dry, and firmly set my glasses back on. I can't deal with their half-hearted pity; it feels too close to 'I told you so' even though they don't mean it that way. 'Let's go get my luggage.'

I lead the way to the baggage carousel, where the bags have just started to come out. Eva comes up beside me and puts an arm around my shoulders.

'I'm sorry, jie,' she says. 'I know this game meant a lot to you.' She leans her head against mine. 'Mummy and I made a celebratory cake that says *We're so proud of you!* If I add an "anyway" to the end it makes a good consolation cake. And it's delicious.'

Although I'm still feeling miserable, the laugh that emerges is genuine. While I hate that I'm so helpless in front of her, such an obvious failure in front of her, I lean into her for comfort anyway.

I feel utterly worthless. Why did I think I could break out of the role that's been my mould my whole life? Even if I thought I was being so bold, so ambitious, so different, I really wasn't. I don't have the ability to make my own path.

After all those years, I'm left with a handful of nothing. It's possible to create a great game right out of high school – Aneeshka is a prime example of that – except I'm not one of those people.

When we get back home, I trudge to my room with my bags and shut the door. My parents understand, I think, because they give me space.

The artwork on my walls mocks me with everything I'll never be, and I rip it all down. Figurines are stuffed into an empty bag and shoved to the back of my closet. The *Portal* gun joins them. The art books come off the shelves and go into a donate pile. The game design books too. I'm going to dedicate my all to this intense scholarship course, and forget about games.

It seems I'm not cut out for the indie dev world after all.

There are missed calls and new messages from Jay. I swipe the notifications away without responding.

Jerky McJerkface

Hey, what happened?

Jerky McJerkface

Are you alive and kicking?

Jerky McJerkface

I assume so since my parents talked to
Aunty Deonna who talked to your aunt
who said your parents said
you're back from Sydney now

Jerky McJerkface

If you're alive stop ignoring my calls and
messages because I don't accept your
terms of surrender.

Jerky McJerkface

Can we at least talk about what
happened? You're talented; this doesn't
have to be the end of the line for you.

Jerky McJerkface

We could find a way to make the game
dev thing work, there's so many paths
you can still take

After a day of this I send a message back.

Sam

> I'm done, understood? I don't want the
> ticket, I don't want the game; they're
> all yours. There's no longer a need for
> competition. I don't want to 'make the
> game dev thing work'. There is nothing
> for you to fix and no paths for you to find.
> Please leave me alone.

I don't want to be the girl he 'helped' to pick herself up, and is now ready to go to uni, get a good job and settle down to start a family.

Even if I can't make it as a dev, I *can* make it as an independent woman.

To my relief, there's silence from Jay after I send that message. I'm grateful he respected my request for space. Damn if I don't miss him and his banter. He knows how to push my buttons in a way that distracts me from everything else, and all I have at the moment is a quiet I want to avoid because that's when the doubts and whispers invade.

Over the next few days my phone fills up with messages from Aneeshka, all of which I try to respond to quickly so she doesn't suspect anything. Excitement over meetings set up with various publishers, interview requests from gaming sites . . . a world I no longer want to be a part of, though I can't bear to tell her.

I suddenly have vast swathes of time on hand, time that I used to spend on *Vinculum*. I don't even have any schoolwork to distract me. Instead, I stay in my room and stare at the ceiling, or flip through random books. Listen to angsty music. I can't game, because it hurts too much. Every game is a reminder of what I'm missing. At one point I get so desperate I start looking up the first year courses in the scholarship program – I've ripped up the application to defer – and start reading up on the topics they cover.

Might as well make sure I graduate with First Class Honours so I can get the highest paying corporate job. If I'm going to sell my soul, it'll be to the highest bidder, thanks.

Oh hey Sam, welcome to the real world.

CHAPTER 27

On Saturday morning, Eva casually mentions that she wants to try out a bakery that does incredible croissants for breakfast.

'I haven't made breakfast, you should go,' our mum says.

She's way too transparent about this double-team. Since when has she encouraged Eva to go out more?

With the two of them pushing me, I end up driving Eva there. She talks about how much her friends have raved about the croissants and how the pastry chef has won a lot of awards. She keeps the mood relaxed, not expecting me to respond. Instead, there's space to process and engage on my own terms. The mention of a fish roe croissant does get my attention, though.

Even when we've arrived at the cafe, placed our orders and seated ourselves at the table, Eva doesn't push me. She's not like our mum, constantly asking if I'm okay and trying to convince me that this is a good thing. With her, I don't need to worry about the dreaded words: *Isn't it good you still have your scholarship?*

'Did I tell you Mummy and Daddy agreed to let me go on the holiday with Tamara's parents?' she says as someone arrives with an espresso for her and a chai latte for me. 'Her parents called them again to assure them they would take very good care of me, they'd protect me like their own daughter, all that.'

I give her a small smile over my latte. 'I'm glad they're being more reasonable.'

'Thanks for talking to them, jie.' She takes a whiff of her espresso, and there's an ill-concealed bitterness in her expression that matches the scent. 'They actually listen when you tell them stuff and don't assume you're too much of a kid to know anything.'

'Hah.' It's something I would've been privately pleased about a week ago. That seems like another life now. 'Yeah, I'm real good at anticipating what people want and doing what they ask. Not so great at thinking for myself, apparently.'

'Well, it means you're the daughter every Asian parent wishes they had.' She presses her lips together for a long moment and looks away before adding, 'Almost every time when Mummy and Daddy are going on about their amazing daughters to some aunty or uncle, they mean you. The one who gets good grades and wins prizes and is always at home and working.'

I never realised she felt that way, wrapped up as I was in my own world. 'Then let me tell you now, none of that was worth it. Apparently it makes me a very good future employee and housewife, and a terrible creative. Meanwhile, you're out here making these brilliant music arrangements and composing music – which, by the way, was the game element that got the most consistent compliments all weekend. So, congrats.'

I'm tired of putting on a good face, tired of pretending I'm not upset and jealous and frustrated and bitter about it all. I simply don't have enough emotional energy to whip out the 'understanding big sister' role. All I can be before her is ugly, and it's not freeing. It's terrifying. But again, I can't muster the energy to be otherwise.

To my surprise, Eva gives me a wry grin. 'Never thought the day would come when you'd be jealous of me.'

Her lack of judgement loosens the tight feeling in my chest, and I return the grin. 'There's a first for everything.'

The croissants arrive, and I take a bite from one. It lives up to Eva's promises – they're perfectly flaky and crunchy on the outside, but soft and airy on the inside, and I have no doubt a heart-stopping amount of butter has been used for each one. As soon as I finish mine, I order another.

'Pig,' Eva says as she collects every last crumb on her own plate.

'Piglet.' I order one more for her, too.

We don't go home after breakfast. Instead we head to New Farm Park and find a grassy spot near the Brisbane River. It's a brown, turgid thing that reflects my mood perfectly. Eva lies down on the grass, while I carefully seat myself so only my slacks are in contact with the ground.

She throws a twig at me. 'Dirt won't kill you, you know.'

I deflect it. 'The bugs might.'

'Oh no, it's an ant! Run for your life!'

'Wait till you get bitten by an army of bull ants, then see if you change your tune.'

'You're still scared by that?' She flicks my leg. 'You were *eight*.'

'It's an unresolved issue, leave me alone.'

We haven't had much 'us' time in years, in large part due to my single-minded focus on creating games, but also because we haven't had a reason to. We had breakfast together, were driven to and picked up from school together, ate dinner most nights with our parents . . . though now I think of it, outside of that we've been living mostly separate lives. I wonder how much of that is because I was so wrapped up in my own stuff, and how much is because I played into the 'good girl' role at Eva's expense.

'If we're admitting things today, jie,' she says after a long stretch of contemplative silence, 'I really wanted you to succeed so you'd give up your scholarship and uni. Then maybe everyone would stop looking down on me because they're comparing me to you.'

'By "everyone" you mean Mummy and Daddy?'

She makes a face. 'I mean both Gu Jies and Gu Jiongs, all the aunties and uncles at church, all of Mummy and Daddy's friends . . . basically any older Asian person who knows our family.' She reaches over and slaps my thigh, the only part she can reach. 'Sure you don't want to run off into the sunset and make games anyway? Do your favourite younger sister a favour?'

'I don't need to disappear or stray off the prescribed path for you to be acknowledged as the awesome person you are. Or at least, I shouldn't. Anyone who can't see that, well, that's their problem.'

'Thanks, jie.' Her head turns slightly so it's facing me. 'You don't need to for me. How about for you?'

I wrap my arms around my knees and rest my chin on top, staring aimlessly at a patch of grass where a man is casually painting the scenery. 'I thought I was passionate about games. Playing them, designing them, making them. Sure I could tell Mummy and Daddy that I'm not going to uni anyway, but what's the point when I can't remember how it feels to love games anymore?'

How long has it been since I made something for fun instead of calculating how it would create my post-high school career? I can't even grasp the feelings from when I first started making *Vinculum* back in the middle of Year Eleven. All I remember is that I was excited about it then. At what point did it also morph into responsibility, a symbol of Sam the indie developer, an expectation to carry and fulfil?

'You already know you're not interested in uni courses, right?' Eva's not giving up. 'Becoming an indie dev isn't the only option. Can't you find something else you'll enjoy that's not uni?'

The sound that comes out of my mouth is more bark than laugh. 'The entirety of my life since the start of high school has been about making indie games. I have nothing else.'

She pulls herself up with a groan and tries to slap the back of my head. I dodge with a move that's worthy of Jay.

'Then go find it,' she says. 'And if it so happens you fall from grace in the Asian community, well, that's a bonus.'

This time I'm actually laughing. 'I'll keep that in mind. Just for you.'

It doesn't matter if we lean different ways while straddling two cultures, or if there is a divide between our worlds we can't quite cross. Like my game, we stumble along our individual paths, each affecting the other in ways even we might not completely understand, through an unseen bond. The vinculum.

In so many ways I'm still wandering alone in the dark on my half of the screen, but knowing she's on the other half? It helps.

We end up staying out for dinner as well — as it turns out, Eva's pretty good to talk to. When we get home, I head straight back to my room as usual. Despite Eva telling me to find something else I'd enjoy, I wonder if I'll find anything else that fills me with the same fire and drive as developing games did.

There's an elegance to a well-designed puzzle that will never grow old. The moment when disparate elements click in a moment of 'ah-hah!' It's the kind of moment when you can almost believe that things have a clear cause and effect, that logic prevails, and you can make sense of the world if you try hard enough. It's what started my love affair with puzzle games, leading to indie games more generally.

Where do I go from here? This isn't where I intended to be.

My staring at the ceiling is interrupted by my parents, who come in and tell me in no uncertain terms that light exercise will help my mood – ignoring my protests that I've already been at the park all day, even though they don't know I simply sat there with Eva – and we're going on a walk around the neighbourhood together.

My dad simply says, 'You spent all day with your mui and you can't even spare half an hour for your mummy and daddy?'

I give in.

They're silent as we walk down our driveway and along our street, slowing their steps to match my reluctant shuffle. Our footsteps echo in the silence of the suburban streets, with only the occasional rumble of a passing car. The light from the street lamps stretches our shadows behind us, long and thin as though our very substance is being spun out into the darkness, sucked away till there's nothing left save for our meat-shells.

My mum's the first to speak. 'Sun Sun, you know . . . your ba and I never wanted you to stop making games. We only wanted you to have more options, and no regrets in the future.'

I stare down at the asphalt, at my shuffling footsteps. 'Well, you were right, weren't you?' I don't bother with Cantonese. 'I'm finished making games, because there's no point.'

My mum takes my hand as we continue to walk through these streets that are the epitome of suburbia, the kind of life my parents moved here to pursue; the kind of life I should aspire to.

'When I was your age,' she says, 'I'd left school and was teaching music at Yamaha. I dreamed that one day I'd have my own music school that was just as big and famous.'

My dad laughs. 'Then six years later I stole her away, and a few years after that we moved to Australia.'

I make a face at them. 'And you asked me why I didn't want to get involved with a boy.'

'To me, it wasn't a sacrifice,' my mum quickly adds. 'I realised that what I really wanted was to have a place where I could teach people music and show them it could be fun. Maybe I don't have that big and famous music school, but the reason for what I do is still the same.' She squeezes my hand. 'I thought it would be one shape, except it was another.'

'People don't have fun playing my games, apparently.' I sound like a sulky, petulant child. I don't care.

'You enjoy making your games, don't you?' she asks.

Do I still? I give them my honest answer. 'I don't know anymore.'

'It's only one game,' my dad says. 'You can make other games.'

He doesn't get it. None of them do. It's not about making other games. It's about knowing you don't have the creativity to break out in an increasingly crowded market. It's about not being good enough to do what you love and make it stick. Doesn't matter how many games I make.

'You should be happy,' I mutter. 'I'm attending university for free, then I'll make a lot of money. Everyone wins.'

After a long silence, my dad says, 'I was fired from my first job. They said they didn't like my attitude; that I argued too much, even though I tripled the sales for our branch. I think they meant I argued too much for a Malaysian, because it was an English company and all the managers were from London. They didn't think someone like me should be telling them they were wrong, even when they were.'

I squint at him. 'You think they didn't want my game because I'm Asian?'

'No, no, I wasn't saying that. I left my second job because they brought in a new regional manager who thought he knew everything about the market and lost the big sale I was about to close. I heard they closed all branches in the region a year or two after I left.'

'So . . . you're saying the game publishers don't know anything about the market.'

'Wait for me to finish, Sun Sun. My third job, I quit before they could fire me.'

'Another bad manager?'

'No, this one really was a bad fit. I did things one way, they did things another. We didn't work out. It wasn't until my fourth job that I ended up at a company I liked, which also liked me. Sometimes it takes a while to find where we belong, my little one.'

He hasn't called me that in a while, and I feel like a child again, wanting to hide away from the world in the safety of my parents.

'I know you really wanted your game to work out. We wanted you to go to university for your sake, not give up on everything you love. As your parents, it hurts us to see you like this.' He ruffles my hair. 'If you don't want to go to university this semester, and would rather take some time to see what you want to do, then we'll support you.'

I sniffle, wishing I'd thought to bring tissues. 'I love you both. But I'm done with making games. I'd rather just take an ordinary path in an ordinary course where you know if you're right or wrong because you either get the A or you don't.'

A good, stable job and a good stable life. As plain white rice, that's the best I can hope for.

'I always hoped you would find a job where you could make good money and look after yourself,' my mum says. 'Except seeing you like this, maybe that's not the right way for you.'

Then I'll make it my way.

'It is. The showcase made me realise I'm not cut out for the creative world.' I don't have the strength of mind, or strength of character. 'I think a normal job would make me happier in the long-term.'

I'm not sure how the situation's turned into my parents convincing me *not* to go to uni, and me convincing them I should. Yet here we are.

'If you say so.' My dad sounds sad. 'Just remember, you can always change your mind.'

CHAPTER 28

In the next week, I dive into learning first year uni content to remind me not to sway in my resolve. On Friday night, when most people would be out having a life, I'm in the middle of watching a video about data-mining algorithms. That is, till my phone rings. I glance at it, expecting it's Jay trying to get in touch with me again. But the name on the screen says *Aneeshka Basu*.

I scramble to pick it up. I don't want her to think I'm ignoring her.

Until today, I didn't know excitement could coexist with crushing disappointment. It's like that ridiculous white/gold or blue/black dress that was popular back in primary school. If I simply glance at it, it's the dark blue/black I see, but if I forcefully flip my brain it's the brightness of the white/gold that comes to the forefront.

Supportive best friend mode, activate.

'Hey!' I say with the most excited voice I can muster. 'How was the meeting with Blackbird Interactive?'

'Sam.' Aneeshka doesn't sound like someone who's met with a publisher whose interest we both dreamed of for years. 'Are you free to talk?'

'Of course!' Oh, no. Did that come out too hyped up? Surely she can't see how my brain keeps flipping back to blue/black without constant attention.

'I remember you said one of the scouts from Blackbird showed interest in your game, right?'

'Right. We had a good talk about it.' It's not really a lie – we did talk, after all.

Her voice is quiet. 'I asked them what they thought of *Vinculum* today. And the strange thing is, no one remembered that name.'

Damn. She wasn't meant to involve me. I was counting on her being so excited about her game, she wouldn't think about mine. Then again, I should have known her better. I'll have to play it off.

'The scout that played it probably wasn't there,' I tell her, scrabbling to remember the name on the lady's tag. Amira? Amina?

'I had them check with everyone who attended, because I was certain they'd know once they heard what it was about. No one remembered having interest in a game called *Vinculum*.' Aneeshka sighs. 'They didn't ask you to pitch, did they?'

When I remain silent, she adds, 'Did any publisher?'

Happy mode. Happy mode. 'Of course! Don't you have any faith in me? I mean, there wasn't anywhere near as much as yours, but there was some.'

'Who?' she asks.

Who wouldn't she have a meeting with? I pull up the showcase site and go to the page of attending publishers, searching for one who might not have approached her.

Aneeshka doesn't sound convinced. 'You can't even remember the—'

'Traction Games,' I say, hurriedly picking a smaller one I haven't heard of. 'Them.'

There's clicking on the other end of the line. 'They're not a publisher. They're a PR firm. Who you pay to handle PR for your games.'

Crap.

'Huh. They misrepresented themselves to me, then.' I take off my fogged-up glasses and rub at my eyes. In these past few days, I've completely lost control of when I leak, and in what quantity. I need to keep it together. 'More importantly, what happened with Blackbird? What did they offer? What cut do they want, or are they going the route of offering *you* royalties?'

'Samantha Khoo.' She sounds like my mother when I'm in trouble. 'Stop deflecting and tell me honestly. How did you do at the showcase?'

'Fi—'

'Don't you dare say "fine". I want the truth, and I thought my best friend would, I don't know, *trust me with it.*'

The words come out in a torrent before I can stop them. 'Yeah, well, you have all your new friends and your new life and the career we always dreamed of, so does it matter if I don't tell you every little thing about my life now?'

'Of course it matters!' I don't need to see her to picture the kind of face she makes when she's frustrated, or the way she clenches and unclenches her fists. 'Because it's not a little thing, it's a huge thing and I thought we were always going to be there for each other even if we're in different cities. What, I'm not allowed to make friends here or do anything other than make games while we chat? I have to be the Aneeshka from high school forever?'

There's the same resentment in her voice that I recognise from all the times she'd complain to me about how she'd like to actually do something without being cross-examined by her parents every time. The kind of tone that was usually followed by, *I can't wait to get out of this city and have my own space.*

'You know that's not what I meant!'

'Do I?' Her words are curt. Cutting.

I take a deep breath, trying to find some words, any words, which express even a fraction of all the conflicting emotions ricocheting inside me like projectiles in a bullet-hell game.

'Look. It was hard when you moved. It sucked that I wouldn't see you almost every day.' My voice starts to tremble, and I hate it for that. 'But it was okay because I was going to make it work. The showcase and the Farrows' workshop were going to be my big break. They were gonna let me join you in Sydney on my own terms.'

Aneeshka's voice is quiet. 'It didn't work out?'

She wants the truth? I'll give her the whole truth. 'It was the ultimate game over, okay? Apparently my work is unoriginal and uninspiring. I am not, in fact, a Chosen One and I am no one of importance at all. I'm not some wunderkind genius. *Vinculum* is no *Turn and Run*. It's bland and forgettable. Apparently I made a "good" game, you know, in the way they use "good" when they don't have a distinctive enough impression to say anything else. I can work hard, but that's all I can do, and it's time to accept that.'

Aneeshka doesn't say anything. I can hear her breathing on the other end, faster than normal.

Eventually she whispers, 'You should have told me.'

'I didn't want to bring down your experience at the showcase.' Why, why won't the tears stop? '*Turn and Run* did well, and it was something to celebrate.'

'How do you think I feel now, looking back on it and knowing you were suffering on your own the whole time? I even invited my friends to dinner to celebrate!' There's an edge of frustration in her voice that she's trying to suppress. 'How to deal with that news should have been my decision to make.'

'No,' I retort, 'it was my decision whether to share my failure with you.'

More silence, as I put my phone on mute so I can blow my nose noisily into a tissue.

Then she says, 'You're right. It was your choice, not mine. I'm sorry for forcing the issue. And we don't have to talk about it if you don't want to.'

I guess I would have wanted to know too, if I was in her place.

'I'm sorry too,' I say, before realising the phone's still on mute. I unmute it and repeat, 'I said, I'm sorry too.'

'I can hear you.'

'Not the first time, you didn't. I left it on mute and ended up telling no one I was sorry.'

She laughs, though a bit tentatively. 'Sounds like peak Sam.'

'Exqueeze me?!' I overplay the outrage so she knows I'm kidding, even though I sound sniffly. 'I'm the least airheaded of us two, thank you very much.'

'True,' she says ruefully. 'I should have noticed something was wrong that night. Now I'm remembering how you were way too hyped up, which I should have known was a warning sign. You always go too far the other way when you have something to hide. I guess I wanted to believe it was real; that you were so excited because we'd reached the next stage together.'

'I clearly missed my calling as an actress,' I say as I step away from my computer, leaning on the windowsill to stare out at the rows of lights dotting the street. 'Think it's too late to change my dream?'

Aneeshka laughs, though it's half-hearted at best. 'I still think you're a talented dev, but if that's truly what you want, it's never too late.' There's a long pause. 'Do you . . . do you

338

still want to be my friend? I hate that a game that took me three weeks to build got all the attention, while the game you've poured your heart into for the past couple of years was overlooked. It's . . . so horribly unfair.'

'You're not thinking of making some noble sacrifice on my behalf, are you? That changes nothing. If anything, it makes it worse for me because I can't ride on your coattails once you're famous.'

'No!' she exclaims, half laughing. 'I wasn't going to say anything like that. Even though it might be selfish, I want to see where this game takes me and how far I can go with it. Even if the situation *is* completely unjust.'

'Good.' I'm still leaking, and everything in me still hurts, but being able to talk honestly with my best friend about this awkward thing between us makes it feel like maybe we can find a new normal. Whatever that is. 'I want to see everyone raving about *Turn and Run* one day.'

'How about *Vinculum*?' she asks. 'What'll you do next?'

'I . . .' A lump rises in my throat, and I fight it back down. 'I'm not ready to talk about it yet. Or about making games. I can't deal with any of that right now.'

Or ever again.

'Do you still want me to tell you about what's happening with *Turn and Run*? Or is that rubbing salt in the wound?'

'Yes! Tell me!' I'm surprised to find I genuinely mean this. Just because I'm struggling, doesn't mean I can't also celebrate with her. And although we might not talk about making games anymore, it doesn't mean our friendship will crumble. I want to believe we're so much more than that. 'Are . . . are we okay?'

'Of course.' She says this seriously, emphatically. 'For what it's worth, I may have made new friends here, and things'll be different to how they were in high school. But my new friends don't replace you, or all the memories we have together, or the friendship and trust and silly jokes we've built up over the past six years.' Her voice is wobbly now. 'Just because I came here to have space from my parents doesn't mean I want space from you. You'll never be rid of me, Samantha Khoo.'

The situation can't be fixed in one conversation. Things will still get awkward between us at times and she's probably already planning how she can soften the blow when it comes to future conversations between us about *Turn and Run*. Still, it's a start.

'You'll never be rid of me either, Aneeshka Basu.'

I wake up puffy-eyed on Saturday morning after chatting late into the night with Aneeshka about every and any topic that's not games. Checking my phone, I discover I've been bombarded with a fresh slew of messages from Jay.

Jerky McJerkface

> We're finishing the competition, Udina. Sunday, same time and place as the very first round.

Jerky McJerkface

> If you don't promise me you'll come,
> I swear to you, I am going to turn up
> at your church tomorrow morning
> with the entire *Negatory* box.
> I'm going to wrap it up nice, dress up
> in my best suit, and go around telling
> every single aunty and uncle I see
> that I'm looking for you because
> I have a present to give you.

Jerky McJerkface

> Every. Single. One.

Jerky McJerkface

> I'll ask them to bring me to you, which
> they will, and which you'll let them
> do because it's certain death to be
> rude to them. Then in front of the
> biggest audience I can gather,
> I will get on one knee and present
> the game to you.

He really knows how to hit my weaknesses. And also how to make me laugh for the first time all week. Even if I'm mortified at the thought of him actually doing that, and furious that he'd turn the tables and blackmail me into participating in the final competition round when I told him to leave me alone.

I see you asking yourself, would he really do that?

My answer is: do you really want to find out if I'm bluffing? You know I won't be satisfied until I'm properly proven to be the winner, which means we finish the final round. And you know what lengths I'd go to, to win.

Why are you doing this? There's no point.

Maybe not for you, but did you ever think what it means to me? This competition, this time with you, ended up being one of the first things I'd truly done for myself without thinking how it would affect my family. I didn't worry about being gwai zai Jay and it was freeing. If nothing else, let me be obnoxious Jay one last time and end this properly.

I never saw it that way before. I don't want to play games, or look at them, or even think about them. I want to see Jay even less, because I don't want to fend off more attempts to 'help' me. But he claims it's for his own satisfaction and his reasoning checks out, so I suppose I owe him this much.

Sam

Fine. One last round.

Jerky McJerkface

Good. And if you don't turn up, I guarantee I will do everything I said the next week.

Keep the break clean. Keep things strictly to the competition.

Sam

Let's get this over with.

CHAPTER 29

Like the first time we competed, Jay's already at the cafe waiting when I arrive. Same table, same outrageous laptop, sans mechanical keyboard this time. He's sipping a coffee and has already ordered a chai latte for me, which he points to when I sit down. I wish he didn't already know small things like my preferred drink, because it makes it harder to walk away.

From the serious set of his face, he's not here to mess around, but if he thinks we're actually going to compete, he has another think coming. Although I may owe him some form of closure, I'm only indulging obnoxious Jay to the point of turning up. I'll go through the motions, then leave my game on the menu screen as a *Screw you*.

If I don't play the game, he can't try a sneaky pity play by throwing the match.

'Ready to end this once and for all, Udina?' he asks as I plop down on the seat across from him.

I shrug, pulling out my laptop and setting it up. 'Sure.'

He pulls out the Bag of Fate. And to think I actually believed it was leading me to a greater place. Hah. It's not wrapped, because I raced out of Jay's house in such a hurry last time. I can't even find the energy to argue about whether he's tampered with it. He can pick any game he wants and it won't make a difference.

Jay places it on the table between us, then reaches in. There's a serious look on his face as he feels around, as though everything is riding on this. Whatever plan he has in the bag, it's not going to work.

He pulls out the paper and places it in front of him. Unfolds it carefully. And . . . it's blank. His wildcard pick. He lets out a sigh of relief.

'Any objections, Udina?'

He's daring me, as though trying to get me to argue back. This is his cocky demeanour, the one that usually gets on my nerves. Not today, though.

'Pick your game, any game.' There's no need to draw it out, not when all I want is to go home.

He takes a deep breath. 'For the final round, the indie game will be . . . *Vinculum*.' He pulls out the USB I gave him. 'Specifically, the build from last Sunday.'

I knew it. I knew he was going to pull some ridiculous stunt like this because he couldn't leave well alone. 'Is this some misguided attempt at pity? Your way of "giving" me the win because you feel so sorry that I crashed and burned so miserably in Sydney? I don't need anyone to feel sorry for me, understood?'

Despite all his talk about me being an opponent he respected and was wary of, the truth is that he sees me as someone who needs coddling. Someone who isn't strong enough to make it on their own. Now I'm grateful I didn't go running to him.

He narrows his eyes. 'Whoever said I was planning to lose?' He holds out the USB. 'Are you going to install this or not?'

I snatch it off him, and clear all current installations of my game before installing that version.

'You can't tell me you seriously think you'll beat the developer at their own game,' I say, as the progress bar ticks towards one hundred per cent. 'Try to hide your Mr Fix-It attempt all you want, I see right through it.'

He crosses his arms and looks at me, deadly serious. 'I told you before, I play to win. Don't think that'll change just because of the game we're playing, or because you're upset about stuff going on in your life.'

The way he says it, I remember how he's never fought me with anything other than a drive for victory, and I believe him. He honestly thinks he can beat me at my own game. The challenger inside me stirs. Sure, I hate this damn game. And sure, I said to myself that I wouldn't play seriously. But I'll be damned if I sit back and let him claim he's better than me at the game *I made*.

He pulls out his controller. 'Your game feels more natural with this in hand.'

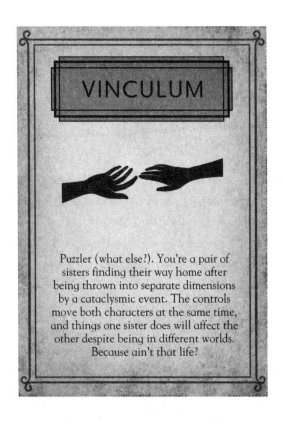

VINCULUM

Puzzler (what else?). You're a pair of
sisters finding their way home after
being thrown into separate dimensions
by a cataclysmic event. The controls
move both characters at the same time,
and things one sister does will affect the
other despite being in different worlds.
Because ain't that life?

How much has he played, to come to that conclusion? I assumed he'd never touched it again after last week. Now I'm even more determined to show him he can't defeat me.

It's on.

I pull out my own controller, still shoved in the bag from last time. 'I agree. Controllers are the best way to experience the game.'

'Ah, I have official confirmation from the developer. Good to know.'

I laugh despite myself. 'The developer also suggests taking time with the game, but I don't suppose that's going to happen today.'

He gives me a look of utter disbelief. 'Are you trying to convince me to throw the game? Not happening.'

We both load up the menu screen and go to the 'New Game' option.

'Ready?' Jay says. 'Go!'

We spin the laptops around, and I'm off. I know my levels inside out. These early levels I laboured over, tweaked endlessly to give a smooth learning curve to players so there weren't any sudden spikes in difficulty. There's a brilliant simplicity to the puzzle design that still gets me. Eva's music is so perfect I pause for a moment, remembering the recording session with our mum, the two of us hovering around her eagerly. The promise of it all. I shake myself out of the memories and push on.

I'm flying through the levels, one after the other. Remembering every design decision I made, why I placed an obstacle *here* instead of *there*. Why I completely revamped this level, and how that one was inspired by a sitcom episode I watched. One after another, I complete them almost by muscle memory. Racing through *Vinculum* as a gamer, not as a dev, it's actually . . . kind of fun?

Across from me, Jay is in full concentration mode. His joystick zips from one side to the other, with a few quick flicks at irregular intervals. Does he realise this is a puzzler, not a platformer? Exact inputs are unimportant. But the way he's focused on his screen as though nothing else in the world exists, he may as well be in the middle of a boss fight where one wrong move will lose the battle. It's gratifying to see him playing so seriously, refusing to underestimate me to the end. Turns out he wasn't lying about taking no prisoners.

Not that it's going to stop me from stomping him. I do make a few mistakes in later levels, the ones I was editing right up to the showcase. I made so many changes that I can't remember what the older versions were like, let alone this very specific version. They force me to pause for a moment and actually think about how I should solve it, and even though I remember the full answer once I start on the right train of thought, it's still satisfying.

Now I remember: *this* is why I started making games in the first place. It wasn't for the games themselves, it was for the joy of the puzzles, of the solving and the logic and the 'ah-hah!' feeling nothing else can quite replicate.

I'm five levels away from the end when Jay spins his laptop around and yells, 'Done!'

I stop, frozen in shock. That's not possible. He can't be that much faster than me. I didn't pause for that long in the later levels, and all the rest were perfectly executed.

He smirks at my expression. 'I told you I was in this to win, didn't I?'

'But . . . how?'

'There isn't only one way to win, Udina. I did a speedrun using glitches.'

He says this so casually, as though speedrunning doesn't require exact timing and a *lot* of practice, not to mention finding usable glitches as opposed to game-breaking ones that force you to reboot the game instead.

'You . . . how long did it take you to get the run down?'

He lets out a sigh and fake-collapses on the table. 'I've been doing nothing else since Wednesday. Ans helped too. No way I could've done it on my own.'

'Why? This is a weird way of making the situation better. Or is this *actually* an obnoxious Jay thing where you wanted to make your victory absolute?'

He doesn't answer the question, instead shifting his chair over so we're sitting on adjoining edges of the table. Then he nervously reaches out and places his hand over mine. When I don't move away, he closes his fingers in a gentle grip. It's warm, and his touch so light, that I feel secure, but not trapped.

'I heard on the Asian Gossip Network that you were done with games. Playing them, making them, whatever. From a surprising source, too – your sister.'

Normally, I'd be annoyed at Eva for butting in because I expect her to know better than to spread my private stuff around. This time, I don't think I mind. 'So you thought you'd make me play the game that made me crash and burn, and beat me while you were at it?'

He laughs. 'It sounds really bad when you put it that way.' He leans in closer, till my gaze is filled with the eyes that seem to see all of me, inside and out. 'But I wanted you to find out for yourself, one last time, if there was really no passion left.'

'What if I ended up hating everything even more?'

'The fact that you're asking me in the past tense means that it worked, right? And if not, you were going to give everything up anyway. I know I messed up when I messaged during the showcase. After it, too. I was scared I was about to lose someone amazing and I wanted to recapture all those moments between us, kinda like taking photos where the moment can't be unmade after. Then Ans told me that he could confront the bullies because he knew I was behind him. Not because I was in front of him.'

He takes a deep breath. 'It doesn't matter if things aren't perfect, because it's not up to me to make them perfect. If you encounter a boss fight in life that keeps beating you down, I don't want to step in and defeat it for you. All I want is to stand beside you and hold your hand along the way. Maybe hand you a mana potion, so you can cast a healing spell and get back into the fight.'

Till this moment, I always thought of being supported as an admission of inadequacy; a debt that had to be repaid when

I reached a point where I could return the favour. Yet this kind of support from Jay, where it's not about 'helping' me but instead pulling me to my feet and pushing me forwards when my own strength fails – that I think I can accept.

'I just . . . I don't want to be the kind of girl who can't stand on her own and needs a guy to sort things out for her, you know?'

He releases my hand, shifting his own to the back of my shoulder as he taps it gently, inviting me to lean in. Although I've never been this close with anyone outside my family before, I've already been laid bare before him, insecurities and all. Everything I am. Physical comfort to complement it feels right. So I lean in, pressing my side against his chest till I can hear the wild *ba-dump ba-dump* of his heart, an echo of my own.

'Hey, this isn't about you being a girl and me being a guy. Everyone's determination needs to be replenished sometimes, and we can't always do it alone. Udina – no, Sam. You challenged me in that GamesMasters store when I was being a jerk, and I partly agreed to the competition because I thought it'd be fun to show you up and prove I was better. But then you didn't stop fighting with every round. Not even when you were playing *Heaven's Complex* hungover.'

He conveniently omits his specific actions, continuing, 'Like I said, I play to win. I wasn't going to let you off easy. Somewhere along the way, I realised I want to play more video games with you. I want to smash more escape room records with you. You saw the Jay behind the gwai zai who's stubborn and has a need to meddle on an Asian aunty level, and wrestled with me the whole way. I want to face whatever the hell life throws at me with someone who isn't afraid to hold me accountable. Who still gets pissed off enough to keep fighting when she's down to her last sliver of her health bar.'

A weight, one I assumed would always be there, lifts somewhat. Enough to breathe. Enough to realise that here is someone I can be weak in front of with no holding back because of subconscious expectations about being a good daughter or older sister or friend. It translates, in a physical sense, into a desire to burrow deeper into the respite he offers.

I take off my glasses and press my face into the crook of his neck. 'Can I tell you that right now I don't even know if I have any fight left and I'm out of strategies to turn things around?'

'Yes.' One hand strokes my back, the lingering heat warming my whole body till the presence of him seems to surround me. 'Yes, of course.'

He leaves it at that, knowing that I wasn't really asking if I could tell him. His response to my actual question is to sit with me, not speaking, not finding solutions, simply letting me process everything in a space where I don't feel under-estimated for who I am or what I'm feeling or what I haven't achieved.

'I do like making games,' I eventually say, and that realisation, that admission, lifts another weight from my chest. 'It's more that I'm tired of always trying to prove myself. To be more. To be enough.' I think about the joy of the puzzles clicking into place as I played my game. 'I like creating moments for players when the pieces suddenly come together and there's the rush of adrenaline as you solve something. I like watching people go "ah-hah!" when things suddenly make sense.'

'Mmm-hmm.'

'And . . . maybe I don't have to do that through video games.'

Wow, that hurts to say. But it's like lancing a wound. I stare into space, contemplating. Recalibrating. Jay strokes the back of my head, and I wriggle closer against him because I trust he'll let me go when I'm ready.

Maybe it's not only others' expectations towards me that I have to overcome. I have to deal with my own as well. Maybe all the paths set out for me, expected *of* me, weren't the only ones out there. Maybe there are more paths I didn't even know existed, which still hold my love of puzzles at their core.

Paths I have to create with my own hands because they don't exist yet.

'What did you think of my game, Jay? Be straight with me.'

'Hmm.' The hum in his chest vibrates against my cheek. 'It wasn't the most original, blow-your-socks-off concept. The puzzles, however, were solid. They made me feel smart when I solved them. The story got me too. After playing through your game – many times, by the way – it made me want to be the one on the other half of the screen, progressing through the levels with you. To provide company for the way home.'

He clears his throat. 'That's all metaphorically speaking, anyway. I'm not sure I'm brave enough to literally accompany you home tonight and face your parents and their five-year plans for our wedding and grandchildren quite yet. Assuming

I haven't misread everything and you do, in fact, want to go out with me.'

'Your reading comprehension gets an A-plus.' I laugh, then push him away playfully as a thought strikes me. 'Wait, you said you were doing nothing except working out a speedrun for *Vinculum* all week. How did you know you'd pick the blank slip?'

He grins. 'We didn't have a chance to cling wrap the bag last time, did we?'

My jaw drops. 'You *didn't*.'

'I might've tampered with the slips last night. Folded the blank sheet a little differently to the others.'

That explains why he was so focused when he was picking a slip, and so relieved when the blank one was revealed.

I cross my arms in mock outrage. 'That's the excuse you give for cheating to win this round?'

He gives me a wry smile. 'I was gonna suggest that we disqualify this round and have another to replace it. The real one that decides the competition.'

While I do want to spend more time with him, whether it's playing games, finding new hobbies such as photography, perhaps, or whatever else the future may bring – winning this competition no longer matters to me.

'The limited edition of *Negatory* and the ticket are yours.' The final piece, severed. It feels right, for where I am now. 'At this point I think attending the Farrows' workshop would mean a lot more to Ansen. Besides, I want to step away from video games for a while.'

'Take your time,' he says. 'Let me know if I can do anything to help.'

I hold out my hand. 'Good game, Jaysen Chua.'

It's the same words esports teams use at the end of a match. A show of respect for an opponent after a hard fight. He clasps my hand in his, and shakes it.

'Good game, Samantha Khoo.'

I don't know where I'm going from here. I don't know what I'll do next, or what an alternative career path could even begin to look like. Will I go to uni after all? Take on a different kind of job? Everything is nebulous, uncertain. My clear vision for the future has been wiped away, replaced by a dense fog that has to be navigated one step at a time.

All I know is that I can have the confidence to charge into the unknown. No matter how many times I fall, there are so many people around me to help me get up again. My parents, Eva, Aneeshka and, now, Jay. All holding me up, sustaining me, and pushing me forwards in their own ways.

I'm not ready to return to my game because it still hurts too much, but it's not the end, either. Because while all the people around me provide me the courage to dream and a soft place to fall, this boy beside me won't let me be when I'm running on empty. He'll tease and provoke and challenge me, however long it takes.

Could I walk on my own? Probably. Is it easier when there's someone to rile me up till I can't stand it and take a step forwards out of sheer annoyance? Definitely.

This is a game that is so much better when played by two.

When Jay releases my hand, I give him my sternest look. 'Don't get ideas about bragging rights. This isn't a full and proper win, it's a match conceded due to extenuating circumstances. You not only rigged the pick, you used speedrunning glitches as well.'

He waggles a finger at me. 'You can't deny I won based on the rules we laid out at the start.'

'I'm pretty sure rigging the pick invalidates that.'

Grabbing his bag, he digs around and pulls out a folded piece of paper. The one I gave him at the start, with all the rules of our competition.

'If you can show me where it says I lose if I cheat when drawing a game, I'll concede.' He pushes the paper towards me. 'Go on.'

He's only doing this because he knows there's nothing there, and it's infuriating. But infuriating is what I need, and he knows this.

I snatch up the paper and crumple it. 'Fine.' He dodges as I chuck it at his head. 'This competition was still won on a technicality, and you know it.'

'Did you hear that?' he asks everyone and no one in general. 'She declared me the winner.'

'I did not! I said *a technicality*!'

'You know what the opposite of winner is? Loser. You lost.'

'I'd rather lose honourably than win through dirty tricks. Which is all you seem able to do. I don't think there's an honourable bone in your body.' Arguing feels good. It feels like my world can go back to normal, even if it takes time.

'Winners don't care about that.'

Even as he reiterates our status as winner and loser over and over, I don't feel like a loser at all. In fact, workshop or no workshop, success or no success, I got more than I gave. I didn't know that I wanted what I got, but it turns out that I did all along.

I've been so obsessed with the idea of achieving my dreams in a very specific way, and under my own power. Maybe it's okay to need help. Maybe it's okay to widen my focus, find something else that still holds my love of puzzling at its heart, and take my time.

I wonder what I'll discover out there?

CHAPTER 3⊙

3 weeks after the Future Devs Showcase

There's a countdown timer over the door of this escape room, but I don't care about that. What I *do* care about is me and Eva finishing all our team's puzzles before Jay and Ansen, and hitting that winner button before them so I can rub it in Jay's face. So what if it's a training game for my new job as a games master at Locked and Coded? This is serious business.

We've already finished all the puzzles in our team's room, as have they. Now all four of us are back in the main starting area, desperately searching for specific words that will get us the remaining wooden dice in our teams' respective colours.

We've both collected four dice each with two to go. Eva and I keep an eye on Jay and Ansen for any clues as we search the room for anything that could be a word for our red team. They do the same. All the other words so far have been linked to either blue or red colours respectively, except none of us can seem to find any puzzles that we haven't already solved.

We're all watching each other in a tense stand-off that alternates between searching the room and ensuring the other team doesn't discover useful information.

That is, until Ansen pulls Jay aside into their team's room and starts whispering as he scribbles something on their team's writing pad. I immediately head over to spy – uh, to investigate. Ansen shuts up the minute he sees me, and Jay stands in front of the writing pad that's on the desk.

'Get out of here, Udina,' Jay says, pointing arrogantly at the door. 'Important blue team business going on here.'

When I lean around him, trying to get a glimpse of the writing pad, he leans with me to block my view. I lean the other way and he follows, so I feint in another direction and make a grab for it with my opposite hand.

He's too fast. He wraps his arms around me instead, pinning my arms to my sides and holding me close enough that I can't even move. He's so close that I can feel the breath from his nose, from his lips. It's so warm, just like his arms.

'Hey, the games master said espionage was perfectly legal.' I stare Jay down, though it's much harder to keep my game face on when it reminds me of that day when he held me close and let me cry into his shoulder. 'But no physical violence or you get a timeout.'

Jay releases me, though he remains right up in my face as he holds his hands out to either side. It's effective for showing that he isn't touching me. The problem is, it also blocks me from seeing the writing pad. 'There. No physical contact at all.'

Behind me, I can hear Ansen's footsteps leaving the room.

'Eva,' I call out while keeping my eyes on Jay, 'follow Ansen. Watch him closely and don't let him get away with anything. I'll handle this one.'

Jay's eyes crinkle in amusement, a teasing in them that's both soft and daring at the same time. 'You'll handle me, huh? How are you gonna do that?'

I lean in just a bit closer and drop my voice. 'How about a bribe? You tell me what Ansen discovered, and I'll . . .'

He doesn't pull back. 'You'll what?'

His low whisper sets off a weird feeling in my chest and a pleasant twist in my stomach that wants to break out, to utterly engulf the boy before me. I've never felt like this before, and I think I finally know what Aneeshka means when she talks about being attracted to someone. About wanting something more.

In that moment as we stare intently at each other, there's no competition, no tussling. Only the certainty that no matter how we spar, or spur one another onwards in ways the world interprets as squabbling or competition, at the end of the day it's each other we turn to when the world rages and roars around us. I always wondered how people could get so carried away and now, I finally understand.

I shift so I'm whispering into his ear. 'Not here. Not with everyone around. Later, though . . .' There's no need to explain what exactly because he knows what I'm hinting at. Stepping back and noting his bright red face with satisfaction, I ask, 'Do we have a deal?'

We're interrupted by whistling and hooting from behind us, because Eva and Ansen observed it all, of course.

'That's my jie, promising, hmm, her first kiss, I'm betting, for valuable information to win the game!' Eva says, then lets out another wolf whistle. 'Thank you for not exposing us all to dangerous levels of PDA right here and now.'

'I changed my mind, I don't want you two to come with me and Petra to PopSplosion,' Ansen says, crinkling his nose in feigned disgust – presumably at us, and not at the mention of his girlfriend. 'I can't imagine how bad you'll be in a few months.'

'Hey, I promised we'll keep well away and leave the two of you to your own devices. We'll only be on call so you won't even know if we spend the whole time making out,' Jay says with a grin, holding his hands up. 'What's to say you won't be like us by then, huh?'

Ansen gives him a Look. 'Ew. No.'

It's then our games master decides to remind us she's here, with a gentle cough over the speakers. Her voice rings out in the character of the game show announcer that's part of our game. 'It seems a very compelling bribe has been put forward by the red team! Will the blue team accept?'

Jay buries his face in his hands. 'Ughhhhhh.' He peeks at me from between his fingers. 'Fine.'

'I can't believe I went to all that effort and you sold me out for the promise of a kiss,' Ansen says, shaking his head with an exaggerated sigh. 'Come on Eva, I'll tell you how to get the word. Blue team gets first dibs on putting it in.'

'I never really understood my sister's obsession with puzzles before today,' she replies as they leave the blue team's room, 'but I think I could get hooked on this.'

Eva deliberately closes the door behind them with a smirk. *As though we weren't just reminded that someone is always watching.*

I groan, and wave at one of the cameras. 'Sorry! Blame this guy; he brings out the worst in me.'

'I think you mean the best.'

A victory sound plays from the machine outside where we've been entering the words we've found.

There's smothered laughter in our games master's voice as she announces, 'Aaaand the blue team has another die with one left to find before they can claim victory! However, their hard-earned information was coaxed from them by the red team in an impressive feat of espionage, and the red team is about to pull even again!'

I glance at the door, but it seems Ansen and Eva have come to an understanding to leave us alone for now.

'Don't try anything,' I warn Jay. 'I'd like to keep working here, if that's all the same to you. They're using games purchased from other companies at the moment, but they want to start designing their own in the near future, and they think my expertise will be useful. Mine!'

It's strange to think that this skill I'd only considered in the context of video games can be valuable in other areas as well. It's like leaving the first town of a game where the gates close behind you and you can't go back. There's a whole world map yet to explore. The real game is only beginning.

Jay's smile is brilliant as he squeezes my hand. 'You've spent your life playing puzzle games, and years designing them. You've played escape rooms and know what works and what doesn't. Who wouldn't want your expertise? And you can put to use all the stuff you'll learn at uni.'

After everything that happened, my parents were ecstatic to hear I'd decided to still do uni, even if it was part-time so I could accommodate this job. They didn't even bat an eyelid when I rejected the scholarship course and went for a game design one instead.

'Yeah, it's a compromise I can live with.' I squeeze his hand back. 'Maybe designing puzzle-y experiences is something I could make a career in, too?'

There's a question mark at the end of that so it's not quite a statement. A disconnect that lingers between the path I'd stuck to so fervently all those years, and the new one I'm tentatively treading on now.

It still hurts sometimes, especially when hearing about how Aneeshka's having more meetings with Blackbird Interactive and there's already been a commitment of substantial funds. That she's putting uni on hold to develop her game. That she's living the dream we wanted to achieve together for so many years, without me, in Sydney. Even though I'm happy for her, even though I want to hear every morsel of news, and support her, it still chokes me up.

Then I remind myself, or Jay reminds me when my own emotions are too much, that it's simply something different. Something that will surely bring new experiences, good and bad, as my world expands.

Like how I'm learning not to interrogate Ansen about how his sketching club is going, or give advice on his relationship with Petra — not that he'd listen to me anyway, Jay said to me the other week with a wry laugh, after we both talked each other down at various points in the day. *And I told my parents to let him sort out more things around the place, stuff they normally come to me for. Imagine their surprise; finding out the younger kid is as capable as the eldest. FREEDOM, SAM. FREEDOM.*

Though it's hard, we're constantly challenging one another. Pushing each other into places just outside our comfort zones, knowing we have not only our communities, but also one another to retreat to.

'This could definitely be a viable career for you.' He sounds so certain now that it bolsters my own confidence. 'I can't wait to play the escape rooms you design.'

The victory sound plays once more, and our games master announces that the blue team and red team are neck and neck once more with one deciding die to go for both teams. We look at each other.

'Better get back out there and crush you before you crush me,' he says. 'That way I can brag for the rest of my life that I defeated the world-famous escape room designer Sam Khoo.'

I don't know if I'm saying this to him, to whatever the future holds, or even the world in general. What's important is that it excites me, and I can't wait to see what happens next. I tilt my head and give him the beckoning gesture that precedes every good duel.

'Bring it on.'

ACKNOWLEDGEMENTS

This journey to publication started over a decade ago and has spanned 6 rough, trunked manuscripts before this. It would never have happened without an incredible support network that I am so, so lucky to have.

Daddy, I wish you were here to see this. Thank you for waiting for me to tell you the news before moving on. Thank you for being my inspiration for dreaming big, taking chances that scared me, and also for introducing me to computers and video games, as well as all the good food. Thank you for always being my support and being the 1 who indulged my random whims like building a custom bookshelf, or making ridiculous poses for photos. I love you and I miss you every single day.

Mummy, for always encouraging me and believing in me when I didn't believe in myself, thank you. Also thank you for being a failure as an Asian parent and supporting me as I chased my dreams despite being pretty broke at times. Home is always, always where you are.

Nat Nut, the best baby sister anyone could ask for. What would I have done if you weren't taking the journey with me through all the good and the tough times in our family? You make me grateful every day that I'm not an only child, especially when I get to raid your drinks stash or get free rides from the airport. (Dave, the best kind of gwei lo, and Zoe, you 2 indubitably get a shout-out too thanks to husband/daughter privilege.)

Puggy, best friend and first reader of everything since high school, my adventure buddy, the entire reason I could move to Sydney and become an escape room creator. I owe you so, so much and your friendship means the world to me.

Jen, sis, you have been such a bright light, such a support, and I'm so grateful our paths crossed.

To the 4 Noble Boingus Horsemen: Phoebe, Soonyoung, Stephanie – you guys are the Victor & Rahim to my Cynthia. The Baron to my Jordan. The Moon (NOT TAESUNG) to my Mara. The Ryden to my Min. Thank you for the random late-night chats, the support, the encouragement, reading every single (!!) snippet I spam you with, and teaching me so much about friendship and communication.

Aaron, you're awesome, especially when you make things go bang. Thanks for being the best co-owner who understands when I drop off the face of the earth for book and family stuff. Readers, if you want to make him (and me) happy *and* try the alien artefact or competitive escape rooms mentioned in the book, come check out Next Level Escape in Sydney!

Andrea Cascardi at the Transatlantic Agency, thank you for believing in this story and getting it through all the revisions and rewrites before and during submission. Anna McFarlane and Nicola Santilli at Allen & Unwin, thank you for your enthusiasm for these ridiculous kids and taking them so much further than I ever thought possible. You 3 never let the story be 'just okay', and have brought an incredible editorial eye to my work and shown this story so much love and care. This book is what it is thanks to you.

To my extended family and cousins, thank you for your support and also providing great comedic fodder over the years. Wenjie, all the late-night chats have been so nourishing for dealing with both ordinary and creative life too!

Em Chan, you are now officially part of a book's acknowledgements because the hippo decreed it so! I still have all our old fanfic writings and I treasure them. You deserve a high-5 every day!

Monsieur Pim (best DM period), Kath (the sharer of grief, but also joys), Ellie (she of the awesome art and fellow musical nerd), Emma (now a Real Writer on a remote island, so supportive of EVERYTHING), Alex (holy crap debut buddies?!), Adam (ever-patient despite my terribleness at emailing), Ayida (random Twitter connections turning into friendships are amazing), Karen (agent sibs ftw!), Tamar (mentor sibs ftw!), Justine (webtoon buddy!), Jason (I AM WAITING FOR THE NEXT ONE!): writing can be such a long and hard journey, and I'm so grateful to have met each and every one of you along the way. Whether it's talking craft or talking shit, I have learned so much through our friendships. I will thank you all personally outside of these acknowledgements otherwise this will go on for ten pages at least!

I'm also grateful for the many writing programs and events that really helped me along this journey. Thank you to Alexa Donne for creating Author Mentor Match where I really grew as a writer and met so many friends, and the team behind Diverse Voices, Inc. and DVPit, where I connected with my agent Andrea.

Thank you to Lucy Wang aka @stillindigo for the incredible cover illustration of Sam and Jay (check out her webtoon *Trinity*, I LOVE IT SO MUCH). And thank you to Mika Tabata for the wonderful cover and internal text design. Also thanks to Vanessa Lanaway, proofreader extraordinaire!

There were also a number of autistic authenticity readers that helped ensure Ansen was a fully-rounded character. Thanks to Sarah Pripas who provided feedback on a very different early draft, and to James Matthews at A_Tistic and Jess Flint, whose feedback was invaluable. Any issues that still remain are entirely my oversight and not theirs!

Thank you to Wai, Cat, Tobias, Kay, Michelle, Leanne, Bec, Nina and Grace for your lovely endorsements that may have had me tearing up! It means so much to have awesome authors I love say nice things about my debut. Your support as established authors is so kind and invaluable.

It takes a village to produce a book (please check out the credits!), and to everyone I've yet to mention who's been working tirelessly behind the scenes to bring this book into the world, I am so grateful for all your efforts because I could never have done this on my own.

And finally, to everyone who reviewed and championed and spread the love about this book, to everyone reading it now, thank you for all your support. Thank you for trusting me as a writer and giving my over-competitive kids a chance to become part of your world too. If you're still working out your path, I hope they encourage you to keep searching, keep trying, keep pushing on through all the twists and turns. Maybe there are more paths you never knew existed, that are waiting for you.

P.S. Did I add a cheeky little puzzle in these acknowledgements? See if you can find the six-letter word – your hint is that there's a clear order, and it's always the first letter after.

Four of the games in Sam and Jay's competition are
nods to popular classic indie games.
If you think they sound fun, why not check out the real game?

If you liked . . .

Why not try . . .

TIME-TWISTER

BRAID

HEAVEN'S COMPLEX

THE TALOS PRINCIPLE

If you liked . . .	**Why not try . . .**

WE CAN'T KEEP MEATING LIKE THIS

SUPER MEAT BOY

THESEUS

THE SWAPPER

Credit: Myles Kalus

Leanne Yong is an Asian–Australian author of Singaporean and Malaysian heritage who loves writing the diaspora experience into contemporary and fantasy YA fiction. She started her career as an IT business analyst (boring) and is now an escape room creator (much more interesting). She has designed internationally recognised games with her partner that weave unique puzzle mechanics with narrative. Leanne currently resides in Sydney for work, but Brisbane is where her home, family and heart (i.e. her cat) are. *Two Can Play That Game* is her debut novel.

CREDITS

AUTHENTICITY READERS
Jess Flint
James Matthews

CONTRACTS
Liz Kemp

COVER ARTIST
Lucy Wang (@stillindigo)

DESIGNER
Mika Tabata

DIGITAL (EBOOK)
Diana Oliva Cave
Emma Singer

EDITOR
Nicola Santilli

LITERARY AGENT
Andrea Cascardi
(Transatlantic Agency)

MARKETING
Prue Foster
Deborah Lum
Josie-Lyn O'Malley
Simon Panagaris
Lauren Ulmer
Carolyn Walsh